Circles in the Water

Prairiescape Books

Circles in the Water

a novel

by Robert Hays

Prairiescape Books
an imprint of
Herndon-Sugarman Press
Savoy, Illinois U.S.A.

To Mary, as always

∞ Pleasure is oft a visitant; but pain
Clings cruelly to us.
—John Keats

ॐ1॰

THE LINE WHERE the wall and ceiling met was indistinct, the two planes appearing to brush together haphazardly and merge into a geometric illusion that tilted first one way and then another, so that the room seemed to rock and sway like the deck of a ship on the open sea. Broder tried hard to get his bearings. He strained to focus his eyes on a point up and out, through the medical paraphernalia that hung over his bed like a tangle of gleaming metal and plastic vines, anxiously searching for something that looked familiar.

Powerful effigies hammered at his brain and demanded recognition. He struggled to block them, to push them aside and throw up a protective barrier against further intrusion, but they were too strong. In his mind's eye he saw Donnie Shand and Ray-Gene and Colletta, and he felt a confusing mix of euphoria and remorse. Donnie Shand and Ray-Gene were the only close friends he'd ever had. He wanted to hate them for what they did to Colletta, but how could he, when he was the one most at fault? Ray-Gene was gone now and he never expected to see Donnie Shand again, but Colletta had come back into his life, as if by magic, and things could never be the same.

She had materialized as if from nowhere: "Hey, Jimmie. I heard you had a hard landing. How ya' doin'?"

The pure and sweet Carolina accent, the soft, almost timid whisper. Even in his languid, drug-induced stupor he had known it was her. Suddenly he was fifteen again and in

1

love, stretched serenely in the grass beneath the delicate canopy of an ancient chinaberry tree in Colletta's backyard on a balmy spring evening in Conway. Overhead, a pale-shining moon seemed adrift in an endless starlit sky. Donnie Shand and Ray-Gene surely must be somewhere nearby.

But this was all wrong. He was supposed to be on his way to Iraq. That was the mission he had trained hard for, readying himself to jump from an airplane in the inky black of night and join in a swift assault against the enemy. Any enemy. Broder was a good soldier who didn't ask questions, he just followed orders. Orders were what made the Army a safe haven—no decisions to make, always somebody to tell you what to do and when to do it, just don't screw up too big or too often and you've got it made. Life as a paratrooper suited him very well. Life as a paratrooper was the only life he wanted.

And then the once-in-a-thousand-jumps training accident spoiled everything. A sudden wind shift which turned his chute upside down a hundred feet above the ground, the oppressive weight of full combat gear, the thudding impact that left him battered and broken. It was a minor incident by Airborne standards, they said. Sure it was. His right leg was splintered almost beyond repair.

How long had he been here? Two days? Two weeks? He had had too many surgeries and too much morphine, living in a shadow world and slipping in and out of consciousness, barely aware of his surroundings.

What he slowly came to recognize as a human voice intruded on the silence. It seemed to come from an invisible-faced image at the foot of his bed, a silhouette backlit by the dim glow of a fixture on the wall: "Are you Broder?"

"Yes. I'm Broder."

"I'm Lieutenant Colonel Hewlett," the image said. "How are we tonight, Sergeant Broder?"

"I'm doing okay, sir." He would take the image's word. If it said it was a colonel, he would speak to it as a colonel.

2

"Do you know what day it is?" the image was asking.

"Maybe Wednesday, sir?"

"It's Sunday. Do you know what year it is?"

"Yes, sir. It's 2003."

"Do you know where you are?"

"Sir, I think I'm in the hospital."

"Do you know which hospital?"

"I guess I'm still at the Fort Bragg hospital, sir. I don't remember being moved."

"Yes, you're still at Fort Bragg. You've not been moved. Do you recall what got you here?"

"Sir, I had a bad jump."

"That's what I'm here to talk to you about, sergeant. That bad jump. How much of it do you remember?"

"I think it just went wrong all at once, at the last second. There was nothing I could do. Am I in trouble, sir?"

The silhouette had taken a more complete form. Broder could make out the likeness of a face, but it was unfamiliar, a face he didn't recall having seen before. The face spoke with authority, the way a colonel would speak.

"Of course not," the face replied. "Accidents happen, no matter how hard we try to avoid them. Nobody is blaming you. We always investigate training injuries."

"I understand," Broder told the face, "but I don't know if I can be of much help. I don't know what happened, but I'm afraid I didn't handle it very well, sir."

"There will be time enough to sort all that out, sergeant. I'll come back in a couple of days, after you have had time to get your head cleared up a little. And you'll be talking to Captain Oates, the safety officer. Meanwhile, get some sleep. You got a nasty break in that leg and that's all you need to worry about for now."

"Sir . . ."

"Yes, sergeant?"

"When will I be able to jump again?"

"All in good time, sergeant. For now let's just worry about

3

getting you up and back on your feet. Both feet! Okay?"

"Okay, sir."

The image disappeared and Broder sank back into his hazy dream world. His mind conjured the exquisite pleasures of the jump. He imagined the familiar sensations spawned by the torturous velocity of a fall through empty space and the buoyancy of floating above the earth and granted his senses free reign to revel uninhibited in the breathtaking rush of cold air and the paradoxical noise of the wind and silence of nothingness. This was the world in which he found serenity. It was a peaceful, calming world, solitary, inhabited by no strange-faced images who said they were colonels and free of disturbing effigies from his past.

When he woke the next morning, Broder would not recall speaking with Colonel Hewlett. But he would remember that Colletta had been there and that memory would bring him pain.

THE TEAM WAS at loose ends, sitting hunched together on the rickety back-porch steps at Ray-Gene's house and facing another monotonous day of sultry Carolina summer. Jimmie poked at the dirt with a stick and Colletta gazed off to the east, intent on a wispy cloud formation miles away, over the ocean. Donnie Shand swatted at a fly.

"Jaybo found a dead rat back there by the fence last night," Ray-Gene said, to no one in particular.

"I hate rats," Colletta declared. "They're dirty. And they eat people."

"Rats don't eat people," Donnie Shand scoffed.

"They do if they're hungry."

"No, they don't. Where did you ever hear such a thing, Colletta?"

"Yes, they do. Rats ate off my grandpa's toes and fingers and part of his nose."

"How could they? Why didn't he fight 'em off?"

"He was dead. He died and nobody knew it and he had

4

laid there for a long time before they found him. And the rats had been chewin' on him. My daddy said so."

The boys still were skeptical. Colletta didn't make things up, but occasionally her gullibility got her in over her head. They found her stubbornness irritating sometimes, especially when she insisted on defending positions which they saw as indefensible, but on the whole they grudgingly respected her for the way she stuck to her guns.

This hadn't always been the case. When she first showed up early in that summer after third grade and commenced to tag along the boys had made clear that she wasn't wanted. It was not that they took offense to her dirty face and tousled hair, her ragged dresses, or her bare feet with soles calloused tough as leather — these things were common in their small world, and in any case not important. But she was a girl and this was a boys' team.

A less persistent girl might have been disheartened but Colletta had hung on tenaciously, her confidence undiminished. She knew she could do anything they could do, and pledged to herself that she'd hold her own with any one of the three in a fair fight, toe-to-toe and nose-to-nose. Fighting was not in her nature, though, and in fact her sweet disposition made it fun for the boys to have her around; they soon learned to tolerate her without complaint. From there it was only a matter of time until they came to take her presence for granted.

Donnie Shand had been the first to welcome her to the team, properly. "It don't matter anymore that you're a girl," he announced matter-of-factly. "We like you good enough, Colletta."

Donnie's acceptance was crucial. He was their leader. His full name was Donald Jackson Shand, and more often than not he was simply "DJ" within the group. He was the oldest of the three boys and would have been a grade ahead of the others except that he'd been held back for missing too many days of school. This didn't matter much, he insisted, because

5

he had a mind of his own and school did not affect him a whole lot one way or the other. In the eyes of Ray-Gene and Jimmie and, now, Colletta, DJ could do no wrong.

As to Ray-Gene and Jimmie, they had been best friends for as long as either could remember. They took a blood oath at least once a month that they would be best friends forever, a pact that in the beginning had involved the ritual scratching of forearms followed by the swapping of blood-smears. They had replaced that ceremony with a mere verbal pledge after Ray-Gene got a nasty infection and Grandma Freeman ordered an end to their "behavin' like mindless fools."

Their relationship was stronger, no doubt, because there were no other boys their age on the block. It meant nothing to them that they lived on opposite sides of the street even though the grownups around them seemed to consider this enormously important. Symbolically, their street was a dividing line and Conway, South Carolina, was a tranquil place where black people and white people respectfully tolerated each other in their ordinary day-to-day lives but still preferred to sleep at night in homes among their own.

"My daddy would skin me alive if he found me playing with a nigger boy," Colletta said, looking Ray-Gene straight in the eye.

"Your daddy's a good-for-nothing drunk," Jimmie said fiercely, quick to defend his friend.

"You oughtn't to say stuff like that," Donnie Shand said. His tone was stern, but softened quickly. "I know you really didn't mean nothing by it, but you oughtn't to say that kind of thing about Ray-Gene."

Colletta looked hurt and, this time, said nothing more. She'd only hoped to change the subject from rats, which she considered filthy and disgusting. Ray-Gene took no offense. The problem was Colletta's daddy's, not hers, and Colletta had never been mean to him or said disparaging things. He could tell that she liked him and she cared nothing about his skin color. He liked her, too, and he already had come to feel almost as close to her as he did to Jimmie and Donnie Shand. These three people were the ones who mattered the most to Ray-Gene, with the possible exception of Grandma Freeman, and he could easily enough ignore the slurs of the adults as long as his friends treated him as an equal.

As on any other day, skin color was not nearly as important in this little coterie as the never-ending struggle to find something interesting to do.

"Somebody needs to come up with a good idea," Donnie Shand urged. "Just settin' around here sure ain't much fun."

"I wish we had us a way to get to the beach," Ray-Gene said. "It don't seem right that we got all summer and don't have a chance to go to the beach like everybody else."

"Everybody don't get to the beach," Donnie Shand said, "but yeah, I guess it'd be fun if we could. My dad might take us some weekend, but y'all know we ain't going to get to the beach today so forget about it."

"Then maybe we could go back to the creek again."

Donnie Shand was not quick to answer. He took it as his personal responsibility to provoke his three followers, not to become a follower himself. He made a big show of weighing Ray-Gene's suggestion solemnly while the others waited hopefully. "Okay, I guess we could," he said at last. "We ain't been to the creek for a while."

Jimmie and Colletta already were up and starting around the house toward the street. Ray-Gene hurried to catch up. Colletta paused at the sidewalk and Jimmie and Ray-Gene stopped beside her to let Donnie Shand take the lead.

"Grandma Freeman, she sends Jaybo down to the creek to hunt frogs sometimes," Ray-Gene said. "DJ, did you ever spear a frog?"

"Of course I have. Nothing to it."

"I get confused about Jaybo, Ray-Gene," Colletta said. "I know he ain't your brother. Is he your cousin or what?"

Ray-Gene answered patiently, "Jaybo's my uncle. He has lived with Grandma Freeman longer than me."

7

"How old is he?"

"Fifteen."

"Is he nice?"

"He used to be kind of mean to me sometimes, but now he's not so bad."

"How come you're named Ray-Gene Kepley when your grandma's named Freeman?"

"Because my daddy was Landon Kepley. My momma's name was Freeman before she got married."

Donnie Shand had set a quick pace. Jimmie stayed almost at his side, step by step, while Colletta and Ray-Gene were beginning to fall behind. Colletta still had questions.

"How come you live with your grandma?"she asked.

"Because my daddy's dead and my momma lives in Detroit," Ray-Gene said. "But she's gonna send for me and my sisters someday."

"I've got a little brother named Hunter."

"We know that, Colletta."

"My Grandma Saylor's got owls-shiners. She don't even know me anymore."

"How can your own grandma not know you?"

"I told you, she's got owls-shiners. She don't even know my momma most of the time."

"I never heard of anything like that," Ray-Gene declared. "You sure you know what you're talking about, Colletta?"

Donnie Shand turned and looked back at the two stragglers with a severe frown. "If you two don't shut up you'll have all the dogs in the neighborhood chasing us before we get in a half-mile of the creek," he scolded. "Can't y'all just be quiet for a while?"

Donnie's rebuke was effective. They traipsed silently on past the last block of houses in town, skirted the edge of a barren slough, and made their way through a small thicket of scrubby live oak to the bank of the creek. The stream was slow-running and stagnant, a reflection of the hot and dry summer. DJ led them ahead toward the best wading hole.

Jimmie suddenly halted and grabbed Donnie Shand's arm. "I saw somebody," he said, almost in a whisper. "Somebody's up there by them trees."

"Be quiet!" Donnie Shand said. "Walk slow and be quiet till we see who it is."

It was Jaybo. He stood with his back against the trunk of a thick cypress tree, his pants down around his knees, with a full erection pointing like a stout lance toward the approaching intruders. He barely paid them heed. The younger boys slipped silenty closer. Their gaze was firmly fixed on Jaybo's penis. Colletta stayed back a step further, but also stared at Jaybo.

"Don't act like you've never seen one before," Jaybo said, hardly looking up. "You little boys come on up close and see what a man looks like."

"I've seen yours before," Ray-Gene said. "And I know what you're doin.' You're gonna squirt like a fountain."

"Y'all just don't get too close," Jaybo warned. "I don't want nobody to get splattered. 'Cept you, little girl. You come over here and put your hand on it."

"He can't boss you, Colletta," Donnie Shand whispered. "You don't have to do what he says."

Colletta hesitated, but stepped forward bravely. "I've seen my daddy's,"she told Jaybo, "and I ain't afraid of yours."

"Get hold of it then!" Jaybo demanded. He seized her small hand and forced her to grab onto his hard flesh. He made four or five quick thrusts and ejaculated in an explosion that left the four onlookers awestruck.

"Keep your mouth shut, Ray-Gene," Jaybo said. "You tell your grandma anything about this and I'll break your neck. You got me?"

"I ain't telling nobody, Jaybo."

The older boy hitched up his tattered trousers and pushed off through the underbrush toward town.

Colletta studied the milky excretion, dripping through the blades of tall grass. "It looks like runny-nose snot," she said, wrinkling her nose in an expression of disgust.

"Don't step in that, Colletta, it's nasty," Donnie warned. "I wouldn't step in that stuff!"

"Now look here, y'all," Donnie Shand said, eager to regain control, "if we're going to have any fun we'd better get at it. We ought not to be gone too long or else we'll be in trouble." He motioned his followers forward with a wave of his hand and, creeping stealthily along the creek bank, led them on to the strand of clean, usually thigh-deep water that was their target. Thick stands of cypress and willow grew right to the water's edge along most of the creek, but here a wide sand bar forced the stream away from the bank and made it easier to spot the menacing cotton mouth moccasins that lurked among the willow roots, nearly invisible.

They splashed lethargically in the water for a time, but the creek was too low to offer much respite from the dreary heat that had built up by mid-morning and the confrontation with Jaybo had dampened their spirits. When Donnie Shand said they'd better go, the others promptly fell into line without a murmur of dissent and started back the way they had come, like a little ragtag army trudging home after a defeat in battle.

An ill-defined sense that their little wilderness no longer offered sanctuary would go unspoken. It wasn't as if they had been accosted by dangerous strangers, nor even that they had been particularly offended by Jaybo's crude behavior. But he oughtn't to have made Colletta touch him, and the boys felt guilty that they had made no move to protect her.

They were half-way back to town before Ray-Gene broke the long silence: "I wish we could make us some money. There's lots of stuff we could do if we had money."

Colletta picked up quickly on Ray-Gene's proposal. If she had money she'd buy them all Baby Ruth candy bars. Maybe they could work for somebody, and she'd be willing to work for almost anybody and do just about anything for money, and she knew there was stuff they could do, and didn't DJ think that maybe they could find work if they went out and looked? She was ready and eager to try and she knew that Ray-Gene and Jimmie were, too.

"Don't be stupid," DJ chided. "We ain't old enough to work, not for pay anyhow."

Colletta was not so easily deterred. "Maybe we could sell flowers," she said. "They sell flowers all the time over by the road where people go to Myrtle Beach."

"Where would we get the flowers?" Jimmie asked.

"There's lots of Queen Anne's lace all around that cotton field over there," Colletta said, gesturing toward the west. "Nobody'd probably care if we got a ton of it and we could sell it real cheap."

Jimmie shook his head and frowned. "Them's just weeds," he said.

"No they're not. Queen Anne's lace is flowers, Jimmie."

Donnie Shand stopped walking and the others promptly halted, too, in lock step, and stood by while he traced a wide, smooth arc in the dust with the toe of his shoe. This was the signal his team wanted, the response they always hoped for when they needed Donnie's careful reasoning. Their leader was about to come up with a plan.

"Sometimes my mom pays me a little bit for work in the yard," DJ announced presently, his satisfaction with himself clear in his tone. "She might have some stuff for us to do if y'all wanted to help."

"I'm willing to work," Ray-Gene said.

Colletta and Jimmie agreed.

Donnie was cautious: "I ain't promising nothing, understand, but maybe she'd at least give us a dollar."

"That's more than we've got now," Ray-Gene said. "You can't get less than nothin'."

Donnie Shand set out for home, walking even faster than usual, but his followers eagerly fell into his quick pace. The sudden prospect of having money to spend brought a sense of exhilaration. Their day might turn out good, after all.

❧ The Shand house, a run-down two-bedroom dwelling, was a block over from the street where the other three lived and two blocks toward downtown. The front of the house was heavily shaded by a scraggly sweetgum tree and overgrown butterfly bushes formed a wall of textured greenery against the faded white clapboard siding. The south side of the house was nearly hidden under an overburden of ivy vines. A narrow sand path led from the sidewalk to the front door.

Angling across the yard, Donnie Shand halted abruptly beside the sweetgum tree and raised a hand to signal those coming behind. They heard loud, angry words and saw DJ's mother and father, apparently oblivious to their approach, embroiled in heated argument at the doorstep.

While Donnie and his followers looked on, helpless and afraid, Langly Shand struck his wife full in the face with a closed fist and knocked her back, hard, against the door. Blood poured from her nose and she looked stunned, but only for an instant.

"You good-for-nothing son-of-a-bitch," she screamed. "I'll kill you this time, I swear I will."

She picked up a brick from beside the step and charged him, landing a blow on his head that caused his knees to buckle. She struck him again and Donnie's father slumped to the ground, blood spouting from a gash over his left ear. He tried weakly to raise himself up. She lifted her arm high and brought the brick crashing down on his skull a third time and he lay still.

❧ 2 ❧

IEUTENANT COLONEL Eldon Hewlett stood at the foot of Broder's bed, ramrod straight, much younger looking than Broder would have expected. He was tall and gaunt, not an impressive figure, with a pock-marked face and an ugly two-inch scar on his left cheek. Broder was two days off morphine and his head was clear at last. He knew Colonel Hewlett's reputation. Hewlett was Airborne through and through. He was tough as nails and drove his men hard. If paratroopers were trained right, Hewlett preached, they would win their battles in combat and, even more important, survive to fight another day. His men did not like him much, but they respected him immensely.

Broder also knew that high esteem had not been easy for Hewlett to come by. Too many men in the division, especially among the senior NCOs, still held a deeply ingrained mistrust of black officers. And according to the ever-active Fort Bragg grapevine, the colonel refused to go out of his way to cultivate friendships; defenders praised him for not being an ass-kisser, but detractors charged that he was not a team player.

Although he had no recollection of their meeting, Broder had been told that the colonel had visited him a few days earlier. He had been worried about what might have taken place. What could he have said to Hewlett, addle-headed as he'd been? And why would he warrant this high-level attention in the first place?

"I've talked with your doctors," the colonel was saying.

He smiled as he spoke and the smile softened his piercing black eyes, catching Broder thoroughly off guard. "They say you've come through surgery with flying colors. You'll be in and out of rehab before you know it. Do you have a family, sergeant?"

"No, sir, I'm single. Well, yes, my parents. And I have an older brother in Tennessee. They don't know anything about this, though."

"Where are your parents?"

"They live in South Carolina."

"They tell me you had a visitor. A pretty young woman?"

"Yes, sir. She was a friend a long time ago."

"It's good to keep in touch with old friends, Broder."

"Yes, sir."

"Now, if you feel up to it, sergeant, I'd like to ask you a few questions about your accident."

"I'm okay, sir."

"Good. How well do you remember what happened?"

"I guess I remember everything up until right before I hit the ground, then it's a little fuzzy after that."

"Tell me what you remember."

Despite his direct language, the colonel's manner was cordial, not demanding, and Broder sensed for the first time that Hewlett truly might be after the facts and not concerned about placing blame. "It was a routine jump," he said. "The jump master released us right over the target and everything looked good. I saw the guys in front of me hit the ground without any problem and I had everything tucked in, ready to land. Then—I don't know how to explain it, sir, all at once it seemed like I was upside down and that's the last thing I remember."

"You don't recall the actual landing, don't know what position you were in when you hit the ground?"

"No, sir. I don't remember hitting the ground at all."

"That's okay. More of it may come back to you. Do you know what happened to the men behind you?"

"No, sir. Nobody's told me anything."

"Well, it may make you feel better to know that a couple of them were caught in the same updraft. They had more time to deal with it, though, and came out of it a lot better off than you. One got a sprained ankle and the other escaped with a few cuts and bruises."

Confirmation that his bad jump was a result of unusual wind conditions came as a great relief to Broder. Ever since he had become clear-headed enough to think about his accident, he had been concerned about the possibility that no witness would affirm his account and he would be found at fault, guilty of poor performance at best and maybe something more. Selfishly, he might have felt better if they had told him that other jumpers also had been seriously hurt. But he told the colonel, "I'm glad to hear that, sir."

"What we're interested in, sergeant, is finding out everything we can from your experience," Colonel Hewlett said. "How can we prevent this from happening again? Maybe a change in equipment, or is there something we could add to our training that would help the next man deal with it better than you did? That sort of thing."

"I guess I didn't handle it very well, sir."

"Don't misunderstand me. You've got a damned good record. Nobody is blaming you for what happened, Broder. You got a freaky gust of wind at the worst time possible and you didn't have a chance to recover. The same thing could have happened to me or to anybody else. Plenty of people saw it, and nobody thinks it's your fault. Do I make myself clear on that?"

"Yes, sir. Thank you."

Hewlett stepped around to the side of the bed. He put a hand on Broder's shoulder and said, "Captain Oates will be talking with you more about this, sergeant. We all have the same interest in saving the next soldier from what you've been through. We would rather have you out somewhere jumping than lying here on your back."

"The sooner the better, sir. How long do you think it'll be before I can jump again?"

"Let's don't worry about that just yet, sergeant. You've had a pretty rough time. I'm sorry."

"I guess it could have been worse," Broder said, grateful for the sympathy.

"Are they treating you well here?"

"Yes, sir. They've been great."

"Good. Take advantage of your time off. Get some rest. Make it a vacation, like you're in one of those exclusive resorts up in the mountains. I'll be around to see you again." Hewlett turned to go, but hesitated. "That old friend who came to visit — is she anything special to you, Broder?"

"No, sir. Nothing special. Just an old friend."

As Colonel Eldon Hewlett disappeared through the door to the hallway, Broder felt a sudden onrush of remorse. How could he have said that Colletta was nothing special? But on the other hand, how could he begin to tell the colonel all the things that Colletta had meant to him, how much he'd loved her, how their lives had been intertwined, how circumstances had wrenched them apart? How could he tell these things to anyone, when there was so much that he'd tried to forget, so much that he didn't understand, himself?

  IN THE END, Donnie Shand's mother was not charged in the killing of her husband. The county prosecutor, always sensitive to public pressure, wanted to bring her to trial but police argued that this was a clear case of self-defense and the broken jaw Langly Shand inflicted before she hit him with the brick was compelling evidence in her favor. Then there were the half-dozen police reports that screamed out a record of systematic abuse. She had been hauled to the emergency room more than once by the sympathetic officers, who now contended that she had been driven to smash her husband's skull in a sudden fit of rage that was the shocking but perhaps inevitable breaking point of a woman who had suffered too long without fighting back. They felt guilty for not having put Langly away and sparing her the trauma of taking his life.

Wilma Shand found little solace in escaping action by the authorities. For her, the fact that she had not intended to kill her brutal husband only made matters worse. The incident and its aftermath left her an emotional wreck, barely able to cope with even the simplest demands of daily life.

Donnie Shand never talked about what happened. When he wasn't around, Ray-Gene and Jimmie spoke of little else. They recounted every detail of the killing and reviewed the gruesome event over and over as if it were a horror movie they could not wait to see again even though it left them feeling helpless and afraid. Colletta tried to avoid the subject and refused to join in their discussions. For her, it was a tormenting memory that she had a hard time putting out of her mind. The mere sight of a red brick made her ill.

They didn't see much of their leader during the remainder of that memorable summer. When he did appear he usually was with his mother and sisters, and he often went a week or more without leaving the Shand house at all. They sought to reassure one another, said don't worry, school would be starting again soon and they'd see him every day and things would be back to normal. But when school days returned in the fall, they knew at once that something was different. They perceived a trait in Donnie Shand they hadn't observed before and it was a trait they didn't like. Colletta called it meanness. Jimmie and Ray-Gene hated that, but could not come up with a better way to describe it. Donnie was not malevolent, but there was an edge, a cold detachment that was new.

Jimmie brooded about this until it was beginning to keep him awake at night. Finally, he turned to his mother for advice. He knew that Donnie Shand always had been something of an enigma to her, but he had sensed that she was especially sympathetic toward DJ in his current plight.

"Your friend's been through a terrible thing," his mother said. "No child should be witness to something like that. It wouldn't be natural if it didn't change him some."

"I just wish that terrible thing had never happened, and we could just go back to like it used to be."

"You can't unbreak an egg, Jimmie. What's done is done. You will just have to give him enough time and I'm sure that he'll come around."

He marveled at his mother's patience, as he always had. It never would occur to him that patience was nothing less than an instrument of survival for Allou Broder, that the obligation she felt to balance his volatile and uncommunicative father and keep the family on an even keel had taught her the necessity of being slow to anger and even slower to condemn. He hoped that his mother was right. He wanted things to be like they were before and yearned for the day their little team would be guided once again by Donnie's steady hand. He tried to be patient, like his mother said.

Through the weeks of fall and into early winter, DJ maintained his cold and uncaring façade. The holidays came and went and school started again with no apparent change in his attitude. Ray-Gene, in particular, worked hard to draw Donnie out and make him talk about his feelings, hoping every morning that this finally would be the day DJ came around. But at the end of every day, after nothing changed, he went home disappointed.

☙ COLLETTA AND JIMMIE were on the front row, watching intently as dramatic events took place before their eyes on the brilliantly lit screen of one of the school's ubiquitous television sets. They and a couple of hundred fellow students, bunched together in the gymnasium on a crisp, clear January morning, stomped their feet and cheered wildly as the rocket-boosted Challenger space shuttle lifted skyward and arched gracefully over the Atlantic Ocean.

Classes had been dismissed so that they could witness

first-hand the launch in Florida because NASA had invited a teacher from somewhere up North to go into space with the astronauts. Their principal thought that putting a teacher in space was an occasion not to be missed.

"It's beautiful," Colletta whispered. "I want to go up in space someday. Wouldn't that be great?"

"It would be kind of scary, though," Jimmie answered. "I don't know if I . . ."

Just as he spoke, the Challenger exploded into a massive ball of creamy-orange flame. His words trailed off to silence, his response to Colletta left unfinished. The boisterous cheering around them turned to shocked stillness. Expressions of disbelief marked the faces of teachers and students alike and their principal, shaken and pale, huddled with her faculty and decided it would be best to cancel school for the rest of the day.

Colletta and Jimmie slipped out quickly through a side door, stunned and subdued, and walked slowly away from the building. Colletta's face was tear-stained. "That was terrible," she said. "You know they were all killed. I've never seen anything so bad before."

"I feel real sorry for that poor teacher. She looked nice, didn't you think?"

"Yes," Colletta sniffed. She started to say more, but her eyes brimmed with tears and she clamped her teeth together hard to keep from sobbing aloud.

"I wish we wouldn't have seen it," Jimmie said. "Don't cry, Colletta." He took her hand and they moved on without speaking.

Donnie Shand came behind them, walking faster. "How come y'all are so slow?" he mumbled.

"We were feeling bad about that teacher," Jimmie said. "Wasn't that awful?"

"Who cares about that teacher!"

"But don't you feel sad about her, DJ? She looked real happy about going into space, and now she's dead."

19

"Why should I feel sad about her? I didn't know any of them people. They all probably will get a million dollars or something. Why should I care?" Donnie Shand quickened his pace and turned the corner toward his house, saying nothing more.

"How could he not care?" Colletta said, more bewildered than angry. "How could anybody not care? Everything was so beautiful, and then they all just blew up. I don't know what makes DJ tick, and I don't like him anymore."

"I wish he was still nice, like he used to be," Jimmie said. "My mom still says we have to give him time. She says it's not easy to get over what DJ's been through."

"Maybe so. But I don't think what happened is any excuse for him acting the way he does."

"It's hard for me, too, but I guess we have to be patient a little longer."

During the days to come, in spite of their determined efforts, Ray-Gene and Jimmie had little success in overcoming Colletta's bitterness. She insisted that it was DJ who had changed, and DJ was the only person who could set things right. Donnie kept his distance, although occasionally they noticed small signs that he missed the steady company of his teammates and wanted things to be normal again. Ray-Gene and Jimmie spent much of their time analyzing the situation. Besides the understandable impact of losing his father, they worried that they had overlooked something less obvious, some subtle but critical key to comprehending Donnie's troubles better and setting things back on the right path.

Their failure to find an easy answer—any answer at all, for that matter—was very much on their minds as they left school on a blustery Friday in late February. The span of daylight hours had grown noticeably longer and a cold rain that had marred much of the afternoon had blown off to the east, over the ocean. They were in no hurry.

"You don't have a daddy, either," Jimmie was saying.

"How come it never seems to bother you too much?"

"It's different for me," Ray-Gene replied. "My daddy was killed on a loggin' truck right after I was born. I can't even remember him. But DJ had a daddy and then lost him. That would be a lot harder."

"Yeah, that's what I been thinking. And then he had to worry about his momma going to prison or something. Remember how scared he was? That'd be hard, too."

"Sure it would. Me and you and Colletta have got to stick together and help him out. His sisters are busy takin' care of their momma and nobody's looking out for him. DJ needs us to be his friends."

Although the brightening weather had made them even more reluctant to rush, when they spotted Donnie Shand just ahead they stepped up their pace to catch up. Donnie reacted coolly to their greetings but he did not speed up the way he did when he wanted to be alone. Jimmie and Ray-Gene took this as a promising sign. They fell into step, one on each side.

"Come on with us to Ray-Gene's house," Jimmie urged. "You don't have to be home yet."

"I don't know," Donnie answered. "My mom gets worried if I'm late."

"You won't be that late, DJ," Ray-Gene said. "It's Friday and Grandma Freeman always makes pies on Friday. We've been walking slow so they'll be ready when we get there. She won't care if there's three of us."

"I guess I could go," Donnie Shand said. "But just for a little bit. I don't want to make my momma nervous."

Jimmie looked sideways at Ray-Gene, who grinned and winked and delivered a thumbs-up signal behind his back. They took a shortcut that angled across a trash-strewn vacant lot, ducked under the low branches of an overgrown cherry laurel at the corner, and ran the rest of the way to Grandma Freeman's house. Jaybo sat on the steps, blocking their way. He surveyed them with cold eyes.

21

"What you little shits want?" he demanded.

"Grandma Freeman made us a pie," Ray-Gene said. "She always lets us have some when we get home from school."

"She got sick and didn't make any pie. Don't bother her."

"We'll go in and see her, then."

"I told you, y'all can't bother her." Jaybo stood up, towering above them on the top step. He was large for his age, already a good six feet tall, powerfully built. "Anyway, I got something important for you to do."

Donnie Shand and Jimmie had stayed back, reluctant to get too close to the menacing Jaybo. Ray-Gene was not intimidated. "What do you want us for?" he asked. "It can't take too long, because Jimmie and DJ ought to be getting home before dark."

"It won't take long," Jaybo said, his attitude less sullen. He pulled two twenty-dollar bills from his pocket and thrust them toward Ray-Gene. "Go to the Barbecue Shack and give this to Sam. Tell him it's for my stuff. Don't give it to nobody else. If Sam ain't there, bring the money back to me. Understand?"

"Sure, Jaybo. We'll get it for you."

Jimmie felt immense relief to get away from Jaybo without further harassment and it was clear by the expression on Donnie Shand's face that he felt the same way. Donnie still claimed to have reservations, and said maybe he ought to get on home just in case his mother needed him, but relented quickly when they renewed their pleas. The three of them hurried to the Barbecue Shack—mindful that Jaybo was waiting—and found Sam wiping tables.

Sam was a huge man with a clean-shaven head and heavy black beard, wearing a dirty apron over dingy white pants and sweat-stained T-shirt. Each of his hairy forearms was marked by a garish indigo tattoo of a stout chain that ended with a ship's anchor just above the wrist. His wide face visibly brightened as the boys entered and he greeted them pleasantly: "Hey, Ray-Gene. Who're your friends here?"

22

Ray-Gene flashed his irresistible smile. "Hey, Sam," he said. "This is Donnie Shand and Jimmie Broder."

"Good to meet you, fellows," Sam said. He swabbed a beefy hand vigorously with his rag and extended it toward Jimmie.

"I've been here before," Jimmie told him. "My dad likes your barbecue a lot."

"Who is your daddy?"

"He's Popeye Broder. Maybe you know him."

"Yes, I believe maybe I do," Sam said. He solemnly shook hands with both of the two new boys, then turned again to Ray-Gene: "How's your pretty sister?"

"You mean Ravonelle?"

"I reckon. Is she the one that your grandma usually sends along to get meat?"

"Yeah, that's her. She's okay."

Sam took Jaybo's money and went to the back. He returned in short order and handed Ray-Gene a slim brown-paper bag, its top rolled down tightly. "Tell Jaybo I appreciate his business," he said. "How is Jaybo? It seems like I ain't seen him in a while."

"Jaybo's doin' good," Ray-Gene answered. "I'll tell him what you said." He clutched the bag firmly. "We best be gettin' back."

They left the Barbecue Shack and walked at a fast pace. Ray-Gene was afraid to be too slow to get back to Grandma Freeman's house with Jaybo's merchandise. Donnie Shand and Jimmie split off at Donnie's street, slowed to a leisurely pace, then stopped to look at movie posters in the windows of a video store that used to be a Walgreens. Jimmie noticed that DJ seemed more relaxed, apparently no longer feeling any pressure to rush home to be with his mother.

A gangling, black and white mixed-breed dog limped across the street and slunk toward them, cautiously, a mixture of fear and hopeful expectation in its eyes. Jimmie instinctively reached for it and the dog was about to submit

23

but suddenly snapped at him instead, clamping its jaws onto his outstretched hand. Its teeth punctured his flesh like little daggers. Jimmie wailed in pain.

Donnie Shand sprang forward. He grabbed the dog by the throat and squeezed until the animal released its grip. Blood dripped from Jimmie's fingers.

"Call and get us help," Donnie demanded of an old man coming out of the video store. "Hurry up. This dog might be mad."

The dog struggled against Donnie's choke hold. Its fight almost was successful, and Donnie frantically regained his grip only after the dog had inflicted a nasty slash in the flesh of his left forearm.

"Turn him loose, DJ," Jimmie yelled. "Let him go or he'll hurt you bad."

"No he won't. He'll calm down." Donnie Shand panted from exertion, but kept a firm hold on the dog. "If he gets loose you'll have to get rabies shots."

The old man, meanwhile, after standing mutely for what seemed to the boys an eternity, finally had gathered his wits and run back into the video store, where someone called for help. A police car was on the scene within minutes, followed almost at once by an animal control officer in a white van. By the time they arrived, though, the dog sat placidly at DJ's feet while he gingerly stroked its neck and spoke to it with soothing words. The fear was gone from the animal's eyes. It surrendered obediently to the animal control woman and patiently allowed itself to be muzzled. When she led it into the heavily screened van it offered no protest.

The police officer directed the boys into his patrol car and rushed them — red lights flashing — to a hospital emergency room, where their wounds were cleaned and dressed and they got tetanus shots. "You're a brave fellow," he told Donnie Shand. "Most people would have let the dog get away. I'm not saying what you did was especially wise, but it sure was brave."

24

Donnie Shand would talk for weeks about how swift the police response had been, how the crisis was dealt with like an important emergency.

"It was like there'd been a bank robbery, or a big accident where people got killed," he told Colletta, who listened in wide-eyed excitement. But all Jimmie could talk about was how DJ had come to his rescue, how courageous he'd been to take on the dog bare-handed the way he did, how he had hung on even after the dog slashed his arm, how he'd been in control of the situation from the beginning. Ray-Gene said this demonstrated being cool under fire, just what they should expect of a leader.

They looked up to Donnie Shand more than ever, made him their common cause. Donnie never would know all the scheming and plotting that went on among the other three in their resolve to make him happy. Colletta mothered him to a point that embarrassed Jimmie and Ray-Gene, but they in turn were deferential to him far beyond their usual manner. No decision was made, no question settled until Donnie had been consulted. They were confident they could see results and told one another that DJ was coming around, responding exactly as they hoped he would. He'd soon be his old self again, their leader, the Donnie Shand they remembered from an earlier time before his momma crushed his daddy's head with a brick.

ᢒᢙ3ᢚᢙ

THE ORTHOPEDIC ward of the Fort Bragg medical center was almost empty. Broder was happy for the solitude. Medical people came and went. Only Rondell Wilson, the stout orderly who had become both the hope and the dread of his life, showed up regularly at his bedside. Wilson was a gentle soul with the hands of a brain surgeon and the arms of an Olympic weight lifter and it was clear lately that Broder's physical well-being had become his top priority.

After some tough days, Broder had reached a point where his level of pain no longer overrode his ability to look ahead. He lay quietly and pondered what was to come. He wished he could be in a C-130 at this very minute, checking gear, coming in low and fast over a precariously tight drop-zone, readying himself for a jump. Absorbed in his aimless contemplation, he was startled by her voice.

"Hey, Jimmie. Feelin' better today?"

"Colletta."

Her name was all he could manage. Colletta had hardly been out of his thoughts since that first night, when she had materialized like an apparition out of nowhere, but now he was struck as speechless as a bewildered child by her sudden close presence. He had wondered when — or if — she would come again, desperately hoping she would and fearful she might not. So many questions he wanted to ask, so many answers he was afraid to hear.

"I would have got back sooner but I've been awful busy at work," Colletta said. "You look like you're feeling a little

27

better. Have you been up and around some?"

"Yes."

He wanted to say it was good to see her, that he'd missed her. He wanted to let her know that merely having her brush against his life again, if only in a few fleeting strokes, had reawakened old feelings, brought a flood of memories. He wanted to speak to her as freely and easily as he might have at some instant years past, a time before those things happened, those terribly destructive, hurtful things that turned their lives in different directions.

But it was Colletta who spoke again, who asked, "You're not going to overdo it, though?"

"I just do what they tell me."

"Of course you do. You're a soldier."

How could he have forgotten how pretty she was, or how easily he lost himself in her soft brown eyes? He wanted to reach out to her and have her come to him the way she once had and pretend that the intervening years had never taken place.

"How did you know I was here?" he said.

"You made the headlines. There was a little story in the post newspaper about the accident. I knew it was you."

"It could have been another Broder."

"I knew you were here, Jimmie."

"How?"

"I saw you — three months ago."

"Where?"

"I work at the Mexicana in Fayetteville. You came in one night, you and a couple of other guys. You had on civilian clothes, but I saw the Fort Bragg stickers on your Mustang. That is what you always wanted — a red Mustang. I'm glad you got one."

"I never dreamed that you were within a thousand miles of here. Why didn't you say something, let me know . . .?"

"I didn't know if you'd want to see me, how you'd act."

"After all this time, Colletta, I hardly know what to say.

How is life treating you? How have you been?"

"I've had some rough spots here and there, but I've done okay. I'm clean, Jimmie. Things are working out."

Colletta hesitated, as if uncertain how to answer, and Rondell Wilson barged in just at that awkward moment and spared her the need to reply. Much as he hated to interrupt, Wilson announced, there was a schedule that must be kept; it was time to cover Broder's leg-cast with plastic and drag him into a hot shower and after that push him through a punishing round of physical therapy. Wilson pretended gleeful blood-lust for the pain he was about to inflict on his favorite patient, an act Broder had come to expect and even appreciate.

"Damn, Wilson, I thought I might get by today without your torture," Broder said, not entirely in jest. "I'm sorry, Colletta. It looks like I've got to go. Wilson has his orders, and Wilson's a man who always follows orders. Will you come see me again?"

"Yes. Whenever I get the chance." She leaned in quickly and kissed him lightly on the cheek. "Don't let 'em hurt you, Jimmie."

The two men stood and stared after her as she glided from the room. The stab of disappointment Broder experienced was not far removed from true physical pain, like the proverbial sensation of a cold steel dagger in the chest, but this was balanced by the white heat of anger he felt toward himself for his own hopelessly bungling ineptitude.

"You're a lucky guy, Broder," Wilson said, almost in a whisper. "Man, what'd you ever do to deserve a woman like that?"

"There's nothing between us. Not anymore."

"Eyes confess the secrets of the heart, Broder, and your eyes tell me you're crazy about that girl. You gonna tell me about her, or not?"

"Nothing to tell."

"You keep on saying that and your tongue's going to get

all tangled up in your own lies. You might as well tell me the truth."

"It's a long story, Wilson."

"You and me got all day, Broder."

But Broder knew that Wilson wouldn't push it. There were secrets in his past he did not want to talk about, and Wilson would respect his silence—for now. His new friend would wait patiently, confident that he would need to talk sooner or later and determined to be there when that time came. In his awareness of this, Broder found some small solace.

❧

❧ *THE HOT CAROLINA* summer of 1989 would transform the lives of Donnie Shand and his three young compatriots in ways none of them could have imagined. They would come to look back on this dark season and ask how they could have permitted it to happen, how they could have let the innocence of childhood slip away so easily. But it was not complicated. Rather, it merely was a case of one thing leading to another in an unplanned progression of events until there was no undoing the damage.

Hot weather had come early to the Carolina coast, with spring rains sparse and signs of serious drought apparent by mid-May. Jimmie remarked that beach traffic already was at a volume normal for July and August. DJ said yes, he had noticed, and they ought to take advantage of it as soon as school was out for the summer. He had been working on a plan. And then, "We can get a ride to Myrtle Beach," as if somehow this should be understood as the first step in an elaborate if still-secret scheme.

"What do you want to go for?" This from Ray-Gene, the one who always would ask the obvious question and unintentionally red-flag the fallibility of DJ's designs.

"I'll tell you when we get there."

"How are we goin' to get a ride? We don't have a car and none of us could drive one if we did."

"My sister's boyfriend works for a dealer and moves cars around, Ray-Gene. Sometimes he goes to Myrtle Beach. He'll give us a ride." Donnie Shand stated these facts in a tone that warned against further discussion.

Ray-Gene meant to say more but thought better of it. He wouldn't press Donnie too hard without support, and none was forthcoming. Jimmie squeezed Colletta's arm, a cryptic signal they had developed that said — in this circumstance — "Let's just wait and see what happens."

Donnie's word proved good. Two weeks after the end of school, he announced that he'd arranged their first trip to the coast and the next day a slender, blond, acne-faced teenaged boy named Luther picked them up in an old but immaculate white Chrysler sedan and drove them to Myrtle Beach. Luther followed Donnie's directions without question. He went several blocks out of his way to drop them off on South Ocean Boulevard, just yards from the water's edge.

"Meet me back on this corner in an hour or you'll have to walk home," he advised sternly. "And be on time. The boss doesn't cut me much slack."

Parking lots of the better beach-front hotels were nearly full, with license plates from East Coast states, the Midwest, and Canada predominate. The clean, wide beach was busy with people but not crowded, and Donnie Shand led his followers down to the surf line and stood gazing out over the calm Atlantic. To anyone who noticed, they might have been awe-struck visitors, seeing the endless stretch of blue ocean for the first time.

Colletta looked at Jimmie with a quizzical expression. Jimmie shrugged his shoulders. Whatever DJ had in mind, they would wait for him to initiate any discussion.

A formation of brown pelicans skimmed the surface of the sea and Donnie watched in apparent fascination until one broke ranks and dived after a fish. Then, almost as if the plummeting bird had been the signal he needed, he turned his back to the water and looked to his right and left, up and down the broad expanse of tannish-white sandy shore. "There are a lot of rich people here," he said. "I'm fixin' to find a way we can make us some money here this summer, if y'all are interested. Let's just look around for a little bit and check things out."

He led them back to the high-tide mark, beyond which the dry sand was deep and loose and pulled doggedly at their feet. An old couple lay asleep on blankets in the shade of an enormous beach umbrella. The rhythmic roar of the surf drowned out the music from a radio that lay face-up between them. A bulky beach bag sat close beside the old woman's arm, a blue calfskin wallet clearly visible among an assortment of keys, lotions, tissues, glasses cases, other personal items. Without breaking stride, Donnie stooped and plucked the wallet from the bag.

Colletta gasped but said nothing. Neither Ray-Gene nor Jimmie uttered a sound. Donnie walked as fast as he could in the restraining sand, bounded up the half-dozen wooden steps that led up to street level, and collapsed onto a sun-bleached bench under a scrub palmetto.

"You can't do that!" Jimmie whispered hoarsely. "You can't steal from that old lady."

Donnie was visibly excited. His hands shook, his breath came in spasms like a spent animal's. "I don't know why I did it," he said. "I didn't mean to. I just saw it layin' there in plain sight. Anybody could have took it. Those old people ought to be more careful."

"That's no excuse," Colletta said. Her eyes flashed with anger. "We don't steal, DJ. We've never stole anything in our lives, and you know it. You've got to take it back."

Donnie Shand opened the wallet and poked through its contents, fingering a New Jersey driver's license and a Visa bank card, and charge cards from Saks Fifth Avenue and Bloomingdale's. There were photos of children, and what he quickly counted out as nearly one hundred dollars in cash. This was more money than Donnie had ever seen in a single stack of bills before, much less held in his hands.

"Don't even look at that money," Ray-Gene demanded. "It's not ours. Colletta's right, DJ, you have to give it back. You're gonna get us in all kinds of trouble."

"Shut up," Donnie snapped. "I'm not asking any of y'all to get involved. I took it and it's up to me to decide what to do with it." His voice rose in pitch, defiant, determined. "If you're scared, go on up there by the street corner and leave me alone."

The others knew that nothing they said would make any difference.

On the ride back to Conway, Ray-Gene, Colletta, and Jimmie slumped in the back seat of Luther's luxurious old Chrysler as if in mourning. Donnie Shand sat sullenly in the front passenger seat, staring silently through the side window, pretending interest in the passing scene.

"Did y'all have fun at the beach?" Luther asked.

No one responded.

"Y'all are a right gloomy lot. Excuse me for trying to make friendly conversation!"

"Yeah, we had fun," Donnie said. His tone was mocking, which led the exasperated Luther to say nothing more.

▸ *DONNIE SHAND'S* ill-gotten fortune lasted two days.

Ray-Gene rushed to forewarn him, in a voice quaking with both trepidation and despair, "I blurted out to Jaybo that you had money, DJ. I'm sorry, I didn't mean to do it, it just slipped out. Jaybo's gonna give you trouble, man. He knows you stole it so you can't tell anybody. I'm sorry, DJ. I didn't mean to. I wish I could take it back—"

"You're stupid, Ray-Gene. Why'd you go and tell Jaybo?"

"I told you. I just blurted it out without thinking. I didn't mean to do it, DJ. I swear I didn't."

"So what do you think Jaybo's goin' to do?"

"He said he'd take it. He meant it, too. Don't mess with Jaybo, DJ. Jaybo would hurt somebody bad for money like

33

that. And I'm afraid he might have followed me here."

On the last point, Ray-Gene proved to be wrong. The two boys cowered in a back room of the Shand house for the rest of the afternoon, surreptitiously slipping to a front window from time to time and furtively peeping out from behind the curtains. Jaybo was nowhere about.

But the following Monday, after Ray-Gene stopped by to ask DJ to go with him to the grocery store and pick up some sugar for Grandma Freeman, their luck changed. Jaybo was waiting, sitting menacingly on the curb in front of the house. He stood as they came closer and surveyed them with cold, calculating eyes. "Say, young Donnie, Ray-Gene tells me you come into some money recently," he said in a low voice. "Is he telling me straight?"

"Leave us alone, Jaybo," Ray-Gene pleaded. "DJ's money is none of your business."

Jaybo grabbed Ray-Gene by the collar and pulled him close. "Don't give me no trouble, little man," he demanded. "This is just between Donnie and me." He pushed Ray-Gene hard and his nephew went sprawling on the concrete. "Now, like I was saying, young Donnie, was Ray-Gene here telling me straight? You got some money or not?"

Under Jaybo's withering stare, Donnie Shand's resolve instantly faded. He admitted that he had money, knowing full well that this was something Jaybo already knew. Jaybo threatened to tell Donnie's mother and maybe even call the police and warned Donnie that he was sure to spend time in jail for stealing from old people. Donnie accepted without resistance Jaybo's offer to keep his mouth shut for three-fourths of the money Donnie stole.

"You understand, I'm being generous because you and Ray-Gene are friends," Jaybo said. "I'm not taking all your money. And I think I'll throw in a little something for your trouble."

Donnie showed up at Grandma Freeman's house an hour later with seventy dollars in hand, as promised. Jaybo was waiting on the front steps. He grabbed the money and slapped Donnie on the shoulder.

"You're a wise man, young Donnie," Jaybo said. "Now I won't have to make no trouble for you. You know what? I kind of like you, little man. You and me would get along just fine if we tried real hard. What say we be friends—work together, you know?"

"Sure, Jaybo," Donnie said somberly.

"Now look here, since you were cooperative and all and didn't make it hard for me, I'm going to give you a little something for your trouble." Jaybo drew a small white packet from the front of his shirt and held it toward Donnie. "Here. This is good stuff. Try it and see if you don't like it."

Donnie accepted what he'd been offered without saying anything more. On his way home he threw it in the gutter. He didn't know what it was, but intuition told him that anything coming from Jaybo was not something good. He was furious over the loss of his money, furious at Ray-Gene for telling Jaybo, and furious at himself for giving up so easily. He had only just begun to consider how he would spend the money and now it was gone.

The next day, Ray-Gene, consumed with guilt, told Jimmie and Colletta everything that had happened, beginning with how he had inadvertently let DJ's secret slip and how quick Jaybo had picked up on it. He felt terrible about what he'd done. He knew better than to tell Jaybo, of course, knew that to his bullying uncle his blunder had extended an open invitation to pounce on Donnie Shand and take advantage of the younger boy's predicament. No moral compunction stood in Jaybo's way, and no fear. He knew that he could strong-arm Donnie without the slightest danger of ever having to answer for his deed.

"Don't be so hard on yourself," Colletta urged. "DJ ought not to have stole that money in the first place. There wasn't any good that could have come from it."

"Colletta's right," Jimmie said. "DJ had no right to that

old lady's money. We should have told somebody."

"Yeah, but not Jaybo," Ray-Gene said.

"We should have persuaded DJ to give the money back," Colletta argued. "It's not in his nature to steal. We shouldn't have stood by and let him get hisself in trouble like that."

"But once we got back home there wasn't any way for him to give it back, Colletta," Ray-Gene said. "He couldn't have found them old people if he'd wanted to. And y'all know we wasn't going to tell on DJ, get him in that kind of trouble. I just wish we wouldn't have gone to Myrtle Beach in the first place."

"I have to admit I kinda feel sorry for DJ," Jimmie said. "I don't think he meant to steal that money. It was just too easy. And then once we got in the car and started back, there wasn't anything he could do. He might have done something good with it if Jaybo hadn't took it from him."

Colletta was coming around. She hated to disagree with Ray-Gene and Jimmie. "I feel sorry for him, too," she admitted. "DJ tries hard to do right, but it's not been easy for him. 'Specially since that thing with his daddy."

Ray-Gene put his strong arms over Colletta's and Jimmie's shoulders like Donnie Shand would have and the three stood side-by-side, in a crescent, leaning their heads forward as if in a football huddle. Jimmie let his breath out in a long, audible sigh. "We're all in this together," he said. "DJ's still our best friend and you know he wouldn't let any of us down. We need to help him out."

"Help him how?" Colletta asked. "We can't make Jaybo give him his money back."

"But we can help him get some more," Ray-Gene said. "That's what I'm goin' to do. It's my fault he lost it, and I'm goin' to help him get some more."

"Like I said, we're all in this together," Jimmie repeated. "We'll all help DJ. You with us, Colletta?"

"I am, but I don't know what you have in mind."

"Whatever it takes."

"Jaybo knows how to get money," Ray-Gene said. "He may do bad things, but he knows how to get money. He didn't have to take DJ's 'cause he gets plenty. I don't know how, but I know he always has it."

"But I'd hate to get messed up with Jaybo," Jimmie said. "There has got to be some other way. Colletta, what do you think?"

"Go ahead and ask Jaybo," Colletta said, speaking directly to Ray-Gene. "He might have some ideas we wouldn't think of. If we're going to get DJ's money back, somebody's going to have to tell us how to do it."

❧4❧

APTAIN HOMER OATES had none of Colonel Hewlett's pleasant demeanor. He was almost the colonel's exact opposite in physical stature, short and squat, with broad shoulders and a thick, bull-like neck. He had a large, cleanly shaved head, a wide, flat face marked by a fat nose and narrow gray eyes that were all but invisible behind what seemed to be a permanent scowl.

Rondell Wilson had alerted his favorite patient: "Watch out for Oates, Broder, he's a mean SOB. He always has the red-ass for somebody. Just hope it ain't you!"

From the minute Oates walked into the room, Broder felt himself on the defensive. The captain's tone was accusatory. There was no indication of the sympathy Colonel Hewlett had expressed for Broder's injuries, no underlying appeal for facts that might help save another paratrooper from going through what he had. No, Captain Homer Oates simply was here to place blame.

"There's a lot of ground we need to cover, Broder," the captain said. "And I don't want to have to go over any of this more than once. Understand?"

"Yes, sir."

"Had you been drinking the night you made that bad jump?"

"Absolutely not, captain. There's no way I'd ever drink when we were scheduled for an exercise."

"How about drugs? Do you use drugs, Broder?"

"No!"

"So your head was clear that night? No alcohol, no drugs involved. Is that what you're saying?"

"Yes, sir. That's exactly what I'm saying."

"That's good, Sergeant Broder. Because if I find out you used drugs or alcohol before a jump I'll have you in civilian clothes before the end of the week! Understand me?"

"Yes, sir. I understand you."

Broder was livid. He was astonished by Oates's attitude, the captain's obvious intention to make him liable, somehow, for the bad jump. Hadn't Colonel Hewlett said plainly that no one thought the hard landing was his fault? What the hell was going on? *He's really out to get me. Be careful, he'll twist anything I say and try to use it against me.*

"I don't know what you've heard about me," Oates said loudly, "but I'm the last man in Uncle Sam's Army you want to cross. I play fair, but with me you get hardball all the way. Until I know for sure what happened out there that night everything's on the table. You understand what I'm saying?"

"I understand, captain, but you're on the wrong track."

"Are you a career man, Broder?"

"Yes, sir. I've pretty much decided to stay."

"Even if you can't jump?"

"I'd never considered that—not getting to jump."

"Well, you'd better start thinking about it, Broder. I may not know yet what you did out there, but this much I know for certain: With that leg, your jumping days are finished."

Broder was jarred by the captain's words. In spite of the pain and slow realization that his injuries were severe, he'd refused to think about the possible long-term consequences of his hard landing. Airborne was his life. What would he do if he couldn't jump?

"One more thing," the captain said. "Broder—is that a South Carolina name, sergeant?"

"Yes, captain, I'm from South Carolina."

"I thought so. I know several important people in South

Carolina. I think I'll find out if they ever heard of you."

Captain Oates left the room as he had entered, antagonistic and unrelenting. In his view, it seemed, accidents did not just happen. Someone caused them, and he was determined to point an accusing finger. Like a combative bull terrier, he would not turn loose until his opponent was fully subdued, and it was pretty clear that in this instance he saw Broder as his opponent.

Rondell Wilson had waited outside the door, all ears. He slipped quietly into the room and approached Broder gingerly. "I'm sorry," he said, "it looks like that nasty son'bitch has got it in for you. I was afraid of that. But don't worry, much as he'd like to he can't hang anything on you. It wasn't your fault."

"You know what, Wilson—if I can't jump again I don't care. If they want to blame me for what happened, screw 'em. Screw Oates, screw the 82nd Airborne Division, screw the whole goddammed United States Army!"

"I know how you feel. But I'll bet that Colonel Hewlett will take care of Oates pretty quick. I think the colonel is a fair guy, Broder."

"Like I said, I don't really care."

Broder wanted and needed a long, rough session in rehab, a forced jaunt on the treadmill, anything that would bring on enough physical pain to override his anger and the dejection he felt after the captain's pronouncement on his jumpless future. Unfortunately, though, the day's prescribed activities were finished and Rondell Wilson's duty stint was over.

"Don't let Oates get you down," Wilson said. "And don't get down on yourself. First thing we have to worry about is getting you back in shape, and on that front the battle goes on. I'll be around in the morning to pick up right where we left off."

Broder would be left alone with his thoughts during the long, restless night. He felt isolated and helpless, his mind awash in a roiling mixture of doubt and apprehension. It was as if that single bad jump had stripped his life of every promise. He craved a consoling voice, the simple nearness of another human being. As always, his thoughts soon turned to Colletta. He thought about the child. He wondered where Colletta was and who she was with. Her last visit had been cut short, interrupted by his therapy, giving them precious little time to talk. And he must have looked like a fool in his awkwardness; this was Colletta, but he had reacted to her as he might have to a stranger. He longed to see her again, to have another chance. Would she come back? And if she did, where would it lead?

Sometime between darkness and light, when he should be waking, Broder finally slept.

JAYBO DID NOT offer the money-making scheme that Ray-Gene, Colletta, and Jimmie had hoped for. When Ray-Gene tried to ask, timidly, without revealing that they wanted the money for Donnie Shand, Jaybo laughed at him, told him to get lost. Jaybo already had made clear that the subject of Donnie's money was never to be brought up, and you stayed away from things that Jaybo didn't want to talk about.

But Ray-Gene still was burdened with guilt, and he was adamant with Colletta and Jimmie. "It has been almost two weeks and we still don't have a plan," he complained. "We got to come up with something, right now. I keep thinking about what DJ said, down on the beach—that there was lots of rich people there and he was goin' to find a way for us to make money off 'em."

"That ain't no help, Ray-Gene," Colletta said. "He didn't say how he planned to do it."

Ray-Gene shrugged. "Maybe he'll tell us what he had in mind. Don't you think so, Jimmie?"

"I don't believe DJ had a plan," Jimmie said. "I know it's not right, but if we could get back to the beach maybe we could pick up a dollar or two here and there the same way

DJ did." Colletta and Ray-Gene frowned, but before they could assert their objections, Jimmie shushed them: "Y'all wait a minute. I said it's not right. But we knew it wasn't right, what DJ did in the first place. And we still promised to do something to get his money back, didn't we? I ain't talking about stealing money from some old lady again. I was just thinking we could pick up a little bit at a time, maybe even come right out and ask people for money if we have to."

"How are we going to get back to the beach?" Colletta's question manifested acquiescence. She was reluctant, but she had been as determined as Jimmie or Ray-Gene to get Donnie Shand's money back and she had come up with no other ideas about how to do it.

"I s'pose we could call Luther again," Jimmie said. "I'll bet he goes over there about every day. Don't you think he'd give us a ride, like before?"

"You know how to get to Luther?" Ray-Gene asked.

"I know where he works."

Ray-Gene and Colletta, however much they might protest later, were relieved. They had vowed to get the money for Donnie Shand and agonized over the challenge until it loomed insurmountably large, and for the time being they were willing to ignore all the conspicuous pitfalls in what Jimmie proposed.

Colletta had insisted in the beginning that they not tell Donnie what they meant to do; they should wait and surprise him with the money. The boys had voiced no objection then but now they weren't so sure. This was something new, and Donnie Shand was the one they always had relied on to lead them into untested waters. Certainly waters as murky as these.

Jimmie began to rationalize: "None of us knows Luther. DJ's the one that knows him."

First Ray-Gene, then Colletta fell into line. They ought to bring Donnie in on their plan in any case, because he'd feel better just knowing they wanted to get his money back. He would be their leader again. They hadn't the temerity to admit that they needed DJ to help them figure out how to approach people and ask for money, though they all knew that if there was anyone who had a knack for such things it would be Donnie Shand.

☙ *LIKE JAYBO*, unfortunately, Donnie did not respond the way they had hoped. "It'd just be begging," he proclaimed. "Y'all probably would get throwed off the beach, for starters. They don't allow no beggars on the beach. Don't you know anything?"

"We wanted to get your money back, is all," Ray-Gene said. He was not defiant, and Colletta and Jimmie detected a note of supplication in his voice. "We just couldn't think of any other way to do it."

"Well, that way won't work," Donnie told him, this time more softly.

For his part, DJ already had made up his mind. He intended to get his money back the same way he got it the first time, with or without the help of his friends. Stealing cash from the old woman on the beach was an act he had committed on the spur of the moment, with no prior intent, but he'd been astonished at how easy it was. His initial pangs of conscience had evaporated quickly once the money was in his hands. And his team would play along, whatever their individual reservations.

Jimmie, in desperation, already had declared himself willing to snatch money from people on the beach. Colletta had promised to help and would stick to her word. Ray-Gene felt strongly that what they were about to do was wrong, but it was his fault that Donnie lost the money to Jaybo in the first place and he considered himself more obligated than anyone to help get it back. He would not let DJ down again. They were a team again and this would be a team action. The scheme no longer was open to discussion.

44

ʘ DONNIE SHAND proved masterful at the plotting and planning necessary to get them to the coast, conning rides from Luther when he could, sometimes mandating that they hitchhike. They set their sights on South Carolina's crowded Grand Strand beaches, careful not to be seen frequently on the same stretch of glistening sands because, as Donnie explained, "We don't want anybody to get to rememberin' us."

The team approached its dishonorable endeavor like toddlers taking tentative first steps, and after three days on the beach had little to show for its effort. Donnie demanded a review session. What had they done wrong? What had they done right? How could they do it better? By the end of the week they had perfected their method and not only become confident, but in some instances recklessly daring. Harried women with little ones to look after were an easy touch for Colletta, who made a fuss over the cute children and distracted proud mothers while the boys ambled by and stealthily made off with purses and beachbags. They took only cash, even the nickels and dimes, and hurried on along the beach like other frolicking teenagers.

Donnie Shand kept careful account of the money. None of the others dared ask how big their take had been, though by the end of the third week they'd begun to wonder if they weren't getting close to replacing what Jaybo had taken. When Donnie signaled an end to the day's work, they huddled in the shade of a barnacle-encrusted fishing pier, just above the high-water line of a gently lapping surf. Donnie grinned in a satisfied way they hadn't seen for a long time.

"It's time we divided up the money," he said. "I never intended to keep it all myself—just to take care of it till we had enough to worry about. Well, y'all are going to be surprised to hear we made nearly a hundred dollars this week. With what we already had, that makes more'n fifty dollars apiece."

Colletta flared. "Damn you, DJ! Why didn't you tell us

when you got your money back? You know that's what we all agreed to. You had no right to keep us out there stealing once you got your seventy dollars!"

"I never agreed to any limit like that!"

"You did and you know it. Do you think we're a bunch of complete fools?"

"Now look, Colletta, I admit that's all I planned to do in the beginning. But you've seen how easy it is! How else're we ever gonna have a chance at money like this? You ain't ever had fifty dollars in your whole life."

Colletta spun on her heel and marched swiftly up the beach, away from the three boys.

"She's right, DJ," Ray-Gene said. "You should've let us know when you got back your money. That's all we ever promised to do." Jimmie nodded in agreement.

Donnie Shand stood awkwardly, his face marked by an expression of uncertainty. Waters of a rising tide swirled around his bare feet. He clamped his jaw firmly, a sign of determination Ray-Gene and Jimmie were familiar with, and they knew Donnie's mind was made up. Fire and brimstone would not dislodge him from the stance he was about to reveal. "Y'all can do whatever you want," he said. "I'm not fixin' to quit. I can do it by myself and keep all the money, or we can be a team like we've always been. I don't care one way or another." He turned and walked after Colletta. After a moment's hesitation, Ray-Gene and Jimmie followed.

Luther picked them up at the prescribed street corner at the appointed time in a sky-blue Mercury. They rode back to Conway in painful silence.

Donnie wasn't seen again for days. In the meantime, his team commiserated over the way they had been duped and promised one another that they never would be fooled by Donnie Shand again. But no one mentioned the subject when Donnie eventually showed up; he said nothing of the money and they were afraid to ask. Colletta's newest threat never to associate with him again soon was forgotten, along with his pledge to keep on stealing on the beach without them. Jimmie and Ray-Gene chose to pretend that none of the summer's shameful activities even had taken place. In any case, they soon were overwhelmed by a startling new and unexpected turn of events.

  ✍ *"WE'RE MOVING,"* Colletta told them tearfully. "My daddy says we're moving back to Georgetown so he can get a job on a fishing boat. But I don't want to leave y'all, you're the best friends I'll ever have."

The three boys sat as if dumbstruck until Donnie Shand felt obligated to speak: "How come it took him so long to decide?"

"When my grandma died, they sold her big old house in McClellanville. Daddy said as soon as we get the money, we will move to Georgetown."

"How long will it take to get the money, you think?" Ray-Gene asked. "Are you goin' to be moving right now?"

"I don't know how long. But Daddy says the sooner, the better."

Jimmie said nothing. He suddenly felt as though all the air had been sucked from his lungs and the blood from his veins. Colletta had been a constant element in his life for almost as far back as he could remember. He was closer to her than to either Ray-Gene or Donnie Shand, although this was something he had not realized until this very minute. Ray-Gene and Donnie were friends, but Colletta was dear to his heart.

He understood, for the first time, that he *loved* Colletta. Not just as a friend, but as a girl.

✄5✄

R ONDELL WILSON worried about Broder, who for the past week had grown more moody and dispirited by the hour and only half-heartedly went through the motions of the demanding physical therapy that was his only hope for full recovery. The young sergeant did as he was told, but Wilson no longer saw the determination that had marked Broder's early days on the orthopedic ward and made Wilson proud to be part of his rehab team. Wilson was close to Broder. Too close, in fact. He was beginning to find it hard to maintain the professional detachment he needed in order to do his job.

"You're never going to get out of this place, Broder, if you don't work harder," Wilson threatened. "Do you know what I think? I think you're lazy!"

"Think whatever you like," Broder replied, his voice flat and without feeling.

This was not the kind of response Wilson had hoped for. He wanted Broder angry. He could work with anger, stretch it into something powerful and mold it into tenacity. A tenacious patient could be energized to work harder toward rehabilitation, and rehabilitation was Wilson's job.

"You up to a good workout today?" he asked.

"Whatever you say."

"I could use a little more enthusiasm."

"Tell me what to do and I'll do it."

"Heard anything more from Captain Oatmeal?"

"No."

"When's your girlfriend coming back?"

"I don't have a girlfriend, Wilson. I've told you that."

"You know who I'm talking about. And you're not fooling me with that 'There's nothing between us' crap."

"Like I've said before, there's nothing between us."

Wilson had bided his time, willing to wait until Broder wanted to talk to him about Colletta. But given the extent of his patient's injuries, full rehabilitation was a challenge under the best of circumstances. If Colletta was at the heart of Broder's problem he was reluctant to wait any longer.

"Okay, Broder," he said, "let's lay it on the line. Something's eating at you. My guess is it's one of three things. Either it's Captain Oates's petty little smear campaign, or the threat that you'll never jump again, or it's the girl. You're pissed at Oates, you're worried about your future in Airborne, and that girl you're crazy about hasn't been back to see you. Am I on the playing field?"

"Okay, so I'm pissed at Oates," Broder said placidly. "Me and about half the other guys in the 82nd Airborne Division, no doubt."

"So that's your problem?"

"If you insist I've got a problem, that's my problem."

"And the girl?"

"There's no girl to talk about, Wilson."

"Yeah, well let's get you down to PT and you can try again to sell me on that one. But I already told you, you're not fooling me. Now get a move on!"

It was no secret to Wilson that Broder's first early morning steps on the treadmill were still pure torture. He'd heard too many times from too many patients how the pain shot up and down a patched-together leg like a high-voltage electrical impulse. He had seen the tears that stung Broder's eyes, watched him grit his teeth to hide the hurt. Even so, Wilson kept up his tough front. He badgered his patient mercilessly, challenged him to do more: "Come on Broder, put out! Act like you're Airborne! How in the hell did they ever make a paratrooper out of you, anyway?"

When the long session ended, Wilson was encouraged. Broder had shown an occasional flash of fighting spirit, more determination to tackle the hard work he'd have to do to regain use of his crumpled leg and get back on his feet. Broder very well might understand his little game but that didn't matter so long as he responded.

Rondell Wilson fancied himself unusually perceptive in understanding what made other people tick. It was pathetically simple in this case; he could read Broder like an open book. Although Captain Oates and the threat he posed to a future in Airborne had Broder worried, Oates wasn't the real problem. It was Colletta who caused Broder's melancholy and endangered his will to recover. Or, more accurately, the absence of Colletta. Every day, Wilson had hoped fervently that she would show up again.

But it was not Colletta who waited for them upstairs. It was Captain Homer Oates, who stood scowling in a corner of Broder's room. "Stay cool, man," Wilson whispered. "I won't be far away." He stayed just outside the door, straining to hear. The captain made it easy, wasting no time on small talk but going straight to the point in a loud voice that to Wilson sounded almost gleeful.

"I've found out some interesting things about you, Sergeant Broder," Oates said. "It seems there's a certain Judge Pillory down in South Carolina who knows you pretty well. I know things about you that I'll bet you didn't tell your momma!"

❧

❧ RAY-GENE, in his usual sweet manner, tried to put the best face on Colletta's news. "It'll be fun moving to a new place," he told her. "And we'll all come see you sometime. I'll bet old Luther could drive us over there if we asked him to. Maybe you could even get us a ride on that fishing boat your daddy's going' to be working on!"

"Sure, Colletta," Donnie Shand said, "You're going to like

Georgetown. When my dad was still here we used to go there all the time to visit my mother's Aunt Pearl. There's plenty of boats in Georgetown, too."

"I can see all the boats I want on the Waccamaw River," Colletta said. "I don't need to go to Georgetown for boats. I don't think you even care I'm moving away!"

"I care," Jimmie said. "We all care, Colletta. We care a lot. Right, DJ?"

"Sure we do. I didn't mean it like we don't care. I was just trying to make you feel better, Colletta. If your daddy says you've got to move you don't get a say and you might as well make the best of it. That's all I meant." It clearly had hurt Donnie to be misunderstood, but he brightened again with a new idea. "We'll get you a present before you go. Maybe even have you a party."

"Sure, Colletta," Ray-Gene said, "we'll all get you a nice present before you go."

"Y'all don't need to do that," Colletta said. "It's good of you to think about it, but you needn't go to all that trouble. I'd like it if you could come see me in Georgetown, though."

Nothing Donnie Shand or Ray-Gene could say would bring solace to Jimmie. Merely the thought of not seeing Colletta every day was unbearable. He lay awake that night until almost daybreak, hurting in a way he never had hurt before. Now he understood a simple truth: The promise of seeing Colletta had been his reason to get out of bed in the morning, to go to school when it was in session, to look forward to the next day when he went to sleep at night. Colletta had become the center of his happiness. If she moved away, he could hardly imagine that he would want to go on living.

Every day, Jimmie expected the worst. Colletta would say the time had come. Although she still was there when school opened for the fall semester it was only because the sale of her grandmother's house had fallen through when the buyer's loan application was turned down. But another family was interested and Mr. Saylor said he was confident that the house was about to sell; he warned his daughter to be ready to leave Conway forever.

Jimmie was grateful for the reprieve, even if it might be short-lived. He walked with Colletta to school every morning and back home in the afternoon. When they were in a classroom together he always took a seat alongside or right behind her. They sat side-by-side in the cafeteria at lunch. He ached to tell Colletta how he felt, that he was in love with her and would rather die than have her move away because life without her would be unbearable.

Day after day he struggled to get up his nerve, but day after day his courage failed. What if Colletta thought him foolish? What if she laughed at him?

For her part, Colletta kept him up to date about what was going on. "My daddy and momma are going to Georgetown tomorrow to look for somewhere for us to live," she told him on a Friday afternoon, apprehension lining her face.

"What if they find a place?"

Colletta quickly looked away, but he already had seen that her eyes glistened with tears. He took her hand and held tight, then put his arm across her shoulders. Colletta leaned against him and her slender body began to tremble with the force of her sobs.

"Don't cry, Colletta," Jimmie urged. "It will be all right. Please don't cry."

"It won't be all right. I love you, Jimmie. I don't want to move away from Conway. What are we going to do?"

"I love you, too, Colletta. You know I do."

"I don't mean like a friend, Jimmie. I mean I really love you."

"I know. I really love you, too. If you moved away I don't think I could stand not seeing you every day."

They stood for a long time, holding each other tightly. Colletta lay her head on his shoulder. Jimmie felt an elation such as he never had experienced before. For this moment in time, the future he dreaded so terribly much didn't matter. He held Colletta in his arms and she loved him the same way he loved her.

* *JIMMIE WALKED* on air. Ray-Gene noticed, and said he looked all cheerful for some reason. Jimmie said it was Ray-Gene's imagination.

"Yeah, well, you're happy about something," Ray-Gene insisted. "I know you, Jimmie Broder. I can see it on your face, whether you own up to it or not. Anyway, there's stuff I need to talk to you about. Me and DJ have been talking about getting that present for Colletta. Y'all want to do it too, right?"

"Sure I do."

Ray-Gene was visibly excited. He'd never given a present to anyone outside his family, and then only at Christmas. He had jewelry in mind, something nice, something silver or gold. Ravonelle had told him that girls could keep jewelry forever and always remember who gave it to them and he liked to think about Colletta having their present forever and remembering years from now that it came from the old team in Conway, and didn't Jimmie think that was a good idea?

"Yes, it sounds good," Jimmie said.

"DJ said don't worry about the money," Ray-Gene told him. "He's still got plenty."

"That's the money we helped him steal, Ray-Gene."

"That doesn't matter now, Jimmie. If we're going to get something for Colletta we have to pay for it. Some of that money ought to be hers, anyway."

The discussion was hard for Jimmie, because it forced him once again to face the reality of Colletta's leaving. He had refused to look ahead to that day, even though he had come to accept its inevitability, particularly after the Saylors found a place they wanted in Georgetown and Mr. Saylor said they could get it as soon as the sale closed on the house in McClellanville. Jimmie tried hard not to let Ray-Gene see the pain he felt in his heart.

The next day, the three boys went to a mall and paid almost forty dollars for a pretty sterling silver bracelet. A helpful saleswoman assured them it was an appropriate present for someone moving away. Donnie had it wrapped and tied with yellow ribbon. They took their gift to Colletta, who was deeply moved and promised to keep the bracelet as long as she lived and said she would never, ever forget them. Even Donnie Shand, usually stoic, became emotional. "The team won't be the same without you, Colletta," he said, then turned and walked away quickly to hide his distress. Ray-Gene promptly followed.

Colletta and Jimmie were left alone. They sat in the lush grass under the chinaberry tree in Colletta's backyard, close together so that their bare arms touched. The day was hot, although the sky was overcast, and oppressively humid.

"They say there's a big storm coming," Colletta said.

"Are you afraid?"

"I don't even care. Jimmie, all I can think about is having to move away."

Jimmie put his hand on Colletta's smaller one. "We can write every day," he said. "I'll find some way to get down to Georgetown to see you, and it won't be long before we're grown up and I'll have a car and everything and after that nobody can keep us apart."

"That seems so far off. But I'll write, too. Every day."

"I just wish you didn't have to move."

"I don't want to. If I had a grandma or somebody who lived in Conway, I'd stay. Even a cousin. But there's nobody for me to live with."

"I wish you could come and live at our house."

"You know I can't do that."

"We'll get married as soon as we're old enough."

"Promise?"

"Of course I do. I promise, Colletta."

Robert Hays

WHEN THE BIG storm hit, Conway was spared its worst fury. Hurricane Hugo slammed into the coast further south and wrought massive damage. McClellanville was virtually annihilated.

The storm destroyed the grand old house Colletta's father had hoped to sell and left only a vacant lot that was of little value and mounds of rubble to be disposed of. With no insurance on the property, Jacob Saylor saw his dreams of a cash infusion and a chance to start over in another town dashed in Hugo's destruction. He leaned heavier than ever on his old crutch, the bottle, and grew uglier in disposition with every passing day. Little Hunter was terrified of him, and even Colletta came to fear him when he was at his worst. The occasional dark mood they'd learned long ago to be wary of became his normal, everyday state.

Colletta was too embarrassed to tell anyone what was going on. She worried about Hunter, though, and in the end that worry led her to confide in Jimmie.

"You don't really think your daddy would hurt Hunter, do you?" Jimmie asked. "Your daddy's never been like that before."

"He wouldn't do it on purpose," Colletta said, "but when he's drunk sometimes he loses control. He gets awful impatient with Hunter and I'm scared he might do something he didn't mean to and Hunter might be right in the middle of it. Hunter's still such a little boy, Jimmie. It wouldn't take much at all to hurt him bad."

Jimmie's ecstasy that Colletta wouldn't be moving away was tempered by a new anxiety. He was not so much afraid for Hunter as for Colletta. What if her concern for Hunter caused her to do something reckless? What if she tried to interfere with Mr. Saylor in one of his drunken rages? His mind flashed back to that gruesome scene years earlier in front of Donnie Shand's house. He imagined Colletta being the one struck instead of Donnie's father, and in his mind's eye he saw her lying crumpled on the ground, not moving.

56

It was a haunting image he could not shake.

He felt sure he should tell someone about Colletta's situation—an adult, a person who could do something to help—but Colletta had asked him not to and he'd agreed to keep her secret. He'd be careful not to say anything to DJ or Ray-Gene. He was enormously conflicted, proud that Colletta trusted him enough to tell him what was going on but very much afraid something bad would happen. He could never forgive himself if it did. How could he live with the fact that he might have prevented it but did nothing?

Over time, relieved that she had someone to share things with, Colletta came to talk more freely with Jimmie about her homelife. She told him when her father lost his job, and how her mother didn't earn enough to support the family working part-time at an IGA supermarket. She admitted that sometimes there was little or no food on the table.

Jimmie turned to his mother. Allou Broder would never abide letting a child go hungry.

"Yes, you can bring Colletta home for supper any time you want," she told him. "We don't have a lot, but we share what we have. She's always welcome at our table."

"Can she come tonight?"

"Yes, of course."

"Can she bring Hunter?"

"Yes, Jimmie, she can bring her brother. Tell them to be here at six o'clock. I'll cook some ham hocks with blackeyed peas and make grits and biscuits and gravy. There will be plenty to go around."

❧6❧

RONDELL WILSON hurried to catch her in the corridor before she could get to Broder's room. He greeted her lightly, "Hey, Colletta. Nice to see you again."

"Hey, yourself, Wilson. How's your favorite patient?"

"Broder? He's no favorite of mine." But Wilson's broad grin gave him away.

"Like hell he's not," Colletta said. "You like him as much as he likes you. And he likes you a lot. He told me so."

"Sure he did. Anyway, who believes anything he says?"

"No kidding, Wilson. How's he doing?"

Wilson turned serious. He put a hand on Colletta's arm and looked her straight in the eye. "He's still in for some hard time, Colletta," he said. "He is at that point now where there's not going to be any dramatic progress. In the beginning, just being able to walk was a huge accomplishment. Now, it's slow going. Broder's tough, but he's like everybody else: He gets discouraged. He worries a lot about his future. Do all you can to cheer him up, okay?"

"I'll do my best."

She waited at the door while Wilson, in his rambling, long-gaited walk, made his way on down the hall, away from Broder's room. She waited an instant longer, inhaled a deep breath, and made sure she wore her best smile when she entered. Broder lay with his face toward the window. She thought he was asleep but as she slipped quietly past the foot of his bed he looked up, his eyes widening.

"Hey, Jimmie. How ya' doin'?"

"They say I'm making progress. Some days it's hard to tell. Wilson knows, though."

Colletta stooped and kissed him softly on the forehead. "You're looking great," she said. "Wilson says you're coming along real good."

"I didn't know if you'd come back."

"I told you I would. I would have been back sooner, but it's hard to find the time. I've had to put in a bunch of extra hours at work. I can't afford to turn it down when I get the chance."

"I'm glad you came, Colletta. I wanted to see you again."

"Me, too. We didn't have much time to talk when I was here last."

"How's the boy?"

"He's doing good. I wish you could see him"

Broder took her hand. "How've you been? Really? It has been such a long time . . ." He stopped in mid-sentence, let his eyes run over her face. She still looked like a schoolgirl, hardly changed from those long-ago days in Conway before their lives had been so abruptly ripped apart.

"I'm clean now, Jimmie, if that's what you're asking. It will never be easy, but I'm in control of my life again and things are going okay."

"I didn't mean that, but I'm glad. You couldn't begin to know how often I've thought about you, wondered how things were working out."

"I've thought about you, too."

Broder pulled himself up to a sitting position and swung his heavy leg-cast over the edge of his bed. He grasped the hospital robe that Wilson was careful to place on a chair at his bedside, within easy arm's reach, and pulled it around his shoulders. He asked Colletta to retrieve a pair of aluminum crutches that stood against the wall in a corner of the room while he struggled up from the bed. He fitted the crutches under his arms and motioned toward the door.

"Let's take a walk down the hall," he said. "I'm supposed

to do this more often than I do but I usually don't have anyone to walk with me. And who wants to walk alone!"

"Doesn't Wilson get you up and around?"

"Yes, but he's got other things to do. He says he can't be
nursemaid to me all day."

"Oh, yeah, I can hear Wilson saying that. He pretends to
give you a hard time, I know, but he seems to take his work
very seriously. I'm glad you have somebody good to look
after you."

They made their way deliberately down the hallway,
past a quiet nurses' station and patient rooms, mostly empty,
to a small visitors' lounge. Even though no one was in the
room, a television set blared from the corner, broadcasting a
used car commercial to any who might "need new wheels
from the man who deals." Colletta turned it off. She held
Broder's crutches while he gingerly lowered himself onto a
vinyl-clad sofa, leaned heavily against the arm and extended his leg-cast sideways toward the opposite end. She
pulled a chair close, facing him.

"Is there anything you need that I can bring next time I
come?" she asked.

"No, but it's sweet of you to ask. They take pretty good
care of me here."

"How's your momma, Jimmie?"

Broder told her about his mother's recent health problems, minor so far, and injuries his father had suffered in
an accident that involved a drunk driver, how his father
had missed work because of it and had trouble getting a
settlement from the insurance company. He made conversation with these personal family reports, but it was not
personal conversation.

"I didn't know," Colletta said. "I remember your daddy
always worked so hard. And you know how much I loved
your momma. She was always good to me. Did you know
she sent me money when I was in Wilmington?"

"No. She never told me."

"She stayed in touch for a long time. That's how I kept up with your whereabouts in the beginning. But I hadn't heard from her in several months before I moved last time. I worried that something might have happened. It's been a long time since I was back there."

"Back 'there'? Meaning Conway?"

"Yes. I'm not so sure I could face it, Jimmie. Too many ghosts."

"We had some good times, too. I wish we could go back and do it all different, take away that terrible thing, but we don't get to live our lives over again."

She paled at his words. Her reaction was barely perceptible, but Broder saw. He had been thoughtless and said the wrong things. He wished he could go back and begin over, this time be more careful. He had wanted so desperately to see her, waiting and hoping through empty days, and now that she was here he'd surely made her sorry she came.

Colletta looked away. "We were foolish children," she said. "We did things we knew were wrong because we could get away with it, and then it all caught up with us. We can't blame anyone else, Jimmie. We never gave ourselves much of a chance. Still, if I'd been stronger . . ."

"I'm sorry. I didn't mean to open painful wounds."

"You can't open a wound that's never healed. Pain is like a circle in the water, Jimmie, after something makes a splash. It just keeps on growing, like it'll go on forever."

"But in the end it runs itself out."

"Yes, but if the splash is big enough it can pull you under at the start."

"You didn't get pulled under, Colletta."

"But I wanted to, and I almost did."

≈

DONNIE SHAND dropped out of school early in ninth grade. Once he had a driver's license, no amount of pleading from his mother, no logical argument from his sisters, no admonishment from school authority could persuade him otherwise. He inherited Luther's job at the auto dealer soon after that.

Money in his pocket and a car. These had always been at the top of Donnie's priority list. Now he had both.

Ray-Gene and Jimmie envied him, happy that he had what he wanted. They lived vicariously through the assorted automobiles they saw DJ driving like his own.

Even Colletta was impressed when he showed up one day at the end of school in a two-year-old Mustang coupe, bright yellow with black racing stripes, and announced that it would be his until the dealer sold it on the lot or shipped it off to a Charlotte wholesaler's auction. Ray-Gene and Jimmie crawled into the cramped back seat of the Mustang and let her sit up front.

Colletta and Jimmie were supposed to go by the IGA after school and pick up groceries, and DJ was proud to offer them a lift. "She can get her stuff and then I'll give her a ride home," he said. "That's better than packin' a heavy sack of potatoes all the way to her house, right Jimmie?" It was clear that he wanted to appear nonchalant as he chauffeured them to the supermarket. He and Ray-Gene waited in the Mustang while Colletta and Jimmie hurried through the store, then DJ dropped off the others at the Saylor house.

As DJ drove away, slowly, as if reluctant to leave, Jimmie pledged to Ray-Gene and Colletta that he would have a car like that someday. "When I get a job and earn enough money," he said, "the first thing I plan to do is buy me a red Mustang convertible."

❯ *DONNIE SHAND'S* absence had helped draw Jimmie and Ray-Gene closer. Jimmie admired Ray-Gene's even temperament and envied his patience, and often was astonished by his ability to rise above things and make the best of a bad situation. Ray-Gene easily might have been overrun in the frequent squabbles that broke out among his sisters, his grandmother, and the oppressive Jaybo.

He stood his ground firmly, though, and had come to be the mediator they relied on. Jimmie gave him great credit for the deceptive level of harmony outsiders saw in Grandma Freeman's household.

Ray-Gene, in turn, counted Jimmie's goodwill among the things he treasured most. He believed that he was privileged to have a truly personal, insider's view of the relationship between Jimmie and Colletta. Ray-Gene loved Colletta, too, with the innocent love of a childhood friend, and deemed it an honor that he'd been witness to their romance from the beginning. He had been there since the day the two of them first met and was still close to both, and in his mind nothing ever could jeopardize this circle of friendship; he and they and Donnie Shand still formed an inseparable team.

Colletta's home situation was worse than ever. Her father no longer made the slightest effort to deal with his demons except to drown them in alcohol, and while she'd learned not to fear him, she held little hope that he would ever give up his drinking binges.

She took care of Hunter while her mother worked long hours at the IGA store. Her mother had warned her that Mr. Saylor was likely to leave home one day and not come back, convinced that it was inevitable that he would fall into the Waccamaw River some night and drown, get hit over the head and killed in a deserted alley, or suffer some other such ignoble fate invited by his condition. Colletta had come to accept her mother's dire predictions.

"I feel awful to say it, but to tell you the truth it's just a big relief when he's not home," Colletta admitted to Jimmie. "I know that's bad of me, but I can't help it."

"It's not bad of you," Jimmie said. "There's nothing you can do for him at home, and no place else if he won't try to help himself. It's not your fault, Colletta."

"I know you're right, but I still feel guilty."

Ray-Gene knew about some of the most serious problems Colletta faced at home, although there was much he was not aware of. He extracted a solemn promise that Jimmie would let him know if a time came when he could help: "What kind of friend would I be if I wasn't there when she needed me?"

o• *THE DAY AFTER* Donnie Shand auditioned the yellow Mustang, Colletta came home from school to an empty house. Hunter, always there first, was nowhere to be found. She was frantic. She paced the floor for an hour, watching out the window and listening for the rattle of the doorknob, then set out toward Hunter's school and carefully traced his usual route home. Still no sign of her brother. She ran to find Jimmie, very much afraid.

"I'll bet he's at the IGA," Jimmie told her. "He probably went to see your momma, and she kept him there until she gets off work."

But Colletta said Hunter had clear instructions never to go to the store alone and usually did as he was told. She wanted to hurry and tell her mother, although she did not expect to find Hunter there. They were half-way to the IGA when they met Ray-Gene.

As Jimmie had, Ray-Gene tried to be reassuring: "Don't worry, Colletta. Hunter is old enough to get around on his own. No way that boy would get lost in his own neighborhood!"

"But if he's not lost, where is he?" Colletta answered. "That's what scares me, Ray-Gene."

Colletta was over-protective, but Jimmie and Ray-Gene understood why. They reinforced her caution much of the time, themselves. Hunter was pallid-looking and timid, frail from chronic poor health, and like his sister they wanted to shield him from the world as much as they could.

No one at the IGA had seen Hunter. Wanda Saylor called the police station, where a pompous desk sergeant told her there really was not much he could do until the boy had been missing for twenty-four hours. He would have a squad car cruise the neighborhood, which he seemed to think was a quite generous concession. In what she would later describe as a most condescending tone, he suggested that she was an over-wrought mother who should run along home, where she'd no doubt find the little boy sitting on the steps waiting for his supper. They all held their breath, hoping the desk sergeant was right, but when they got back to the house it still was empty.

& ULTIMATELY, HUNTER'S disappearance was solved with help from an unexpected source. Jaybo reported gleefully that he'd seen Hunter with the boy's father earlier in the afternoon, at the Shark's Tooth tavern three blocks away.

Colletta and the boys were greatly relieved, but Colletta's mother was furious. "I can't take any more of that man!" she declared, her usually sallow face reddening. "I wish he'd die and burn in hell! God forgive me, but I really do."

Ray-Gene and Jimmie, who'd never heard Mrs. Saylor raise her voice before, pretended not to notice the outburst, hoping to spare Colletta's feelings. "Jimmie and me'll go get Hunter," Ray-Gene whispered. "Don't worry Colletta, and tell your momma that everything is going to be all right. We'll come straight back in no time at all. Is that okay?"

"Are you sure y'all want to be involved in this?" Colletta asked. "You don't have to. It's not your problem."

"Sure we do," Jimmie told her. "You stay here and try to calm your mother down some. It won't take us long."

"Thank you, both of you. But be careful. When my daddy's drunk he can be awful mean," Colletta said. "I don't think he would do anything, but he can say terrible things. Hunter's probably scared to death."

The boys found the Shark's Tooth nearly deserted. A lone bartender looked up when they entered and signaled them to stop. "No minors allowed in here," the man said gruffly. "You fellas move on along, now."

"We just want to pick up Hunter," Jimmie told him. "He's Mr. Saylor's little boy and somebody told us he's here.

We just want to get him and leave. You don't want him in here either, do you?"

"Okay, then," the bartender said. He motioned with a nod of the head toward the back. "They're back there. Be careful what you say to Saylor, though. He's not in a very good mood."

It took a moment for their vision to adjust to the darkened interior. When they could make out the rear of the room more clearly, they saw Colletta's father slouched in a booth by the wall, far back, and Hunter's head barely visible over the back of the seat. They walked closer and Jimmie said, quietly, "Your momma wants you to come home now, Hunter."

Hunter turned and a look of surprise swept his face. He started to get up. His father grabbed at him and missed, but Hunter recognized there was going to be a problem and quickly sat back down. "Hold on!" Mr. Saylor commanded. His voice was coarse, his words slurred. "You don't go anywhere until I say so."

"We just wanted to get Hunter and take him home in time for supper," Jimmie said, still keeping his voice low. "His momma and Colletta will be waiting supper for him. They expect us to be right back."

"Is that you there, Jimmie?" Jacob Saylor said, scowling through bleary eyes and trying to shade his face from the dim overhead light with a wavering hand. "It is you, boy. What'n hell you doing here?"

"We just came to get Hunter, Mr. Saylor."

"I ain't said he could go. Hunter and me are having a nice talk. He don't spend time with his daddy like he used to."

"You ought to let him come with us, Mr. Saylor," Ray-Gene said. "Hunter's probably hungry. Don't you want to get home for supper, Hunter?"

The man shaded his face again, trying to focus his eyes on Ray-Gene. "Who are you?" he demanded. "I know you.

You're that little nigger boy that's always hanging around Colletta."

"This is Ray-Gene, Mr. Saylor," Jimmie said calmly. "He's a good friend of me and Colletta both and he's been to your house lots of times. You remember Ray-Gene, don't you?"

"Ain't that what I just said? I know him. I told Colletta not to have no part of him."

"Sir, we don't want to cause any trouble," Jimmie said. "We just want to take Hunter home for supper. If you'll just let him leave with us we won't bother you any more."

"Take him, then," Mr. Saylor said savagely. "I'm through talking with him anyhow. You two don't come around here again. And you, nigger boy, don't come around my house, either. I've got a gun and I know how to use it."

❧7❧

B
RODER'S DAY had gotten off to a better-than-average beginning. There still was a great deal of pain, but it was less intense now and easier to control; a couple of little pills and his torment could be made bearable for hours at a time. He'd actually looked forward to the arrival of Rondell Wilson, who charged into his room at precisely 0700 hours, pretending enthusiasm for their early morning routine of raw physical therapy.

"Nobody but the Army would turn a sadistic brute like you loose on innocent patients this time of day," Broder said.

"Innocent? You? Give me a break, Broder," Wilson shot back. "And we need the early start, because I'm going to run your sorry butt through about a week's worth of hard work before noon."

Wilson had insisted from the outset that the most reliable measure of progress would be Broder's performance in these morning therapy sessions. For Broder, this had led to a virtual roller-coaster ride of emotions. He had made great strides in the early days of his confinement, but after that he had gone through a prolonged slow period when he seemed to make little if any headway. He had advanced rapidly of late, though. Forced motion that would have been excruciating scarcely a week earlier hardly merited a groan, and now it was Broder who became the pretender.

"Go easy, Wilson," he complained. "You're never satisfied until I beg for mercy."

"You're doing great," Wilson said, finally being serious.

"Before you know it, they're going to pull you out of here and put you back on duty."

"Can't say I look forward to that. What the hell are they going to do with me if I can't jump?"

"Have you heard anything more from Colonel Hewlett or Captain Oatmeal?"

"Nothing. You know a lot more about this than I do, Wilson. What do you think? Is there any chance of me jumping again?"

"I wish I could tell you. It's just that most of the guys who come through here are not hurt nearly as bad as you were. As far as I know most of them go back to jumping, but the truth is, a lot of the time I never know what happens after they leave here. They might make 'em truck drivers, for all I know."

Broder had come to know Rondell Wilson better than he had known any other man he had claimed as a friend since going Airborne. He knew that Wilson was the fifth and youngest child of two Philadelphia school teachers, that his father had served in the U.S. Navy and his mother had once hoped to become a concert pianist, that two of his three sisters and his older brother were married and had seven children among them and Wilson loved his nieces and nephews like they were his own. He knew that Wilson had enlisted in the Army as a way to pay for a college education, and still entertained hopes of going to medical school "some day." He knew, too, that deep down Wilson peceived that medical school probably never would happen, and that was a shame because Rondell Wilson was smart and competent and had the level of compassion for his fellow human beings that every doctor ought to possess.

After about their third day of contact, Broder had come to realize that Wilson was the perfect grownup image of his boyhood companion, Ray-Gene. Wilson's gentle nature was so like Ray-Gene's that he had to remind himself from time to time that this was not his long-lost friend from Conway, that he never would see Ray-Gene again and those days were gone forever except in his memory.

He was not sure why he had come to feel such closeness with Wilson after only a brief acquaintance. Wilson's likeness to Ray-Gene was part of the reason, no doubt, and so was the fact that Wilson was crazy about Colletta. But there was more to it than all that. The two of them were compatible and he would have counted Rondell Wilson a friend, trusted him and leaned on him, even if there'd never been a Ray-Gene or a Colletta or a Conway, South Carolina.

"You've got to face the possibility of being grounded, you know," Wilson was saying. "They are not going to kick you out, but they may say you can't jump again."

"You know how I feel about that, Wilson."

"Yeah, I know. If you can't jump, you don't want any part of this damned circus. I know how you feel, and I understand. Believe me, I do."

"Did you ever jump out of an airplane?"

"Me? Are you kidding? Never in a million years will you see this man jump out of anything higher than a ground-floor window. You got to be crazy, man, to want to jump out of airplanes!"

Broder had never tried to explain why he loved jumping. Could he explain it? You had to experience the exhilaration, the sheer terror of the low-level night jump, all the known and unknown possibilities, the conquering sensation of relief when an emphatic jerk of the harness told you the chute had opened, let all these liven your senses the way nothing else ever could. He never would be able to put into words how the jump purified, how it offered an escape to a sheltered world where painful memories and worries about the future could never intrude.

Jumping had been his salvation and he worshipped at its throne, but this was not something he cared to try and explain to Rondell Wilson. "I simply think if you haven't done it you'd never understand what it feels like," he said.

71

"Okay, let's say they threw me out of a C-130 and I liked it," Wilson said. "Even so, I wouldn't care to come floating down somewhere in enemy territory with people shooting at me. Doesn't that idea scare you a little?"

"That's what I'm trained to do, Wilson. I don't pretend I wouldn't be afraid, but I'd be ready for it."

"Better you than me, man. I'd just as soon stay back here and help put the pieces back together. But I'm glad somebody's willing to do it so that I don't have to. Now let's talk about something else. When do you expect Colletta to come see you again?"

"I haven't a clue."

"Can't you call her or something?"

"She never gave me a number, and I don't think I should bother her at work. Besides, what excuse would I have for calling?"

Rondell Wilson fixed a deliberately exaggerated stare on Broder, held it for a long moment, then laughed and shook his head. "I like you, Broder," he said, "but, man, you are one obtuse dude. Let her know you want to see her, beg her to come if you have to. When you get out of this place you can go see her but for now she's got to take the initiative and come to you. Most women don't like that. She needs to know you want her to come, and she needs to hear it from you."

☙ *POPEYE BRODER* was a taciturn man whose formal education had ended with the seventh grade, ensuring a life of hard work at low pay. Popeye was not his real name, of course. His name was Curtis, which he hated. His father—a grandfather Jimmie never knew—nicknamed him Popeye because his bulging biceps were disproportionate to the rest of his body. This physical imbalance had come about through Curtis's determination, as a youth, to be a strong man without knowing precisely how to go about it. His starting point was to stick a metal coffee can onto each end of a three-foot length of electrical conduit pipe, then fill the whole thing with concrete. He worked out vigorously with this heavy homemade barbell twice a day for three years and built the strong arms he wanted while the rest of his body went unattended to.

Jimmie rarely took his problems to his father, and when he did he rarely was satisfied with the response. Popeye Broder was inclined to predict that most problems would go away in time if they simply were ignored. He said as much about Mr. Saylor's gun: "I'd not worry about it too much. He was just drunk. He probably won't remember any of it when he sobers up — if he ever does."

Jimmie had hoped for something more specific, something he could use to reassure Ray-Gene, who had tried hard not to show the sting he felt from Mr. Saylor's words that day at the Shark's Tooth tavern. The racist slur had been nasty and unexpected, but Jimmie could tell that it was the threat of violence that bothered Ray-Gene most. Ray-Gene was afraid to go anywhere near Colletta's house.

Nonetheless, Jimmie repeated his father's words. Mr. Saylor was drunk, probably didn't know what he was saying. Ray-Gene had done nothing to offend him or make him angry and the man had never voiced a grudge toward Ray-Gene before, at least not to his face. "Don't worry about that old drunk," he said. "He's not going to hurt you, Ray-Gene."

"He's mean, Jimmie," Ray-Gene countered. "Sometimes people just say when they're drunk the stuff they're scared to say sober. You don't know that he wouldn't shoot me if I happened by some day when he was in a bad mood."

Jimmie made no effort to refute Ray-Gene's argument. He'd seen the look in Mr. Saylor's eyes that day in the tavern and, for whatever reason, there was real hatred behind the man's threatening words. Colletta's father was malicious. The last thing in the world Jimmie wanted was to have something bad happen to Ray-Gene. He loved Ray-Gene much as he loved his own brother.

The boys had been careful not to let Colletta know there had been a confrontation at the tavern. Neither Colletta nor her mother, overwhelmingly relieved at the mere sight of Hunter, had asked what it took to get him away from his father and they had elected to ignore questions conveniently not asked. Hunter, for his part, apparently had taken the entire episode in stride and found nothing that happened worth talking about, thus inadvertently helping them keep their secret.

Jimmie tried hard to coax more information from Colletta without arousing her suspicion. Merely the thought of Mr. Saylor having a gun in the house was a worry; surely there was real danger that in one of his drunken rages he might shoot someone, either intentionally or by accident. As concerned as Jimmie was for the safety of Ray-Gene and Hunter, he worried about Colletta most of all.

He began to have nightmares, and although his dreams had different settings they all had a common thread. Colletta was in every one, always threatened by some invisible force and calling to him for help. And no matter how desperately he struggled, he always was held back by some equally invisible force, unable to reach her, frantic and helpless, not able to save the girl he loved.

One night the dream was different. In this one he and Colletta, Ray-Gene, and DJ once again were caught up in that terrible quarrel between DJ's mother and father and stood frozen in terror as Wilma Shand smashed a brick into her husband's skull. Jimmie held Colletta tight and tried to shield her, but Langly Shand's blood splattered on her face and hands. Colletta screamed and Jimmie tried to help her wipe it away. The harder they wiped, the more profusely the blood flowed down Colletta's arms and hands and dripped from the tips of her fingers into black, endless space.

Jimmie lay awake the rest of the night, afraid to sleep. He'd been wrong to avoid talking with Colletta about her father's gun. He must confront the issue head-on.

  THEY KNOCKED on doors all afternoon, only to find that nobody wanted fourteen-year-olds. Grandma Freeman told them why. They were too young for a real job, "and who's goin' to pay y'all when they got children of their own to do chores for nothing?" Her explanation did little to lift their dampened spirits.

"Maybe things will get better next summer," Ray-Gene said. "But, yeah, I know, you wanted money now to buy Colletta a Christmas present."

"That's what I was hoping for," Jimmie said.

"If I had money and a car, I'd take Grandma Freeman to Baltimore for Christmas. She's always talked about visiting family in Baltimore once when she was young, and I think she'd like to go back again."

"Why doesn't Jaybo take her?"

"Jaybo said one time he was going to, but he won't ever get to it. You know how Jaybo talks. You know, acts like he could go anywhere he wants to, any time he wants. He just likes to flash his money like he's rich."

"You think Jaybo really is rich?"

"Jaybo's got plenty, but he's not rich."

"I still don't understand who Jaybo works for."

"Jaybo says he works for a company that don't have a name," Ray-Gene said. "He won't talk about it. Ravonelle says he's going to get in big trouble someday, and I don't want to know anything about it."

"Anyway, I was still thinking about that idea of a trip for Christmas. If I could, I'd take Colletta somewhere — maybe to visit her aunt in Wilmington, or something."

Jimmie could not get his mind off Colletta's Christmas present. Christmas spending always had been modest at the Broder house and he never had done Christmas shopping because he'd never had money for gifts and no one ever had expected anything from him. But now he wanted to buy something special for Colletta and he was beginning to fret over it. Ray-Gene wasn't much help.

On Sunday afternoon, he decided to press the issue with his mother. He was afraid to wait much longer. "I suppose we can come up with the money, if you find something that's not too expensive," Allou Broder told him. "Any idea what you want to get her?"

"I didn't start looking yet."

Jimmie wanted suggestions, but his mother didn't volunteer advice and he hated to ask. Besides, no one else knew Colletta nearly as well as he did. He would know the right thing when he saw it.

He stopped by the Saylor house later in the day. Hunter was ill and Colletta worried that it might be something Jimmie could catch, but he insisted on coming in. "I don't get colds and stuff very easy," he argued. "There's more of it in school anyway, and I have to go there every day."

Colletta's mother was working and Mr. Saylor, as best Jimmie could tell, was nowhere about. This might be a good time to talk to her about the gun.

Colletta made hot chocolate, thin because she had to use water in place of milk, and served it in a chipped china mug. Jimmie was hardly company and she was not embarrassed by the shabbiness of her home. She asked about Jimmie's momma, whether he'd seen Ray-Gene.

"I saw Ray-Gene yesterday. Me and him went out looking for a job."

"Any luck?"

"No."

"I don't think you have to work, Jimmie," she said. "I think school's more important, don't you?"

"I guess it is. It would be good to earn some money, though. My brother's got a job now and I think he's going to be moving out on his own pretty soon."

"You mean like moving away? Away from Conway?"

"Probably. He's not talked about it much."

He wanted to steer the conversation toward Mr. Saylor's gun. It would be easy just to ask Colletta right out if there was a gun in the house, but he would hate to explain how he knew about it, how Ray-Gene had been threatened by her daddy that day at the Shark's Tooth tavern. But nothing he could think of would lead them to talk about guns so he gave up and turned to something else. "Ray-Gene says Jaybo works for a company that doesn't have a name," he said. "Did you ever hear of that before?"

"I wouldn't believe anything Jaybo says," Colletta answered. "Jabo's a complete no-account, Jimmie. Don't you think Ray-Gene knows that?"

"He's not afraid of Jaybo anymore, not like he used to be."

"He ought to be. Jaybo's going to get in real big trouble one of these days. I just hope it doesn't affect Ray-Gene too much when it happens."

"Does Ray-Gene come around here much?"

"I don't think he's been here in a month or more."

She doesn't know why, Jimmie thought, but I can't tell her Ray-Gene's afraid.

Colletta stood. She said she ought to check on Hunter, and if he was awake fix him something to eat. Hunter not only was awake, but hungry, and Colletta said she needed to fry eggs and potatoes, and she'd like Jimmie to stay and eat with them. If he wanted to help he could peel and slice some potatoes while she made biscuits and flour-and-water gravy. She already had four sweet potatoes half-baked in the oven, to finish with the biscuits, and she would put a pan of shelled pecans in at the end for toasting.

Jimmie followed her to the kitchen and pitched in with a paring knife. Colletta's larder offered little to work with, but she took her cooking pretty seriously. Any discussion of Mr. Saylor's gun would have to wait.

Hunter came to the table pale and drawn, clearly weakened by whatever ailment he was stricken with. He broke into a wide grin when he saw Jimmie. "Hey, Jimmie," he said. "I didn't know you was here."

"I just stopped by to see how you were feeling," Jimmie lied. "You doing better?"

"I feel pretty good. Better than yesterday, anyhow."

"That's not saying much," Colletta said. "Yesterday you puked all day. You were sick enough to die!"

Hunter had a hearty appetite. Fried eggs and potatoes, biscuits and gravy flew off his plate. He ate one of the large sweet potatoes and shared another with Jimmie. He started to scoop up a handful of pecan halves, but they were still hot from the oven and Hunter groaned from burned fingers.

"My lord, Hunter, you act like you've not eat in a week," Colletta complained.

But Jimmie could see how her eyes brightened when she watched Hunter at the table, gratified that he ate heartily. She and Jimmie started clearing plates. Hunter, waiting for the pan of pecans to cool, looked up with surprise when his father entered the kitchen.

"What 'n hell you doing up, boy?" Mr. Saylor boomed, startling them all with his angry voice. "Ain't you supposed to be sick?"

Hunter froze. Colletta put down the plates Jimmie had handed her, turned calmly toward her father. "He's better, Daddy. You should have been here to see him eat," she said. "You want some supper?"

Mr. Saylor eyed Hunter almost belligerently. There was an instant in which he seemed to be confused, then his face softened. He scuffed Hunter's hair roughly with his big hand and smiled. "I'm glad you're better," he said. "Good to see you're up and around, boy. Thanks, honey," he said to Colletta, "but I don't believe I want any supper right now."

Jimmie had stood by silently, expecting some show of displeasure from Mr. Saylor upon finding him in the kitchen with Hunter and Colletta. Mr. Saylor looked toward him and nodded, mumbled his name in what apparently was intended as a greeting, and turned back toward the front of the house.

"I'd better go," Jimmie whispered to Colletta.

"No, please stay. At least for a little while. Daddy's not in a bad mood today. He'll be glad to have you visit."

"Are you sure?"

"I'm sure, Jimmie. You'll see."

Hunter, meanwhile, had relaxed, and went back to his pursuit of toasted pecans. He spread a handful on the table and attacked them vigorously, as if he still was very hungry. He chewed with a loud smacking noise that made Colletta laugh.

❧8❧

RODER HAD looked forward to this face-to-face meeting with Colonel Hewlett. He had great hopes that
a confrontation with the colonel would bring some
relief from the anxiety he had been left with after sessions
with Captain Oates, sessions from which he had emerged
angry and discouraged. He had been in the military long
enough to know that if Homer Oates was out to get him,
for whatever reason, the captain could do things that made
his life very unpleasant. He was out of the medical center for
the first time since his bad jump, pushed in a wheelchair by
Rondell Wilson down the block to division headquarters.
Simply being outdoors again raised his spirits.

They were ushered promptly into the colonel's office,
where Wilson left him. Broder was not sure of the correct
military protocol, dressed as he was in washed-out hospital
pajamas and robe and not able to stand at attention. He
saluted smartly from his sitting position and hoped that he
did not look too foolish.

The colonel looked up from the paperwork on his desk
as if only now aware that he had a visitor. "We can dispense
with all the formalities, sergeant," he said, casually brushing
aside the salute with a wave of his hand. "I appreciate your
coming here. I wanted to talk to you and my schedule is
crowded this morning. I'm supposed to be off to check on a
field exercise and need to be in the air before noon."

"Thank you for seeing me, sir."

"First off, how's the rehab coming, Broder?"

"I'm doing well, sir. I hope to be back on duty soon."

"All in good time, sergeant," the colonel said, "all in good time. The reason I wanted to see you—and what I say here does not go beyond these walls, understood?"

"Yes, sir. Understood."

"The reason I wanted to see you is—and I'm sticking my neck way our here—I've heard some things about Captain Oates that disturb me. Now, hear me out. I have looked at your record and I believe Oates is barking up the wrong tree. I saw nothing that should prompt anyone to look for alcohol or drug use on your part, yet that seems to be what Oates wants to and thinks he can find. Does this square with your experience?"

"Yes, sir, it does. In fact, Captain Oates virtually accused me of being either drunk or high on drugs when the accident happened."

"And you have no idea why he would think that?"

"No, sir. No idea."

"I have to ask you, Broder, and you'd damn-well better be straight with me. Have you ever jumped after drinking or using drugs?"

"No, sir. Absolutely not."

"Never?"

"Never."

"I believe you, Broder. Like I said, I looked at your record. You're a good soldier. There's something going on here that I don't like and I intend to find out what it is. If you're willing, I need your help. If I'm wrong we could both be in a world of hurt. The last thing I want is to see a good career ruined, and that goes for sergeants as well as captains. But if my suspicions are valid, there's something rotten going on that has to be dug out and crushed.

"If you don't want to get involved, I understand. If you do, I'll stand behind you all the way, though I have to tell you up front we both could get shot down in the end if we're not very, very careful."

Broder hardly knew how to respond. This was not what he'd expected. He was completely in the dark as to whatever the colonel was asking, but under the circumstances, especially given the good things the colonel had said about him and the implied trust, how could he refuse?

"I'll help, sir," he told the colonel. "Just tell me what to do and I'll do my best."

"For now, do nothing. If I'm on the right track, somebody else will make the first move. And don't worry, Sergeant Broder, I'll know what's going on. And I'll be in touch when I need to. Nobody's going to abandon you."

"Yes, sir."

Colonel Hewlett stood, pushed an intercom button on his phone and directed that Rondell Wilson be sent in. The meeting was over. Wilson appeared promptly and vigorously wheeled Broder from the colonel's office.

"Well, what did he say?" Wilson demanded, as soon as they were out of the building. "Have they done their investigation, or what?"

Broder was hesitant. He obviously could not reveal what went on in Colonel Hewlett's office but he hated to lie to Wilson. How could he tell Wilson anything? "I guess they're still working on it," he said. "But I think everything's going to turn out okay." To his great relief, Wilson didn't push for more detailed information.

Broder was confused and scared by what he'd just heard and the obvious questions began to form in his own mind. What was the "something rotten" the colonel was afraid of? He had gone into the meeting with Hewlett merely hoping to hear the colonel say that his training accident had been investigated and he had been cleared of any fault. It seemed now that he was being dragged into something as sinister as it was mysterious, something that had nothing to do with his bad jump or his own future, and something that, for now, he had no choice but to keep to himself.

&- *JUST BEFORE* Christmas, Donnie Shand lost his job. Ray-Gene heard about it first and told Jimmie. "DJ and his boss had a big argument," Ray-Gene reported. "It's going to be hard for him now. He liked having a car and money. You think he'll get another job as good as that one?"

"I doubt it. Me and you found out how hard it is to get a job, Ray-Gene. DJ won't ever be able to buy a car like that Mustang," Jimmie said.

"You think it's his own fault they sacked him?"

"I think we'll never know. You know how DJ is."

Jimmie guessed that Donnie would not admit to being wrong, if in fact the problem was of his own making. Ray-Gene claimed to have seen first-hand how nasty Donnie's boss could be; he was inclined to give Donnie the benefit of the doubt. They agreed that if DJ did not want to talk about his abrupt and unexpected unemployment, they wouldn't pry.

They had not seen Colletta since school let out for the holidays, almost a week earlier. Jimmie said she would be just as upset over DJ's misfortune as they were.

"You ought to be the one to tell her," Ray-Gene advised.

"Suppose so. I hate to have to give her bad news, but I don't want her to hear it from somebody else. I need to go over there anyway and take her my Christmas present."

He had bought a red sweater for Colletta, a beautifully knit, soft and feminine garment that his mother said any girl would like. Colletta would be surprised. He fidgeted with anticipation on his way to the Saylor house, eager to see her response. The door opened slowly to his knock, just a sliver. Hunter peered cautiously through the crack, grinned when he saw Jimmie and threw the door open wide.

"Hey, Jimmie."

"Hey, Hunter. You get all well?"

Hunter looked healthier than he had for a long time. There was color in his face and an aspect of vitality that had been absent for several months.

"I'm feelin' real good, Jimmie. You okay?"

"Sure, Hunter, I'm okay. Is Colletta home?"

Hunter shook his head, indicating not. "She's went to Momma's store to bring home some stuff for supper. She ought to be back d'rectly," he said.

"Are you here by yourself, then?"

"Yes."

"You're getting big enough to stay by yourself, I guess. I just didn't know if Colletta would leave you."

"She don't like to, but sometimes she has to. You want to come in and visit a while, Jimmie?"

Hunter stood to one side, further extending his invitation. Jimmie stepped into the living room and Hunter closed the door. "You can set over there," Hunter said, pointing to a worn sofa that sat with its back against the front wall, under the window. Jimmie did Hunter's bidding, gingerly placing the paper bag that held Colletta's present on the floor at the end of the sofa and settling himself onto a bumpy cushion.

Hunter sat close beside him. When Jimmie put his arm on the arm of the sofa, Hunter moved closer to the opposite end and raised his small arm into a similar position, unconsciously mimicking every move of the older boy.

"Where's your daddy today?" Jimmie asked.

"He's at work."

"Where's he work at?"

"I don't know," Hunter said. "He started there just the other day. It's someplace our mom found out about."

"How is your daddy these days, Hunter . . . I mean is he acting better, you know, and not being so tough on you and Colletta?"

"He's been real good, Jimmie."

Hunter started to cry. He tried to hold back, and at first there was only a soft whimper, but then he could no longer control himself. His distress gushed forth in violent spasms. Jimmie moved closer to the little boy and put an arm across his quaking shoulders. After an awkward couple of minutes,

Hunter slipped from under his arm, got off the sofa and ran from the room. In a moment he came back, wiping his nose on a dingy piece of cloth, and sat close beside Jimmie again, saying not a word.

"Are you all right now?" Jimmie asked. He felt self-conscious, as if he somehow was invading Hunter's privacy. "I hope I didn't say something wrong."

"No, you didn't say nothing wrong. I'm sorry, Jimmie. I oughtn't to have acted like that, crying like a baby."

"Everybody feels like crying sometimes, Hunter. Nothing wrong with it."

"Do you ever cry?" There was pleading in Hunter's voice that directed Jimmie to respond affirmatively.

"Sure I do. And I'm a lot bigger than you."

His answer brought an expression of relief to Hunter's pale face. He smiled and started to speak, but his words were clipped short by a fierce hiccup that jerked his body and sent him instead into peals of laughter. He hiccuped again, laughed even harder, and ended up sliding from the sofa and rolling on the floor, laugh-tears streaming down his cheeks. Jimmie laughed too, uncontrollably for a time, and rolled on the floor beside the younger boy. They had wrung out their emotions before they tried talking again.

"I'm wore out, Jimmie," Hunter said finally, "but I feel good."

"Me too. Laughing does that to you."

"I'm sorry I cried, Jimmie." Hunter looked somber again, suddenly withdrawn.

"I told you, don't worry about it."

"Want to know why?"

"If you want to tell me. You don't have to."

"It was because we're not having no Christmas."

"Sure you are," Jimmie said. "Everybody has Christmas, Hunter."

"No we're not. Daddy lost all the money my mom had saved up for Christmas. Then there was bills to pay. They don't know it, but I heard them talkin' about it."

"But your daddy's working now, didn't you say? He'll earn that money back in no time. I'll bet y'all have a real good Christmas, Hunter."

"I don't care. Christmas don't mean much to me."

• *ALLOU BRODER* clearly was moved by Jimmie's generous spirit when he begged that whatever Christmas present was hidden away for him, he be allowed to take to Hunter instead. This was the only solution he could think of, running home with Colletta's present under his arm, not willing to give it when Hunter would be left empty-handed. He told his mother about Hunter's crying and the revelation about the Saylor family's money problems, how Hunter expected no Christmas. His eyes were misty as he repeated Hunter's story.

"Mr. Saylor drinks up all the money they get, Momma. They ought to lock him up or something," he said bitterly.

"Maybe he can't help himself," his mother replied. "But you're right, of course, Colletta and Hunter have to pay for it. And their mother, too, who's doing her best under hard circumstances. But you don't have to give up your Christmas for Hunter. That wouldn't be fair."

"I don't mind. Honestly, I don't."

She would hear no more of it. Hunter would not be left out at Christmas, she promised, and that night they went out and bought a blue, soft wool boy's sweater and a Chinese checkers game, then candy, nuts, and oranges. "You can give Hunter the sweater and checkers," Allou Broder said. "The other things will just be something from our family to the Saylors."

Jimmie felt ten feet tall when he went back to the Saylor house the next day, as early as he dared. Colletta greeted him at the door. Hunter was asleep. Jimmie surmised that no one else was in the house. "I brought you some stuff for Christmas," he told Colletta. "Here are my presents for you and Hunter, and my momma sent some family things."

"You didn't have to do that," Colletta said. "I didn't get you anything yet."

"I don't want you to, Colletta. Please don't get me anything, okay?"

He thought Colletta looked very pretty. She looked older. He wanted to see her in the red sweater. But what if it didn't fit, or she didn't like it? His self-confidence—all the satisfaction he had felt merely buying a Christmas present for her—instantly evaporated. "You can save these until Christmas if you want to," he said.

He was relieved when Colletta agreed. She said she would like very much to open hers now, but she wanted to save Hunter's until Christmas morning and she would not feel right if she didn't wait.

"The other things are for everybody," Jimmie told her. "My mom got them. They're from the Broder family to the Saylors."

"Tell your momma thank you. We appreciate it."

"Are your mom and dad working today?"

The pain apparent in her eyes, the color that shaded her cheeks told him what he didn't want her to have to say in words. But Colletta had long since stopped trying to conceal from him what went on in her house and she would not attempt to deceive him now.

"Daddy's not working," she said softly. "He came in real late last night, and we could smell his alcohol all the way in the back room. When Momma tried to get him up this morning he cussed her and said he didn't have a job to go back to. We don't know what happened yet."

"I'm sorry, Colletta."

"It's humiliating, Jimmie. And it makes it awful hard on our mom."

Jimmie felt a tide of anger rising within, outrage at the man who caused Colletta's distress and Hunter's empty holiday and made his family suffer endlessly because of what looked like nothing more than a father's selfishness and uncaring. How could any man do such things to the people he ought to love most of all?

"*Co-lett-a!*" The furious roar came from another room. "Colletta, dammitalltohell, girl, where are you? Git in here. I need you!"

"I'm coming, Daddy." Colletta barely raised her voice. "I'm coming. Stay right here, Jimmie. I'll see what he wants."

Hunter, looking dazed and sleepy, stumbled into the living room, a barefooted ragamuffin in a tattered, over-sized gray shirt and dingy cotton underpants. He looked around as if uncertain where he was, then spied Jimmie. "Hey, Jimmie," he said placidly, "I didn't know you was here."

"Hey, Hunter. How're you feeling today? No hiccups this morning?"

Hunter giggled and put his hand over his mouth. Mr. Saylor's angry voice erupted again and Hunter was plainly apprehensive. Jimmie took the boy by the arm and led him to the battered sofa against the wall, where they sat side by side. Hunter leaned heavily against his older and stronger friend as if seeking protection.

Mr. Saylor emerged shortly, red-faced and scruffy, shoeless but otherwise fully dressed in work clothes he apparently had slept in. Colletta was behind him, holding back, keeping space between them as if two-steps distance might spare her the hurt of association.

"You didn't tell me anybody was here," Mr. Saylor complained, speaking to Colletta but not looking back.

"It's just me, Mr. Saylor," Jimmie said. "Not anybody you have to worry about."

"You're out early, boy." Mr. Saylor's voice was no longer gruff, but whiny now, pathetic. "You wanna have breakfast with us? Colletta's about to fix me some."

"No, sir. I've had breakfast. I just come by to bring some Christmas presents. My mother sent some things, from the Broder family to the Saylors. She said merry Christmas."

"Here, Daddy," Colletta said, stooping to lift a paper grocery sack that held the separate bag of oranges, the candy and nuts. "This is what Jimmie brought us."

Her father glanced at what Colletta held toward him and turned away. His back was to Jimmie, but there was no mistaking that the Broder family's representative was the target of his stinging words: "Take that stuff and get it the hell out of here! We don't need no charity."

❧9❧

I F THIS WAS the same Captain Homer Oates, he was acting
out of character, smiling and pleasant, conversing with
the young sergeant as if the two were old friends. Broder
tried hard to play the captain's game, whatever it was, and
at the same time keep his guard up. He never had trusted
Oates; he saw no reason to trust him now. I wish Wilson
was here, he thought, he'll never believe me when I tell him
about this. But he had not seen Rondell Wilson since mid-
morning.

Captain Oates painted a rosy picture of Broder's future in
the 82nd Airborne Division and said, "You'll always be Airborne, sergeant, even if you never leave the ground again."

"Yes, sir, I understand that," Broder replied. "But if I
can't jump, I really don't want to stay."

"Nonsense. It takes a lot of men on the ground to support every soldier that jumps. Good men. There's always a
place for a bright and able young guy like you, Broder,
whether you jump or not. That's what I wanted to talk to
you about. It looks like I'm going to have a spot open in
HQ detachment. It's a training cadre position, but I need a
man who can take charge and get things done. More of an
administrative role. This is my slot and I can use it pretty
much as I damn well please."

"I'm afraid I don't follow you, captain."

"I'm offering you a job, Broder. I want you on my team! I can have a hold clamped on your assignment for at least a year, maybe two. The world has not stopped while you've been here in the hospital. Everybody you know has shipped out, scattered all over the Mid-East, and you're damned sure not going to be sent over there to catch up with 'em."

Broder was speechless. Could this be the same man who just days earlier had virtually accused him of lying about his bad jump? The same man who threatened to force him out of Airborne, out of the Army altogether? Captain Oates's startling change in attitude left him surprised and confused.

"Just give it some thought, sergeant," the captain went on. "I don't have to have an answer right now. You're not going anywhere. But when your new orders come through, I'd like you assigned to me. By choice, Broder. I don't want to have to go out and shanghai you. I could do that, you know."

Broder caught the subtle but clear threat, the nasty hint of the real Captain Homer Oates. "Yes, sir," he said, "I'll think about it." He added no word of appreciation. Military courtesy might force him to respond to Oates's phony entreaty, but he would be damned straight to hell before he'd go an inch further than he had to.

Later in the day, Broder reported Oates's proposition to a skeptical Rondell Wilson.

"Man, how do you expect me to believe anything you say if you try to feed me crap like that?" Wilson demanded. "Number one, Oates has never — repeat, never — been civil to anybody in his entire existence. Number two, he doesn't like you, Broder. He thinks you drink and do drugs before jumping, all kinds of nasty stuff like that. Didn't he make that plain and clear before? Come on, man, you must be having more of those funny dreams you get on the pain medicine!"

"Damn it, Wilson, it happened just the way I told you. That's exactly what the man said."

"Okay, Broder. If you say so. Still seems mighty peculiar to me."

"I didn't say it wasn't peculiar. I just told you the facts. Oates acted like a recruiter, trying to get me in his outfit. I have no idea what's going on, but to tell you the truth it scares the hell out of me."

"Don't trust him, Broder," Wilson said firmly. "Oates has a bad reputation, and as far as I can see he's earned it. He scares me, too. For your sake, man, I wish I knew what he's up to. But guess what. You and me have got more immediate things to concern our lazy butts with. It's time for me to take you to the gym and show you some real pain. Think you're up to it?"

"I can take anything you can dish out, Wilson. Let's go."

Rondell Wilson was as good as his word. He pushed his patient hard through a three-hour rehab routine rigorous enough that both were exhausted when it ended. The sheer physical demands of therapy left little time to worry about other things, giving Broder a mental rest. He needed the respite, because the prolonged stretches when Wilson was not around left him no one to talk to and gave him too much time to think.

Broder lay awake that night, contemplating his situation and trying to make sense of what was going on. What had he gotten himself into with Colonel Hewlett? The recent exchange in the colonel's office seemed more puzzling every day. But it was Captain Homer Oates who had tossed him the sharpest curve yet, first treating him like a criminal and threatening to throw the book at him and now talking as if he was a man the captain wanted and needed in his own outfit, and was determined to get.

He had come to accept, grudgingly, that he probably would never jump again and he was close to certain that if he couldn't jump he had no desire to stay in the Army. But what would he do on the outside? Military life was the only life he'd had since he left Conway as a naïve and confused youth looking to find his way in the world. The Army was all he knew.

His thoughts quickly drifted to Colletta. It had been five days since her last visit. She promised to return, though she didn't say when, and he hoped it would be soon. Now that she had come back into his life two days without seeing Colletta seemed an eternity.

He thought about the boy. How old would he be? What did he look like? Surely Colletta had pictures of the child, but she had volunteered none and Broder had not had the courage to ask. In his mind's eye he could see Colletta as a pretty little girl, a guileless playmate with a dirty face. He wondered if the boy might mirror that image.

Broder finally drifted into a light and troubled slumber, but this did not last. His mind was awash in worries, stresses that would not permit the peace of deep and restful sleep.

He sat on the side of the bed and rested his face in his hands. Ahead of him lay weeks of painful therapy, and after that, what? How had he become embroiled in this mysterious, menacing predicament that placed him squarely between Colonel Hewlett and Captain Oates in some corrupt competition in which he wanted no part? He felt as if he had been snared by forces that were about to drag him deeper into a dark hole from which he might never escape.

For the first time, Broder understood that he might be treading dangerous ground. He thrived on dangers he understood—jumping from airplanes in the dark and facing the withering fire of unseen enemies on the ground. He was trained and ready for these, knew how to handle them. But this was a different kind of danger. This was something secret and malevolent and it left him uncertain and afraid.

❧

❧ *RAY-GENE AND* Jimmie lay sprawled on a patch of sparse centipede grass in the splotchy shade of a gaunt pecan tree in back of Jimmie's house, facing another long, hot Conway summer and hoping for inspiration. Ray-Gene swirled a pine stick and poked listlessly at an ant hill. He mumbled to Jimmie, "You've got to paint that scuppernong arbor, right?

"Yeah, sometime I do," Jimmie replied. "I just don't want to start it yet. You seen DJ lately?"

"Yeah, I saw him a couple of days ago."

"What's he doin' these days?"

"He didn't tell me much. I asked did he have a job and got no answer. Believe it or not, he seems to be real friendly with Jaybo these days. The two of them are always going off together, but I don't know where."

"I never thought I'd live to see Donnie Shand and Jaybo friends."

"Well, they are. Least they act like they are. How 'bout Colletta? Seen her recently?"

"It's been almost a week. It makes me crazy not to be able to see her more, Ray-Gene. I was used to seeing her every day at school, but since school let out it's been a lot harder. I'm afraid to go over there most of the time because you never know how her old drunk father is going to act. I can't call her and find out if he's there because they don't have a phone."

"Seems to me like y'all need a signal of some kind," Ray-Gene said. "You know, hang a rag on the door when he's gone, something like that. How come she don't come over here?"

"He orders her to stay home with Hunter and gets mad as hell if he comes home and finds them gone. I told her not to risk it."

"You think he's still mad at me? I've not been close to Colletta's house since he threatened to shoot me. Maybe he's madder at you now than me."

A rustle of footsteps interrupted before Jimmie could answer. It was Hunter, panting and exhausted, his usually pale face flushed and sweaty. "Colletta got a broke arm," he gasped. "She fell in the kitchen, off a chair. She told me to come and find you. Can you come and help her, please?"

Jimmie and Ray-Gene jumped up and Jimmie ran toward the gate. Hunter dropped to the ground. "I don't think I can run any more," he called after Jimmie. "I'm all out of breath. But you go on. I'll get home in a little bit."

"Yeah, Jimmie, go on," Ray-Gene yelled. "I can take care of Hunter but he needs a minute to catch his breath. Is there anything else I can do?"

Jimmie was half way to the street. "Just come on over to Colletta's house as soon as you can," he called back over his shoulder. "I'll figure out what to do when I get there."

Jimmie raced to the Saylor house, bounded up the steps and shoved open the unlocked door. Colletta was slumped on a straight-backed chair in the kitchen, holding her left arm gingerly across her lap, her face tear-stained and white. The scene before him affected Jimmie like nothing ever had before. He was swept by a wave of panic, a sense that he had to act fast coupled with feelings of helplessness and uncertainty.

Colletta smiled wanly. "Didn't I make a fool of myself?" she said. "I'm sorry, Jimmie. I sent Hunter because I didn't know who else to go to."

"You did the right thing, Colletta. I'll help you. You have to get to the emergency room."

"I guess so. But how?"

"I'll call the police or something."

"I don't think the police would come for something like this, would they? There wasn't a crime or anything."

"I'll call for an ambulance, then. How bad does it hurt?"

"It hurts a lot," Colletta said, her lip trembling. "But I don't need an ambulance. I just need somebody to get me to a doctor."

"How 'bout I call us a taxi?"

"You got any money?"

"No. But they oughtn't to charge us in a case like this. An emergency, I mean."

The front door banged open and Ray-Gene hurried into

the kitchen. Hunter was close behind. He looked at Colletta's swollen arm, which was taking on a bluish-purple tint, and began to cry.

"Don't cry, Hunter," Colletta said, in her best soothing voice. "I'll be all right. Jimmie and Ray-Gene will take care of me. You did good by getting over there so fast."

"It looks like it hurts awful," Hunter said. "What are they gonna do, Colletta?"

"We're going to get her to the emergency room, Hunter," Jimmie said. "We were just trying to decide the best way to get her there."

Ray-Gene leaned forward and put a hand on Colletta's shoulder. "I'll run and get Jaybo," he said. "He can get us to the emergency room as fast as anybody could. Y'all wait right here. Jimmie, you can get her some aspirin or something. Better have Hunter get a drink of water and lay down and rest. I'll be right back."

&- IT WAS MID-AFTERNOON by the time the medics released Colletta, her forearm in a heavy cast carried across her chest, close to her body, in a stout sling tied behind her neck. X-rays had offered clear images of a severe fracture just above her wrist. Setting the bone had proved extremely painful but Colletta stood up to it bravely, astonishing Jimmie with her stoic courage. She had permitted no one except him to stay with her through the full range of treatment, forcing Hunter, despite his protests, to wait in a lounge with Jaybo and Ray-Gene.

Hunter had been scared and anxious, even though Ray-Gene assured him repeatedly that Colletta would be all right, and was visibly relieved when he saw his sister. The pain-killers prescribed and administered in the emergency room had worked well. Colletta was giddy, almost festive.

Hunter hugged her and peppered her with questions while Jaybo insisted on signing his name on her cast, in bold black strokes. Once Jimmie and Ray-Gene recognized that

Jaybo's action was fitting, they followed suit. A couple of nurses added initials and a young x-ray technician drew a prominent smiley face at the tip of the cast, where it crossed over the back of Colletta's hand.

Jaybo drove them all back to the Saylor house, pulled his Oldsmobile up tight against the curb for his passengers to alight. Jimmie held the door open, and took Colletta's right arm to help her from the car. "I don't know how to thank you," she said to Jaybo. "I'm really grateful to you, and you too, Ray-Gene. I won't ever forget what you did for me."

Jaybo waited for Hunter to scramble out, and said, "Forget it." Ray-Gene waved silently from the passenger seat as Jaybo drove away.

Hunter rushed ahead while Jimmie led Colletta up the steps and into the house, urging her to walk slowly. All the medicine might make her dizzy, Jimmie warned; this was not a time she'd want to fall. Colletta laughed at his coddling, but let him hold her good arm and guide her to the sofa in the living room. He made sure she was safely seated before leaving her side. Hunter stood at the arm of the sofa, as if on guard.

"I'll get you some water," Jimmie said. "That arm's going to hurt a lot, Colletta. Did they give you enough pills?"

"They just gave me four or five, I think. But I have a prescription for some more."

Hunter looked at Jimmie and frowned. "How much do prescriptions cost?" he asked.

"It depends on what it is," Jimmie said. "But it seems like ordinary pain medicine oughtn't to cost too much. Colletta, do you want me to take your prescription over to the IGA and give it to your mother? She ought to get it filled pretty soon, before you run out of pills."

"Maybe a little later. But I wish you'd stay around for a while before you go. I don't know what I would have done if Hunter hadn't found you, or if Ray-Gene hadn't got Jaybo to take us to the emergency room. I think I might have passed out before Momma got home, it hurt so bad."

"Sure, I'll stay," Jimmie said. "Just as long as you want. Hunter did good. I wish I had found some way to get you to the doctor, but I hadn't thought of anything yet when Ray-Gene said Jaybo would do it. I guess we have to feel better about Jaybo now."

Hunter smiled at Jimmie's words of praise. He still hovered solicitously over his sister. Colletta took his arm, drew him around the end of the sofa and motioned for him to sit beside her. "I appreciate what Jaybo did for me," she said, "but I still don't think he's a good person. I wouldn't want Hunter around him much. That was the first time Ray-Gene had been here in a long time. Was he at your house when Hunter found y'all?"

"We were in my backyard looking for something to do. Hunter took care of that, all right!"

Jimmie came and sat next to Colletta. He wanted to take her hand, but with Hunter sitting on the side with her uninjured arm all he could do was slip his hand inside her elbow, above the cast. She leaned her head on his shoulder and in an instant was sleeping soundly. She was still asleep when Jacob Saylor stumbled coming up the steps, quickly regained his stride, and staggered clumsily through the open front door.

Jimmie heard the noise and roused Colletta, who had slept on his shoulder for more than an hour. Hunter had gone to the kitchen to look for something to eat, so they were alone in the living room when Mr. Saylor entered, stopped in the middle of the room and looked about as if not certain where he was. He was dirty and scruffy, his eyes bleary from drink, his left hand trembling. In his right hand he carried a bottle of liquor only partially hidden in a brown paper bag.

Mr. Saylor looked surprised at the sight of Colletta and Jimmie, as if he'd expected the house to be empty. Then he noticed the cast on Colletta's arm. "My god, girl," he said hoarsely, "what's happened to you?"

"I'm all right, Daddy," Colletta told him. "I fell off a chair and broke my arm but Jimmie and Ray-Gene took me to the doctor. I'll be okay."

Her father stared in disbelief. His eyes suddenly filled with tears. He turned to Jimmie. "You took care of her?" He spoke in a raspy whisper. "You took care of my little girl?"

"It wasn't just me, Mr. Saylor," Jimmie said. "Ray-Gene helped a lot and Jaybo drove her to the emergency room. And Hunter helped, too."

"But you stayed with her," Colletta's father said. "You've been here to look after her. I should have been here when she needed me, but I wasn't. You took care of her."

"Yes, sir. I did what I could."

Jimmie and Ray-Gene took care of me, Daddy," Colletta said. "I wasn't hurt seriously. Nothing really bad happened while you were gone."

Mr. Saylor dropped down on the floor, in a kneeling position. He let loose of his bottle, clasped his hands in front of him and raised them toward Colletta as if in supplication. "It'd be all the same if you'd been killed," he whimpered. "I wasn't here, and you needed me. What kind of father isn't here when his little girl needs him? I'm a worthless father, Colletta. I'm a worthless man."

Jimmie whispered to Colletta: "Do you want me to go?"

"No, Jimmie," she said, "I want you to stay."

Hunter had slipped up to his father quietly from behind. "You ought to have been here, Daddy," he said firmly. "She was hurt and you wasn't here. You should be here when we need you." Jacob Saylor appeared to be startled by the sound of the boy's voice. He tried to turn toward him but lost his balance and fell on his side to the floor. He began to cry, silently at first, then in loud, choking sobs. Hunter knelt on the bare floor beside him, stroked the side of his face, and whispered soothing words into his father's ear.

❧10❧

RONDELL WILSON grinned like a Cheshire cat. Broder, who had stopped and leaned against the wall to rest, turned and looked to see why. It was Colletta, walking toward them, silhouetted against a brilliantly sunlit window at the far end of the hallway.

"It's her, man," Wilson said. "I knew she'd be back."

Broder said nothing.

Colletta approached quickly, smiling, as if Broder and Wilson were the two people in the world she most wanted to see. "Hey, Jimmie," she said meekly, and, "Hey you too, Wilson. How's everybody doin' today?"

"Real good, Colletta. Real good," Wilson said. "Nice to see you again."

Broder stood silently. His heart pounded, and he could find no words. He had hoped fervently that Colletta would come today, felt deep in his bones that she would. But he had not expected her this early; her sudden appearance once again took him by surprise.

"And you, Jimmie," she said, locking eyes with Broder, "still making good progress?"

"Yes. At least I think I am. How 'bout it, Wilson, am I still making good progress?"

"Yes, ma'am!" Wilson said. "He is truly making good progress. And I should know, since I'm the one responsible for the daily care and feeding of him and the other animals on this floor of the zoo." Then, more solemnly, "It really is good to see you again, Colletta. I'm glad you came." He put

101

a hand on her shoulder and squeezed. "I've got rounds to make. But I'll be close if you guys need anything."

"Take care, Wilson," Colletta said, and turned back to Broder. "You honestly do look much better. I hope you're doing as well as Wilson says."

"Well, you know Wilson. You can't believe anything he tells you. But I am doing well. The doctors say I'll be out of here in no time. Want to come into my living room and visit, or would you rather take a walk down the hall? Scenery's about the same, either way."

"Let's go to your room. The halls are busy today."

Broder swung his crutches in a wide arc and circled back toward his room, with Colletta walking slowly at his side. The room was small and crowded and had only a single chair for visitors. Broder backed up to the bed, lowered himself slowly into a sitting position on the edge, and motioned Colletta to the chair. He was in terrible pain but his medicine would kick in soon. In the meantime he hoped not to let it show. "I'm glad you came," he said. "I really did want to see you again. How've you been?"

"I'm doing good, Jimmie. I would have come sooner, but it's hard to get over here during the hours they'll let me in. I'm working all the extra time I can get. It's not easy being a single mother. But you know that."

"How's the boy?"

"You mean Jacob? Or did you even know his name? You wouldn't have had any reason to know."

"Jacob is a good name. I like it."

"I wanted to name him Jimmie. After you. I just didn't know if I could. Aunt Edith thought he should be Jacob, after my father. Jacob Saylor may not have been the greatest father in the world but I loved him. They said he served his time honorably, right to the end. I still miss him."

"I know," Broder said. "He loved you and Hunter, too, even if he didn't always show it. I'm sorry you lost him. I didn't know until a few months ago, when my mother sent me one of those 'Oh, yes, I forgot to tell you' letters."

"Once you leave home, it's hard to keep up with that kind of thing."

She stood and slipped to Broder's bedside. He reached out and took her hands in his and saw and felt the softness of her skin, the tenderness of her woman's touch, the grace of her slender fingers, breathtaking in their elegance, as if for the first time. How could he ever have taken these hands for granted, as commonplace elements in his ordinary life?

"How did we come to this, Colletta?" he said. "I've been going back over things in my mind, over and over, and I just can't understand how we let it all happen."

"You can't always understand the why of things, Jimmie. Sometimes it's better not to try, really. It can make you crazy if you know that doing something different might have changed things, because now you can't go back and undo what's already happened. You can be sorry, but you can't change things. The past has come and gone and it's better just to leave it buried. To try and do otherwise is like going into the graveyard and turning up old bones. No matter how hard you dig, in the end all you've got is old bones."

She freed her hands from his and leaned toward him, clasping his head and lightly guiding him forward until his face rested against her breasts. Broder could feel her heart beating, feel the warmth and depth of this woman he had loved and somehow let slip away. He wanted to pull her tightly to him and hold her forever, as if this might bridge the years they had lost and blot them permanently from his memory.

"You can't believe how much I've missed you," he said.

Colletta started to speak, but before she could make a sound there was a knock on the door and the room suddenly was crowded by the commanding presence of Lieutenant Colonel Eldon Hewlett: "Excuse me, sergeant, ma'am. I'm sorry to interrupt, but I'm on a tight schedule this morning. I only need a minute."

Colletta stepped back quickly, away from Broder's bedside. "I need to go," she murmured, and disappeared into
the hallway. Broder's physical pain was overtaken by the icy
hurt of something precious being pulled away yet again, as
if loss was to be his enduring lot in life.

"I'm sorry, Broder," the colonel said. "Looks like I came
at a bad time, but what I have to say is urgent and I needed
to say it now."

"What is it, sir?"

"Captain Oates has requested that you be assigned to his
HQ detachment and I'd like to go along with it. He said the
two of you talked about it. Is that correct?"

"You could say that, but it was something of a one-way
conversation."

"How do you feel about it?"

"Let's just say it wouldn't be my first choice, sir."

"I figured as much. But I need you over there, Broder. If I
approve his request, you'll be getting orders in a week or so.
If I don't, it won't happen."

"I don't understand why he asked for me, sir."

"Sergeant Broder, do you understand the importance of
perception?"

"Sir?"

"Perception. People see vichyssoise and escargot on the
menu, they think they're getting fine food. Offer them cold
potato-and-onion soup and snails, they're going to turn up
their noses. That's perception, Broder."

"Yes, sir. But I'm afraid I don't get your point. What does
that have to do with me and Captain Oates?"

"Because for some reason Oates has a perception of you
as a screw-up, somebody with a shady past. Something he
can use against you. I know you're a good soldier, otherwise
we wouldn't be having this conversation. But Oates sees you
in a different light. He'll try to use you. You're going to be in
a tough situation. What I really came for, is to offer you a
last chance to back out."

"Colonel, you said you need me in Oates's outfit, right?"

"Yes, sergeant, just like we discussed it the other day. But you have to do it of your own free will."

"Go ahead and let them cut the orders."

As Colonel Hewlett walked briskly away from the Fort Bragg hospital, Broder lay on his bed and agonized over what had just occurred. How sweet Colletta's presence had been, and how unfair it seemed that her visit once again was cut short so ruthlessly when he had wanted and needed so very much for her to stay. And for what? What had he gotten himself into? He had a hunch he'd find out soon enough, and felt a wave of dread wash over him like the surf at high tide collapsing a child's sand-castle on the beach.

ᘓ

ᘓ COLLETTA AND JIMMIE were hunched together on the dingy sofa in the Saylor living room. Her face was distorted with pain. "It hurts something awful," she said, pulling her left arm tight across the front of her body and clasping the rigid cast with her right hand as if squeezing the hard, molded form that encased her fractured bone might somehow lessen the torment. Jimmie gently put his arm across her shoulders. He wanted to pull her closer but was afraid to be too forceful.

"Don't you have more pills?" he asked. "You shouldn't have to suffer so much pain."

"The pills are all gone. Momma was going to call the doctor today and get me a new prescription, but she won't be home till tonight. I'm sorry I'm such a baby with this."

"Don't act crazy. Nobody is being a baby because a broken arm hurts."

A muted knocking at the front door led Jimmie to draw himself away, gingerly, and pull up to a standing position. "Let me find out who that is," he said. "You don't need to move." He crossed the room, walking softly, as if the sound of his footsteps might intensify Colletta's pain, and opened the door carefully.

105

On the porch stood Donnie Shand.

"I heard about Colletta's accident," Donnie greeted him. "I just wondered is she doing all right?"

"She'll be glad to see you, DJ."

Donnie Shand spied Colletta on the sofa and went quickly to her, his face bright with the crooked smile that once had been a constant in their lives. "Jaybo told me what happened," he said. "How ya' doin'?"

Colletta minimized the pain she had confided to Jimmie only minutes before. She told Donnie that she was doing well and said it was good to see him again.

"I'm sorry I don't see you guys as often as I'd like anymore," Donnie said. "I miss y'all a lot, both of you. And I miss seeing Ray-Gene."

"I guess you stay busy, with work and all," Jimmie said.

"Yeah, most of the time. Ray-Gene tells me you and him got your driver's licenses."

"Yes. But it won't likely make much of a difference since neither one of us has a car."

DJ eased himself down beside Colletta. "Jaybo didn't tell me very much about what happened," he said. "How'd you break your arm?"

"Fell off a chair."

"No kiddin'? You ought to know better than to be climbing on chairs! Where's Hunter at today?"

"Back in his room reading a book. Hunter's got real big on reading lately."

"I guess that's good," Donnie said. "Myself, I never saw a book I had any trouble putting down. Are your momma and daddy doing okay?"

"Yes."

If DJ noticed the brusqueness of her reply, he gave no indication.

Jimmie would not have believed that Donnie Shand's presence could make him feel awkward, but their old friend suddenly struck him as out of place here in Colletta's house, like a distant relative who showed up unexpectedly at a family gathering. He wanted very much for Donnie to go; the distant relative was invading their privacy, disrupting their solitude. "Colletta has been in a lot of pain," he told Donnie. "She won't complain, but her arm hurts pretty bad."

"Nobody should have to hurt from something like a broken arm," Donnie said. "Don't you have some pain medication or something, Colletta?"

"I won't have anything until mom gets home," Colletta said, "but I'm doing okay."

DJ's smile became a frown. "You shouldn't be without medicine when you have pain," he said angrily. "Look, I've got something that will help." He drew a small envelope from his shirt pocket and held it toward her. "This is prescription medicine that'd be safe for you to take. It will hold you till your mother gets home."

"I don't think I could take something ordered for somebody else," Colletta said.

"Sure you can. I told you, it's a prescription. Probably the same thing the doctor would give you. It'd be just as safe for you as it would for anybody else. Please take it. You need it. I can get more."

"I don't know if I should," Colletta said. "But my arm does hurt a lot. If you're sure it's okay for me, it might help for a little while. Don't you think so, Jimmie?"

"I don't like to see you in so much pain," Jimmie told her. "If it's drug-store medicine it should be safe. I don't see any reason you couldn't take it."

Donnie Shand gave her the envelope. "Good," he said. "I'm glad I could help. Take two of these now, Colletta, and then take more when you feel it wearing off. You can have them all." Jimmie went to the kitchen and brought a glass of water. Colletta swallowed two of Donnie's pills. He assured her the pills would work fast. "I have to go," he said. "But it's good I come by when you needed me, right? I'll see y'all again soon, I promise."

DJ's pills quickly numbed Colletta's pain. She told Jimmie she was considerably improved, felt better in fact than she had for several days. Her whole outlook was brighter. She was sorry for complaining about her little hurt, which probably was much less than what lots of people endured every day and didn't even talk about. And maybe she had worried too much over all the problems she felt responsible for. Everyone probably considered her foolish for climbing on a chair and they had a perfect right to do so, and she'd experienced enough embarrassment to pay for her mistake and felt guilty about all the hardships she'd brought on her family, the medical bills, her limitations when it came to taking care of the house and looking after Hunter with her broken arm and, worst of all, her father's humiliation and the anxiety her mother had suffered. But now she thought it couldn't have been all that bad, and she wasn't going to think about it any more.

🙠 JIMMIE AND RAY-GENE accepted the first paying jobs they were offered. Their search for work had gone on for months, and they had long since stopped being particular.

Ray-Gene would be the newest grocery bagger and carry-out boy at the IGA supermarket where Colletta's mother worked, twenty hours a week maximum. His schedule for the first two weeks suggested that he would be lucky if he clocked even half of his allowed hours, but it was a beginning. He was optimistic about his future with IGA.

Jimmie took a part-time job with a used-car dealer commonly known as Mack Brown, washing and polishing the automobiles Mack bought or traded for before they went on the sales lot. Mack was a solid and respected figure in the area business community and many of the younger men in Conway had worked for him at some time in their lives. They all knew the story of how his phony name came from an old cowboy movie star and they generally had found him easy to work for and honest with their pay.

Donnie Shand stopped by the car lot on Jimmie's first day on the job, smiling and happy. He joked about a used-up old Pontiac Jimmie was trying to make presentable, but understood the peril of keeping a new employee from his work. He left after only a few minutes, promising to come again soon. Jimmie remembered the ill feeling he'd harbored toward Donnie that day at Colletta's house and felt bad for it. DJ was still his friend, still the leader of the team.

The prospect of having money to spend was new to Jimmie and Ray-Gene. Their earnings would be modest, but to them any amount would have been impressive. Neither had given much thought to what he would do with his first paycheck. Jimmie's mother urged him to save all he could, and Ray-Gene got the same advice from Grandma Freeman.

Popeye Broder warned Jimmie to take his job seriously and never lose sight of the fact that the impression he made on his first boss might follow him all his life. "No foolishness," he admonished.

Jimmie took his father's counsel to heart, determined that his boss would see what a hard worker he was. But two hours into his third morning on the job he was vigorously polishing a faded black Lincoln Towncar, intent on his work and oblivious to his surroundings, when Mack Brown slipped up silently from behind and popped an air-filled paper bag close to his head. Jimmie jumped and yelled, and Mack roared with laughter.

"You're too serious, boy," Mack said, still laughing. "We need to loosen you up a little. Life's too short not to have a little fun along the way."

"You scared me, Mack," Jimmie said. "I didn't hear you coming."

"I can sneak up on anybody," Mack Brown bragged. "My papa used to say I was part Indian."

"Are you?"

"Naw, he just said that because of the way I could sneak up on people. I used to do it all the time when I was a little kid. My grandmother started calling me Cherokee, but I wanted to be called Mack Brown after my favorite cowboy movie star, Johnny Mack Brown. You're not old enough to remember Johnny Mack Brown, are you boy?"

"I never heard of him before. Was he famous?"

"Sure he was. And I could act just like him. Papa thought it was pretty funny and started to call me Mack Brown, just like I wanted. My mother hated it."

"Can you still act like him? Not that I would know, since I never saw him."

"Nobody's around who would know anymore," Mack said. "I probably couldn't do it anyway. I thought I looked like old Johnny Mack when I was little. But he was a solid fellow with nice black hair and I grew up tall and skinny as a stringbean with big thick glasses and this mop of red on top. Well, I guess it's more gray than red now, but it used to be red."

Jimmie had kept on working while his boss talked. Conscious of his father's advice, he was afraid to give the appearance of slacking off.

"Tell you what," Mack Brown said, "I busted my doughnut sack behind your head. How about you running down yonder to the doughnut shop on the corner and getting us another one? And you might as well get a dozen doughnuts while you're at it."

"I thought doughnuts came in boxes," Jimmie said.

"Hell, boy. Lighten up. I'm trying to give you an excuse to slow down awhile and go get us some doughnuts. This Lincoln isn't going anywhere. The sack thing was a joke." Mack Brown laughed merrily. "Here's the money. Go on now. Get us a box or bag or whatever the hell they come in. Any kind you want."

Jimmie got the doughnuts. When he got back to the car lot, Mack insisted they sit in the sales office long enough for his new employee to drink a cup of coffee with his boss, have a couple of doughnuts, and get better acquainted.

110

In the next half-hour, Jimmie surmised several things about Mack Brown. Mack was naturally friendly, wanted Jimmie's company, and had no ulterior motives in asking his hired hand to sit and talk. His boss was easy-going and un-pretentious, far removed from the stereotypical used-car salesman. And Mack Brown knew more about the people of Conway than anyone Jimmie had ever talked to before.

"I've been up here a long time," Mack Brown said. "This town has changed some, but not all that much. And people, they don't hardly change. You ever lived anywhere else?"

"I was born here," Jimmie asserted.

"Well, Conway is a good place to live. I've been here a little more than thirty years. I was born down in Savannah, Georgia."

"What brought you up here?"

"Business. I was looking for a good place to start my own business and found an up-and-going establishment here that was for sale cheap. Been here ever since. I noticed that Shand boy talking to you the other day. Is he a friend of yours?"

"Donnie Shand? Yes, me and Donnie have been friends since we were real little. But I suppose I need to get back to work, Mack."

"I guess we do need to get that Lincoln on the lot one of these days," Mack said, without conviction, making no move to indicate their doughnut break was over. "I suppose you know what happened to the Shand boy's daddy, then?"

"Yes. I was there. Not something I'll ever forget."

"I can tell you one thing, boy. There were a lot of people in this town who thought that Shand woman should have gone to jail. I'm not saying I was one of them, but I knew plenty who said a woman ought not to be able to kill her husband and get off scot-free."

"I know she was awful sorry about what happened."

"That may put her in good stead with the Almighty, son, but it don't usually cut much slack with the law. Mind you I'm not taking sides, just saying what I know."

THE SINCERE and tearful remorse Jacob Saylor exhibited when his daughter suffered the broken arm proved short-lived. He managed a week without a drink, but temptation overcame him at that point and the crash was complete. He disappeared for three days.

"We knew it wouldn't last," Colletta told Jimmie. "He just can't make it very long, no matter how hard he tries."

"I don't think he'll ever change, Colletta."

"Momma says we have to have hope."

"Sure you do. But you have to be realistic about it. Do you really think he'll change?"

"I don't know. But I'm not going to give up hope."

His new job meant that Jimmie had less time to spend with Colletta, which was somewhat ironic because they had worked out a simple system that she could use as a signal when her father was not in the house. After Jimmie told her about Ray-Gene's suggestion, Colletta found an old picture postcard from Florida—a faded photo of a pink flamingo—which she would stand in a corner of a front window to show that her father was gone. Jimmie could feel free to visit whenever the flamingo was displayed. Unlike the rag on the door handle that Ray-Gene had suggested, Mr. Saylor would never notice the postcard even if he came home while it was visible.

On a couple of occasions when he stumbled home earlier than usual and found Jimmie at the house, Mr. Saylor hardly paid him notice. Colletta said their scheme with the pink flamingo wasn't needed anymore, but it had added a sense of risk and daring to Jimmie's visits and for that reason they kept on playing their little game.

❧11❧

HEN ORDERS transferring him to Captain Homer Oates's headquarters detachment arrived, Broder's immediate reaction was a slight sense of satisfaction; Rondell Wilson could no longer doubt his story about the mysterious Oates "recruiting" visit. Wilson had professed to accept Broder's account of that meeting, but Broder suspected his genial caretaker of harboring at least a modest level of skepticism. And Broder, himself, still found that particular session with Oates hard to believe.

But here it was in black and white, orders to report to Captain Oates's unit upon release from the post hospital. His reassignment, on paper, already had taken place. He had the option of a week's leave before returning to duty.

Given the uncertainties that lay ahead, Broder found that he was no longer eager to leave the protective sanctuary of the cramped hospital room Wilson mockingly referred to as his penthouse suite. Even under the best of circumstances, his eagerness for a new assignment probably would have been dampened by the lingering threat that he could no longer jump. Now there was this enigmatic tug-of-war between Oates and Colonel Hewlett, in which he had begun to worry that he might be a powerless puppet whose strings were being pulled from both sides.

Broder had tried to stop agonizing over his new post. Whatever lay ahead, he'd face up to it when the time came, the same way he had dealt with military life from the outset. He had faced a great many uncertainties before he had been admitted to the elite Airborne fraternity, and since he began jumping his training had put heavy emphasis on staying flexible, ready for whatever the day might bring.

He had been sorely tempted to tell Rondell Wilson what went on in Hewlett's office that day. Oates was using him for something he would rather not get involved in, and what were Colonel Eldon Hewlett's motives? He wanted to trust Hewlett and felt he had little choice but to go along with whatever game the colonel was playing. If his trust in the colonel should prove a mistake, he would be in even deeper jeopardy. He would be more comfortable with his situation if someone else, a trusted outsider, knew what was going on. That would be Wilson.

Wilson barely glanced at the paper Broder tendered. He twisted his mouth toward one side of his face and looked up and away, as if he needed to refocus his eyes. Broder had learned to read that unconscious signal; Wilson twisted his face like that when he was anxious about something.

"I hate to see this, Broder," Wilson said, honest concern in his voice. "I really do. I don't know what Oates is up to, but I wish you hadn't been dragged into it. I wouldn't trust Oates as far as I could throw a Humvee."

"I know. You told me that before."

"And I'll probably tell you a dozen times more before you clear out of here. Where is his outfit, anyway?"

"Not sure yet," Broder said, "but I think it's the old Third Training Regiment headquarters."

"Yeah, I know where that is. Will you try to come back around and see me once in awhile, after you get over there?"

"Why bother? You'd be busy, jerking around some dumb meathead silk-jockey like me down in the torture chamber."

"Torture chamber, my ass. Rehab's what got you through this, Broder."

"I'm kidding. You did fantastic things for me. I'll never forget it, man. Of course I'll come see you. I know where to find you."

"Well, you're not gone yet," Wilson said. "Who knows? I may get another whole week to torture you. And we're about to get sentimental here, which I'm sure your Captain Oatmeal would not approve of. Now that you're mended enough to do things like hit the shower all by yourself, I've got to get on down the hall and take care of some guys who need me. See you later."

Broder showered and dressed, still in cut-away pajamas to accommodate his awkward leg-cast. He studied the cast. The time Colletta fell off the chair and broke her arm . . . that's really when her trouble began.

He felt all alone. Slouched in a corner of a starkly unadorned room of the Fort Bragg medical center orthopedic ward, he wished he could be a child again. He wanted to be back in Conway with Ray-Gene and Colletta and Donnie Shand and have nothing more on his mind than how to pass the time on a hot summer afternoon. But those innocent days were a distant past, and ended too soon, fated to be overshadowed by darker times that were every bit as much alive in his memory, trying recollections more difficult to escape and hard to push aside once they surfaced. Happy mental images from the good times inevitably led to malevolent ones from the bad.

The one sure defense Broder had found to keep those dark reflections bottled up in the deeper recesses of his mind was jumping. His very first jump had led to nearly total serenity, and Airborne life had assured a training regimen that helped maintain his equanimity. The shattered leg was not the only casualty of his hard landing.

Broder had fought desperately to discipline his mind the same as he had disciplined his body. He had conquered fear, learned to accept the ridiculous vagaries of military life, and convinced himself that he truly was the master of his own destiny. One bad jump had severely shaken his confidence, but he was not about to give up on himself just yet. He could handle whatever obstacles fortune threw up in his path. As to the current situation, he simply had too much time on his hands and too much time on his hands engendered too much negative thinking. Inactivity had salted the refuge of his hospital room with traps and snares and he needed to be more vigilant.

There were simple tricks. Instead of allowing himself to dwell on somber reflections on all the ways his life had gone wrong, he would force himself to concentrate on the mundane things by which he was surrounded. A variety smells from the hospital kitchen filled his room. What were they? Today it was something pungent and overpowering, unidentifiable, but no doubt a less palatable Army version of wonderful and exotic fare. Pleasant aromas too, but these were less dominant, easily subordinated. He would have no appetite for lunch or dinner.

He thought about his red Mustang, deserted on a parking lot near his old unit. It would be safe. No hard miles being put on it so long as its only driver sat here nursing a mending leg. He had intended to put the Mustang in storage if he received overseas orders, but that was a moot point now.

He would have to move, once he was out and about. His jumping gear would have to be turned in while he was temporarily denied paratroop duty. This was something he had considered before, then pushed out of his mind like those bad memories. Not something he looked forward to, but he'd face up to it early on and get it out of the way.

Broder's solitude was broken, finally, by an orderly who stopped by to deliver mail. "Looks like you're living right, Sergeant Broder," the slender, blond and boyish-looking young man joked. "Got a letter for you today."

"Letters fall on the unjust as well as the just," Broder replied. "I don't remember seeing you around here before. New to this paradise?"

"Been here for a year, sergeant. I'm Kent. You probably haven't seen me much because I've been on leave for three weeks, home in Cleveland."

116

"Cleveland, as in Ohio? I hear it's a beautiful place."
"I know you're putting me on, but the truth is Cleveland is a beautiful place. It just doesn't get the credit it deserves."

"Just like you and me, Kent," Broder said, which sent the orderly on his way in good humor.

He ripped open the letter. He would have recognized its origin even from some distance, with Allou Broder's large, awkward, familiar left-handed scrawl covering much of the front of the envelope. As always, the Conway return address was on the back. The letter had been forwarded by the clerk in his old unit, and he felt guilty for not having written and telling his parents about his training accident and its consequences.

His mother's correspondence was typically brief: Things were pretty much the same in Conway. She and Dad were well, as she hoped he was. She fretted about all the turmoil going on in the world and whether he might have to go to war.

Okay, he needed to write and bring his mother and father up to date, soft-pedal the bad jump and the hurt but let them know he was safe from combat duty any time soon and relieve their minds. He would write this afternoon.

But his mother's letter reminded him again of another place and time and brought back the bittersweet memories he had worked hard to thrust aside. It also led him to an impulsive, but firm, resolution. He had a week of time off coming, and now he recognized how priceless that week could be.

He yearned to find Colletta, see her in her own surroundings, sit across from her at a corner table in a dimly lighted little café, drive along a quiet street with her at his side. He vowed that he would take his leave and do these things. He had new incentive now to gain his release from the hospital. Having a purpose and a plan renewed his spirit, though his mind still was not at ease.

• MACK BROWN hated to sit around on slow business days with no one to talk to. He claimed to despise this more than just about anything else he could think of, with the possible exception of waiting out an ambivalent hurricane warning, and if there was no customer on the car lot he would entice some innocent passerby with a free cup of coffee. Innocent, in this case, meant anyone who had not been trapped into the experience before and therefore didn't know better.

As a last resort, Mack would call Jimmie off the lot and insist that he sit and talk. Or more accurately, listen.

Mack claimed to remember every customer he'd ever had. He could describe in infinite detail the circumstances under which countless individuals in and around Horry County had bought his vehicles, always delineating how he had been too considerate, sold too cheap, and many times taken an outright loss. He purported to know how many Buicks he'd sold, how many Fords, how many Dodges, how many Oldsmobiles and Chryslers, how many pickup trucks, how many foreign cars.

Jimmie calculated that if all the tales his boss told were true there were scores if not hundreds of unfortunates who had profited from Mack's generosity. But Mack rarely included dates, and given the number of years he'd been in business Jimmie supposed it possible that he was guilty of nothing more serious than modest exaggeration. He was inclined to give Mack the benefit of the doubt.

"And by the way," Mack Brown said one morning, "if you need a car some weekend, take that little white Chevy Celebrity over there. It's real clean. Lots of miles left on it. Good tires. Drive it like it was your own, but you have to pay for the gas."

The offer was unexpected. At no time had Mack indicated that use of a car was among the perks of Jimmie's job. Mack kept on talking without waiting for a response. "I forgot to tell you," he said, "Donnie Shand came by looking for you Friday when you weren't here. He seems like a good kid. I guess it must have been pretty hard for him, given what happened to his father and all. You know him right well, didn't you say?"

"Yes. I used to see him a lot." Jimmie hoped that Mack would go on with his own stories and not dwell on Donnie Shand. Mack was a gossip. Jimmie had no desire to give him fodder for the rumor mill.

"I guess you know, then, what happened to his daddy?"

"Yes, I know. We talked about it before."

But Mack Brown was not to be deterred. "Pretty nasty business," he went on, "a man getting his head bashed in by his own wife. You probably wouldn't know it, but a lot of people in Conway thought she hadn't ought to get off so easy."

"Yes," Jimmie said, "you told me."

"Well, I don't claim to know what should be done in cases like that. I suppose the authorities looked into it well enough. If they thought she was justified in what she did, I don't feel like it's my place to second-guess anybody. But like I said, I know there's lots who feel different."

Before Jimmie had time to respond, Mack spotted a potential customer on the lot and was quickly on his feet and out the door. Jimmie took a last bite of doughnut, wiped his hands on the front of his shirt, and went back to work.

Mack was tied up with his customer for the rest of the morning, working hard to make a sale. The man test-drove three different vehicles and lingered over each one after he brought it back to the lot, moving around it deliberately, viewing it from various angles as if to see it in some particular light.

This was the challenge Mack Brown clearly thrived on. He was patient, never attempted to pressure a customer, and didn't mind if a potential buyer spent a week on his car lot so long as the contact ended in a sale. "We've got as much time as Columbus sailing the ocean blue," he'd say, and as a final inducement he'd promise a full refund to any buyer who ever caught him in a lie. If he happened to sense that a six-pack of beer or a half-pint of whiskey might be looked on favorably he would get that little premium on the table right away. Sometimes this was all it took to lock in a promising deal.

So far as Jimmie was concerned, it was a relief to have Mack kept busy. He had no desire to resume their conversation about the death of Langly Shand.

Jimmie had been jittery with anticipation from the instant Mack offered the use of a car and could not wait to tell Colletta and Ray-Gene. He headed straight for the Saylor house when his work on the car lot was finished for the day. He ran half-way, reluctantly slowing to a walk only when he was out of breath.

Colletta answered his impatient knock. Her mother was there also, unusual because she normally would be at work at the IGA this time of day. Mrs. Saylor acknowledged him from the kitchen, barely looking up, said it was good to see him, seemed like it had been a long time. Jimmie said yes, it had been a long time, and he was happy to see her too and he hoped she was well. But he was looking at Colletta all the while he exchanged pleasantries with her mother, and he could see that she was not well.

Colletta stared back at him, dully, as if he were a stranger in whom she had no interest. She was tired-looking, pale and drawn. She said, "Hey, Jimmie," in a weak and drowsy voice. "You not workin' today?"

"I worked. I'm done for the day," he told her.

"I forgot. You get lots of time off."

"I only work part-time, Colletta. Mack doesn't want me around unless he has a lot of stuff for me to do. That's why I've been able to come by here lots of afternoons."

"Oh, yeah," Colletta said, "I forgot."

"Are you sick? You don't seem like yourself today. You don't look good at all."

"It's probably just the medicine I've been taking. It makes me sleepy. Sometimes it makes me a little sick, I think, but I don't know for sure if that's what it is. Maybe it's just a bug or something."

"Do you want me to go on home, so you can lie down?"

"No, please stay. I was hoping you would come."

"Anyway, I just came by for a minute to tell you something. I didn't plan to stay long."

"What is it?" Her question was mechanical, lacking any manifestation of enthusiasm, any real curiosity.

"Nothing important," Jimmie said. He was disappointed to see already that Colletta might not share his excitement. "I was just goin' to tell you Mack Brown said I could use one of his cars some weekend if I wanted to, that's all."

"That's good, Jimmie. I didn't know Mack let you use a car."

"Neither did I. Mack hadn't mentioned it before, else I would have told you. But we can talk about it more later, after you're feeling better."

"I'm okay," Colletta insisted. "I probably just need another pill." She looked past Jimmie into the kitchen, raised her voice only slightly. "Don't you think so, Momma?"

Mrs. Saylor took a few steps toward them, into the room. "I don't like you taking so much medicine," she said. "We don't even know what those pills are."

"That's silly, Momma. It's prescription medicine. DJ said so."

Real concern marked Wanda Saylor's face. "But those pills are for pain, honey," she said. "I wouldn't think they'd be good just because you don't feel well."

"The pain's why I've been taking them, Momma. My arm hurt like everything yesterday."

This was the first time Jimmie had heard Colletta complain of pain since the cast had been removed from her broken arm two weeks earlier and he was surprised. "Are you still taking the pills DJ gave you?" he asked. "I didn't know he gave you enough for that long."

"I used them all up," Colletta said, "but DJ came by a couple of days ago and brought me some more, just in case I had more pain. He said they were kind of a gift from Jaybo."

⮞ JIMMIE FELT like a million dollars as he walked up to Mack Brown's car lot on Saturday afternoon to pick up his first loaner. The white Celebrity Mack had nominated earlier was gone, sold to a man who worked for the city street department, but Mack was equally high on a green Plymouth Reliant he had taken in trade on a big Chrysler. Mack said it was as good a car as Jimmie would ever need and watched like a proud father as he drove off the lot with exaggerated caution and turned toward town.

Jimmie went straight to the IGA store and waited in the parking lot until Ray-Gene got off work at four o'clock. After that, the two drove aimlessly around the city. They had no place to go, but that did not matter; having an automobile elevated them to higher ranks and neither would have dared ask for more.

"Has Colletta seen it yet?" Ray-Gene asked.

"No," Jimmie said, "I just picked it up a little while ago, just before I came by the IGA and got you. I wanted to go by Colletta's, but I think she's sick and sometimes Mr. Saylor tries to stay home long enough to sober up if he thinks one of the kids might need him."

"Like he'd be able to help," Ray-Gene said sarcastically.

"Yeah, well, something strange is going on with Colletta too, Ray-Gene."

"Strange like what?"

Jimmie hated trying to explain his anxiety to Ray-Gene, but for the last three days he had been unable to escape a mental image of Colletta's mother with her worry-etched face. He had been to the Saylor house only once since the day he'd observed Mrs. Saylor's conspicuous apprehension, and although Colletta claimed she was feeling well, she had been moody and restless. This was not at all like Colletta.

"Maybe I shouldn't have said anything," he told Ray-Gene. "I'm probably just over-reacting. Colletta's been sick again and I get worried, but I think she's probably okay now."

"But you just said you didn't take your car by her house because you thought she's sick. You're confusing me."

"Damn it, I don't know what's going on with Colletta."

"Hey, I didn't mean to upset you."

They rode for a time without conversation. Music from a classic rock station played through the car radio, its volume turned low. There was a long commercial break and Ray-Gene laughed at a comic beer advertisement, distracting Jimmie so that he almost drove through a red traffic light. He saw it just in time and hit the brakes hard.

"So DJ's not seen it either," Ray-Gene said finally. "You seen him recently?"

Jimmie was glad for the change in subject. "No, not recently," he said. "The last time I saw him was when Colletta broke her arm. Mack Brown said he come by the lot looking for me, but I wasn't there. He's not been back."

"I was thinking maybe we ought to go by his place and see if he's home. He'd like to see your car, don't you think?"

Jimmie agreed. He swung into the parking lot of a hardware store and turned around, then drove to Donnie Shand's house. The house was dark, and no one came to the door.

Ray-Gene was obviously disappointed. "You got the car all weekend?" he asked.

"Sure. I just have to take it back Monday morning, when I go to work."

"Let's go by DJ's tomorrow, then."

"I was going to show the car to Colletta tomorrow. She ought to be all right by then. You don't have to work?"

"Naw, I'm off on Sunday this week," Ray-Gene said. "Maybe Colletta could get out of the house and go with us."

"We'd probably have to take Hunter, too."

"That's not a problem."
"Okay. We'll do it tomorrow."

❧ *IT WAS EARLY* afternoon when Jimmie stopped in front of the Saylor house. Hunter was in the window and saw him drive up and had the front door open wide even before he was on the porch, calling "Hey, Jimmie" excitedly.

Jimmie said "Hey, Hunter" back and went inside, looking about for Colletta. There was no sign that anyone else was there.

"You got a car, Jimmie?"

"Yeah, I get to use it all I want. Is Colletta here?"

"Colletta went somewhere," Hunter said.

"And left you here by yourself? Do you know where she went?"

"It's okay. Momma says I'm old enough that I can stay by myself now."

"Sure you are, Hunter. There's no doubt about that. Do you know where Colletta went?"

"She went to get her some medicine."

"Is Colletta still sick?"

"I don't know. What kind of car is that, Jimmie?"

"It's a Plymouth. But tell me about Colletta, Hunter. I didn't know she was still sick. If you know where she went we can go in the car and meet her so she don't have to walk all that way. Did she go to the drug store, or where?"

"She didn't go to the drug store."

"Where, then?"

"I don't know. She said she had to have some pills, and she didn't say where. I don't know where she went."

❧12❧

THE MEXICANA was crowded with lunch-time customers. Broder slid into a booth by a front window. From nothing more than habit, he preferred to sit where he had a clear view of the Mustang in the pine-shaded parking lot. He had surveyed the restaurant quickly when he entered, looking for Colletta, but she was nowhere in sight.

It felt good simply to be out among people again. With his cast removed and only a heavy wrap on his leg, he had been able to dress in ordinary clothes for the first time in what seemed an eternity. He walked with the aid of a single crutch, could bend his knee, and even found it possible to get in and out of the Mustang without too much difficulty.

He wore civilian clothes. In a military town like Fayetteville, he would have been recognized as a soldier rather easily in ordinary times despite his dress but the extended hospital stay had left him pale-skinned and his hair was long by Army standards. Only the Fort Bragg registration decals on the Mustang would give him away. Not that he wished to pass for a civilian; he thought of himself strictly in terms of Airborne and civilian life was something he had left far behind, like a world traveler who barely remembered his homeland.

An efficient young man introduced himself as Michael, his server. Michael took his order, rushed it to the kitchen, and returned promptly with a sweating glass of cold sweet tea wrapped in a paper napkin.

"You're busy today," Broder said.

"It's always this way at lunch time," Michael said."Is this your first time here?"

"I've been here before, but not this time of day. Do you know someone named Colletta, who works here?"

"No, but I've not been here very long. I'll ask in back, if you like. What's her last name?"

"Saylor. Colletta Saylor."

"I'll find out for you."

Broder sipped his tea and waited for Michael to bring his cheeseburger basket, chosen over the Mexicana's more exotic specialties. He wondered if Colletta might have grounds for offense at having him inquire. He could think of no reason why she would object, and waited contentedly for his server to return. The wait was short.

"I'm sorry, sir," Michael said as he placed Broder's food on the table, "but the manager said it is against company policy to give out any information about employees." The waiter obviously was embarrassed by what he had to report.

Broder regretted having put him in that position. "That's okay," he said. "I appreciate your effort." Then, to put the server more at ease, "Don't worry, I'm not from the IRS or anything like that. Colletta's an old friend and I just heard recently that she works here. No big deal."

The young man wiped diligently at Broder's table and stacked dishware he'd picked up across the aisle, glancing warily toward the back of the restaurant as he worked. "I know someone who can help you find her," he whispered. "Just sit tight."

Broder smiled. Colletta would savor the intrigue. She also would be surprised to see him, if he managed to find her, because other than a lone mention of the Mexicana she had not left a single clue as to how he might get in touch. He pondered whether her secrecy might have been intentional, and promptly rejected any such notion.

She had no reason to hide. The disjointed, helter-skelter way things happened during her visits to the medical center simply had not encouraged her to talk much about herself.

The day Colletta first showed up, like a wraith from his distant past, he had barely been aware of her presence. All her visits combined would add up only to minutes, not hours, and they had had precious little opportunity for talk. Rondell Wilson often had been nearby, and there always had been an interruption of one kind or another.

He still was amazed that she had come to him at all. Her reappearance at this point in his life probably was the last thing Broder would have expected, but now, sitting here in the brightly lit Mexicana and surrounded by cheerful people in ordinary, everyday encounters, it was as if he waited for Colletta to join him. She would slip into the opposite seat and look into his eyes and smile. "Hey, Jimmie," she'd say softly, "how ya' doin'?" Unthinkable as such a sweet happening may have been only a few short weeks ago, at this moment it would pass as just another of those ordinary, everyday occurrences.

"You the fella lookin' for Colletta?"

Broder was startled. Engrossed in his own thoughts, he hadn't noticed the pretty, dark young woman who stopped beside his table, leaning in close so that she could speak quietly.

"I'm sorry," she said, somewhat louder. "I didn't mean to scare you!"

Broder smiled. "Don't apologize," he said. "I'm the one who should be sorry. My mind was a thousand miles away. Yes, I asked about Colletta. Do you know her?"

"She's a friend. I can tell her you asked, but you'll have to tell me your name. I wouldn't do anything in the world to hurt Colletta."

"Neither would I. My name's Jimmie and Colletta's my friend, too. We hadn't seen each other for a long time, and I just found out recently that she worked here."

The young woman slipped into the seat across the table, where Broder had just imagined Colletta. She extended her hand and returned Broder's smile. "I'm Maria. I know who you are," she said. "You're the guy who's turned Colletta's life upside down. I don't mean that in a bad way, Jimmie. It's obvious you're one of the good guys, and lord knows Colletta needs more of those in her life."

"Do you know if she'll be in today, or could you give me her phone number?" Broder inquired.

"She's not here, Jimmie. She took the week off, said she had to get away somewhere where she could think things through. I think that involves you, but you probably know that."

"Any idea where she went?"

"She wasn't sure where she was going to end up. She just needed to get away."

"Isn't the boy in school?"

"Day care," Maria said. "He can be away anytime."

"Do you expect her back by the weekend?"

"I have to tell you the truth. Colletta sounded awful uncertain the last time I talked to her. I'm not sure she's coming back."

BRODER GUNNED the Mustang east on Bragg Boulevard, oblivious to speed limits and traffic. He merged in and out of lanes, stopped and started with changing signals, driving mechanically, crossed the Cape Fear River into East Fayetteville barely aware of where he was or how he got there. He turned right at Cedar Creek Road and roared toward I-95.

Of all the things that had gone wrong in his life, few had jolted him like Maria's words: "I'm not sure she's coming back."

If Colletta was leaving Fayetteville, it was because she was running from him. It was because she had chosen to withdraw again, after touching his life but briefly, like a bullet glancing off his skull and leaving him dazed and wounded, groping in the dark. What had he done to deserve this? What could he have said that drove her away? How could he have misread her so completely? He cursed the fates that caused his bad jump, that broke his body and put him in the hospital, that brought Colletta to him and took him back in time.

He pushed the Mustang south on the Interstate at speeds of eighty-five and then ninety, raced past Lumberton exits and saw the signs he hadn't really wanted to see. The state line was just ahead. He would be back in South Carolina in the blink of an eye.

And there it was: South of the Border, the sprawling, themed tourist sanctuary, grand and gaudy with its large fiberglass figures, its fast food and trinkets, its welcoming "Pedro" and giant sombrero, an honored stopping place in the miles of desolate pine woods known affectionately by hundreds of thousands of East-Coast travelers. It was a place to which he once had brought Colletta and Hunter, in the cherry-red Dodge Shadow he still remembered fondly — the first truly road-worthy automobile loaned him by Mack Brown. They had come for the simplest of reasons: Colletta had been sick, but now she was feeling much better, and she'd heard of South of the Border all her life, considered it distant and exotic, a sight she'd always wanted to see. And they'd found it a majestic place, where they bought Cokes and hot dogs and Hunter had counted license tags from New York and New Jersey and Virginia and Florida and Georgia and no one had been disappointed.

That had been their longest journey together. Colletta snuggled close in the seat beside him and Hunter played the radio alongside. Broder remembered her sweetness and how in love they'd been and how grown-up they'd felt, pretending they were happy travelers who might be on their way to anywhere in the country and maybe they would be gone for weeks.

That all happened long ago. In the years since, he had driven this highway many times, zipped by South of the Border with scarcely a passing glance.

He had learned to put that day behind him, to let go. But not this time. Memories of Colletta were here.

He wanted to dislodge himself from this small corner of the world and fly to a far-away place. He wanted to jump into an inky darkness, feel the rush of cold wind in his face, lose himself to free fall through the empty space between earth and heaven, forget everything that had gone before. But Colletta had come back into his life and he could not escape the past.

RAY-GENE TRIED hard to stay out of Jaybo's business. Jaybo might be family, but he was the kind of family nobody needed, and even Grandma Freeman, Jaybo's own mother, made a habit of talking Jaybo down. Ravonelle preached the principle that what you don't know won't hurt you, and had warned Ray-Gene time and again to separate himself as far as possible from his uncle's shady dealings. "He'll take you down with him, Ray-Gene," she declared. "Before he's done he'll probably take us all down." So much for principle.

Ravonelle may have offered good advice, though, except that it came too late for Ray-Gene; he already knew too much. He'd tried hard to avoid the truth—even accepting for a time the "company with no name" explanation for the source of Jaybo's money, although he knew it was illogical. But he had seen too many suspicious activities and heard too many rumors. He knew that Jaybo was a dealer who sold drugs all over Conway, and maybe elsewhere. He knew that Jaybo worked hard and made a lot of money, he knew that Sam at the Barbecue Shack was a middle-man between Jaybo and one or more big-time suppliers, and he knew now that Donnie Shand was somehow involved. There was no doubt in his mind that sooner or later Jaybo would end up in jail.

Jaybo made lots of trips out of town, but where he went was his own closely guarded secret. When Ray-Gene asked, Jaybo would say, "I'm going to Aynor," or "I got business in Dillon today," or mention another of the scattered hamlets within an hour's drive of Conway. Ray-Gene could tell that Jaybo expected him to know that it was a lie and understand the message: "Where I go is nobody's business, least of all your's." He quit asking.

There had been a time when Ray-Gene lay awake almost every night and prayed for Jaybo's downfall. As he saw it, the sooner Jaybo was caught, the sooner he could stop expecting police to come busting through the front door at any minute.

Ray-Gene was not afraid of Jaybo, and he'd never feared for Jaybo. He worried about his grandmother and his sisters, first of all, and to a lesser extent about himself. If Jaybo got caught with something illicit in the house they all would pay a price, like Ravonelle said. But he'd never worried about Jaybo's activities affecting Jimmie or Colletta, and it came as a jolt when he heard what was going on. If Colletta got pills from Donnie Shand she had some of the same drugs Jaybo sold on the street.

"You're wrong, Ray-Gene," Jimmie protested. "DJ said it was prescription medicine, just like she'd get in the drug store. Jaybo pushes illegal stuff, everybody knows that."

"I'm not wrong, Jimmie. DJ lied. Jaybo sells stuff that makes people feel good, and makes them want more. DJ's working with him. Whatever he gave Colletta didn't come from a drug store, it came from Jaybo. I don't know what DJ does for Jaybo, but it's not honest."

Jimmie pledged to go to Colletta at once and demand some straight answers. If that didn't work he'd hunt down DJ and if they had done anything to hurt Colletta, come hell or high water he would take his complaint right to Jaybo. Nothing Ray-Gene could say would make any difference.

"You stay here and watch for DJ," Jimmie commanded, more direct than he'd ever been with Ray-Gene before. "Last thing you want is to run into Mr. Saylor, especially if he finds out Colletta has some problem that started with Jaybo. I'll let you know when I find out something."

Ray-Gene would not protest. He had not forgotten Mr. Saylor's threat and, in his mind, any place Colletta's father might be always would be a dangerous place.

    ABANDONING his previous caution with Mack's loaner Plymouth, Jimmie made a fast U-turn in the street and sped back to the Saylor house. Like Ray-Gene, he knew enough about Jaybo to be terrified at what Colletta may have gotten herself into. He was furious at Donnie Shand. Jaybo had been nothing but a petty hoodlum for as long as Jimmie could remember, but he expected a lot more of Donnie.

To his great relief, Colletta met him at the door. She shushed him as he entered. "Don't say anything too loud," she whispered, "Daddy's here."

Hunter was there, too, squirming in a chair and pulling on socks. He had the usual grin for Jimmie. Colletta's father was nowhere in sight, but Jimmie had often enough experienced Mr. Saylor roaring in from another room and taking him by surprise and he was grateful for Colletta's warning. His outrage at Donnie had elevated to a fever pitch as he drove from Ray-Gene's house, but he felt vindicated the instant he got a closer look at Colletta. She was wan and haggard, her eyes hollow and dull.

"You don't look so good," Jimmie told her. "Hunter said you needed more medicine."

"I feel great," Colletta replied. "I'm sorry if Hunter made it sound like I was still sick, because I'm not."

"I need to know, Colletta: What kind of medicine have you been getting from DJ?"

"It's nothing, just some pills. Like Jaybo sent when I first broke my arm. It really helps with the pain. I need some more, but I couldn't find DJ. Have you seen him?"

"That may be dangerous, Colletta! You know DJ sells drugs for Jaybo. If you don't even know what you've been taking, it's probably something illegal. It could hurt you. And besides, you could get in trouble taking stuff like that."

"Oh, don't get carried away. I told you, it's only pain pills. It's prescription medicine, just like I would get at the drug store."

"You don't know that."

"DJ said it was," Colletta insisted, but Jimmie sensed a hint of doubt.

"You can't trust DJ anymore," he said. "Not since he got involved with Jaybo. Ray-Gene says DJ's working for Jaybo, and we think he's selling drugs. You know anything Jaybo does is no good, and DJ's into it now up to his neck."

Colletta's eyes sparked with anger, the first sign of emotion she had shown since Jimmie arrived. Her voice rising, she said, "Damn it, Jimmie, I'm not stupid. I broke my arm, and when it hurts I need pain medicine. Maybe you've never had a broken bone, but it's painful. What's wrong with me getting something for my pain? I don't have any more prescription from the doctor and DJ gave me pills that work really good and I don't think there's anything wrong with that!"

"DJ's not a doctor, and Jaybo sure as hell isn't. How would they know what's the right medicine for you?"

Hunter tugged at Jimmie's sleeve, trying for his attention. "Jimmie," he pleaded, "why don't you take us in your car and find Colletta's medicine, like you said you would?"

Colletta put a hand on Hunter's shoulder, gently pulled him back. "Jimmie doesn't want me to have my medicine," she said. "I guess he thinks I should just have to suffer. Why don't you explain that to Hunter, Jimmie?"

"That's not the way it is, Colletta," Jimmie said. "I don't want you to suffer pain. It's just that I worried that anything DJ gave you might do something bad to you. I thought your broken arm was all healed. Does it still hurt that much?"

"Sometimes the pain is terrible. It hurts so bad I can't sleep at night unless I have something for it. The pills DJ gave me worked real well and I swear they won't hurt me. I honestly do need to find him and get some more."

   ❧ *RAY-GENE DASHED* from the porch, waving his arms, and met them at the curb. He pulled open the back door of the Plymouth and jumped in beside Hunter. "Let's get going!" he yelled. "Before Jaybo gets here. I was waiting outside just in case y'all came back here."

Jimmie stepped hard on the gas pedal. He drove to the end of the block as fast as he dared, then slowed and turned at the corner. Colletta slumped in the seat beside him. He studied Ray-Gene's face in the rear-view mirror, and tried to sound dramatic: "What's this all about, anyway?"

"DJ said for us to meet him over by Mack Brown's car lot at three o'clock," Ray-Gene said. "He didn't want Jaybo to see us."

Had it been his choice, Jimmie would have picked anywhere in town for a meeting place rather than Mack's car lot. Mack didn't sell on Sunday, but almost always went to the lot in the afternoon and moved cars around, cleaned the office, caught up on his bookkeeping. Jimmie did not want Mack Brown to see them rendezvousing with Donnie Shand. It might look suspicious. Mack watched for things like that.

His concern was relieved somewhat when they found Donnie, sitting in a blue Mercury sedan parked in the shade of thick cherry laurel on a street that ran behind the car lot. Mack was less likely to see them here.

"Why don't y'all get in with me?" Donnie greeted them.

Ray-Gene and Colletta climbed into the Mercury while Jimmie turned Mack's loaner around and parked behind Donnie, bumper-to-bumper. He told Hunter to wait in the Plymouth. Ray-Gene was sitting in the front seat of the other car with Donnie and Jimmie got in back with Colletta.

The others had finished exchanging preliminaries by the time Jimmie joined them and Donnie Shand got straight to the point. "I know you want some more pills, Colletta," he said, "but I don't have any. I'll get some tomorrow."

"What is that stuff, DJ?" Jimmie demanded. "You told Colletta it's prescription medicine just like she'd get at the drug store, but me and Ray-Gene think it's the stuff Jaybo sells. I don't want you pushin' Jaybo's drugs on Colletta, DJ!"

Donnie sat with his back to the driver's door, facing Ray-Gene. He turned slightly, toward the back-seat passengers. "I wouldn't do that," he said hotly. "She knows I wouldn't give her anything bad. She needed something for her pain and I gave her some hydrocodone, just like she'd get with a prescription."

Colletta and Jimmie both started to speak, but Ray-Gene talked over them. "Whose prescription do you use, then?" he asked Donnie. "You said it takes a prescription, so how do you get it? Jaybo gets it somewhere, right?"

Donnie Shand went on the defensive. "Y'all don't want to know too much, and neither do I," he said. "Yeah, Ray-Gene, Jaybo gets it. I don't know where. But it's legitimate prescription medicine. Jaybo sells it by the package, just like I gave Colletta, or else one pill at a time, whatever somebody wants. If I didn't know it was good I would not give it to Colletta, okay?"

Colletta put a hand on Donnie's arm in a calming gesture. "I trust you, DJ," she said. "Those pills have helped me a lot and I know you wouldn't give them to me if they weren't good. Don't you have any more?"

"I'm sorry, Colletta, not right now. I'll get some in the morning and I'll bring you some as soon as I can, okay?"

"I've got a little bit of money," Colletta said, "and I want to pay for the pills. How much will it be?"

"I'm not taking money from you, Colletta, not for just a handful of pills. I'll have some more to sell, but yours will be free. Just don't ever let Jaybo know."

Jimmie was still skeptical. "You sell the rest of them to school kids, right? Colletta has a lot of pain and needs the pills, but you sell Jaybo's stuff to kids that don't need them."

Donnie flared. "I don't sell to kids!" he said loudly. "I sell to grownups. Mostly women who have plenty of money, if you want to know. And if they need pills they don't have prescriptions for, what's the harm? Just because they don't want to go to their doctors don't mean they oughtn't to have the medicine if they want it. I'm not doing anything bad, Jimmie. It seems to me like you ought to be happy I can get the pills for Colletta!"

Ray-Gene threw up a hand in a signal of alarm. "Cops!" he said. "Everybody be quiet."

A Conway police cruiser rolled up close behind the Mack Brown Plymouth and stopped. They all sat motionless as an officer got out and walked around to the passenger side of Jimmie's loaner, where Hunter was barely visible in the back seat.

"You'd better get back there quick, Jimmie," Ray-Gene said softly. "We don't want him talking to Hunter."

Jimmie scrambled from the back seat of Donnie's Mercury and drew the officer's attention.

"Do you know anything about this car?" the policeman asked.

"Yes, sir, I'm driving it," Jimmie told him.

"Is it one of Mack Brown's cars, off the lot there?"

"Yes, sir."

"How come it's parked back here?"

"Me and some friends were just settin' and talking, is all. I work for Mack. He lets me drive the car on the weekend."

"You sure that's all there is to it?"

"Yes, sir."

"I want you to move along, son. Your boss helps us out sometimes and I don't want to hassle him or any of his boys, but we get too many complaints from the residents about him parking his cars on the street. If his lot's not big enough, he needs to get rid of some of his cars. If you're driving it I won't give you a ticket, but you and your friends need to find somewhere else to park and talk."

"Yes, sir, we'll move," Jimmie said, certain the relief in his voice was obvious. He'd been hit by a wave of panic at the sight of the police car and it had taken all the nerve he could muster to talk calmly with the officer.

The policeman turned as if to go back to his cruiser, then hesitated. "Who's in that other car?" he asked.

"Just my friends," Jimmie said. He tried hard to keep his tension from showing.

The officer brushed past him, walked around the front of the Mercury and approached the driver's window. When Donnie Shand started to get out of the car, the officer put his hand on the door and told him to stay inside. Jimmie's hands shook as he watched the officer lean down and stare into DJ's car and look over the occupants deliberately, one by one, as if he suspected them of being wanted criminals. "Could I see your driver's license, son?" the officer asked Donnie.

DJ said yes, and fumbled for his wallet. He produced a license and handed it to the officer through the window. The officer studied it for what seemed an inordinate amount of time, then returned it.

Jimmie stood on the grass beside the Mack Brown loaner and watched with great trepidation, certain that the police officer was suspicious. What if they knew that Donnie Shand was a dealer? Maybe Donnie had been under surveillance, and maybe Jimmie, Ray-Gene, and Colletta had just been snared in their net. His chest tightened until he could hardly breathe. He could feel his pulse pounding in his temples.

The police officer was gone as suddenly as he'd arrived, after delivering a stern warning to the young citizens to stay out of trouble and wishing them a good day. Donnie Shand was completely dismissive, said "all the Conway cops suck" and "Jaybo says you can do a bribe and get out of anything" and "they got nothing better to do than go around hassling people like us while the big-shots can get away with any-thing." Ray-Gene, like Jimmie, was totally unnerved by the encounter, while Colletta showed no emotion.

"He'll come back around and check," Donnie cautioned.

"We better move along. Don't worry, Colletta, I'll bring you some pills in the morning."

And to Ray-Gene and Jimmie, "See y'all soon, okay?"

Hunter, meanwhile, had crawled from the Plymouth and stood beside Jimmie on the grass, looking slightly bewildered. He grasped Colletta's hand when she came up beside him.

"You doin' okay, Hunter?" Colletta asked.

"Sure. You okay too, Colletta?"

"I'm okay, Hunter. Get back in the car."

Jimmie opened the front passenger-side door, anxious for Ray-Gene and Colletta to get in the car. He wanted to leave this street fast. DJ said the police car probably would come around again, and Jimmie assumed that this was based on experience. He did not want to still be here and face more questions should the officer return.

In his apprehension over the police officer, Jimmie had forgotten his other great concern. He was quickly reminded.

"Hey, Jimmie," Mack Brown called, pushing through a gap in the cherry laurel. "What's going on?"

☙13❧

IT HAD BEEN dark for almost an hour by the time Broder got to Wilmington. He stopped on the outskirts of town and filled the Mustang's gasoline tank, crossed the long bridge over the Cape Fear River and followed U.S. 76 until it took on street names, first Dawson and then Oleander. He had no plan, no destination other than the city.

This was his first visit to Wilmington in years, and nothing looked familiar. He recalled it as a place of striking old homes protected from the ravages of Atlantic storms by a few miles of sand and mud flats, the kind of locality they made movies about and a city he once had decided was where he wanted to live. But that all seemed a lifetime ago, and now he wondered if coming here made any sense at all.

Wilmington was more than mere whim, though, not an unthinking act of desperation. A stint of aimless driving on the deserted back roads of South Carolina had brought him a modicum of peace and, more important, given him time to think. He tried to lay out the situation logically and devise a plan, give himself some rational basis for what he might do next. During her entire life, Colletta had lived in only three different places. The last was Fayetteville. He knew that she would not have gone back to Conway and this left Wilmington. He believed that if he could find her Aunt Edith he would find Colletta.

But now came the bitter realization that he had no clear means to bring that about. He did not know Aunt Edith's last name, did not have a street address or a phone number, and knew nothing about the rest of Aunt Edith's family. The proverbial needle in a haystack looked like an easy find compared to what lay ahead for him in Wilmington.

Jagged daggers of lightning and long, muffled rumbles of thunder had been moving in off the coast for the last hour, emphatic omens of an approaching squall. Broder had paid them little heed, obsessed as he was with his search for Colletta, and when the storm struck he was not prepared for its ferocity. The rain swept down in wind-blown sheets, taxing the capacity of the Mustang's wipers. He could see almost nothing. He was afraid to keep on driving and afraid to pull over, afraid to move at any speed and afraid to slow down too much lest he be struck from behind.

He did not see the boy until it was too late.

There was a thump, a flash of bright clothing, something brushed aside. Broder knew he had hit a pedestrian.

Now it was instinctive. All his Airborne training, all the rehearsals for life-and-death situations came into play. He slammed the Mustang to a stop, put on the warning flashers and, ignoring the crutch on the seat beside him, ran to the back of the car and looked frantically for his victim. Blinding headlights were coming fast toward him. In an agonizing flash, he imagined the person he had hit lying in the street, invisible to the oncoming driver. He raised his arms over his head and waved them like warning flags. Tires screeched as the approaching pickup truck skidded to a stop on the rain-slick pavement.

"Get out of the way before you get run over," the driver yelled angrily. "I could have hit you!"

"I already hit somebody," Broder shouted back. At that instant he saw the boy, lying motionless at the edge of the street. "Oh, god, it's a kid. Help me!"

The body lay against the curb, face-up in a gutter deep in rushing rain water. Reflecting patches on the child's sneakers glistened silver in the brilliant beam of the pickup's head-lights. Broder, followed by the truck driver, rushed to the victim, expecting the worst. They were greeted by a barely audible moan. Then an arm straightened slightly and the boy began to raise his head.

"Don't move," Broder warned. "How bad are you hurt?" And to the other driver, "Can you get to a phone and call police and an ambulance?"

"I'm right on it," the man said. "I've got a cell phone in the truck."

Broder was running fingers over the boy's limbs, systematically, feeling for broken bones. The boy started to move again. "Lay still until I see how bad you're hurt," he urged. "Did you hit your head when you went down?"

"I don't think so," the boy said meekly. "I don't feel like anything's broke, or anything like that."

"An ambulance ought to be here at any minute now. Lay still, in case there's something serious. I'm the one who hit you and I'm really sorry. I never saw you at all, in the rain. We'll get you to a hospital just as fast as possible, and call your folks. But please lay still."

The driver of the pickup truck returned with an umbrella, which he unfurled to protect the boy from the rain. Police and an ambulance were on the way. "How's he doing?" the man asked Broder, who was still on his knees beside the boy.

"I can't find any broken bones and he says he didn't hit his head when he fell," Broder answered. "But I'm scared to death until we get him to an emergency room. I swear to God I never saw him at all, not until I hit him."

The other man leaned over them and held the umbrella and put a friendly hand on Broder's shoulder. "You couldn't see anything," he said. "Why in the world would he have been in the street on a night like this? If you hadn't hit him, I probably would have."

❧ BRODER, COLD AND shivering in his wet clothes, sat in a waiting area adjacent to the hospital emergency room while a Wilmington police officer filled out an accident report.

Emergency room doctors already had assured them the boy was not seriously hurt. The other driver testified that Broder was not at fault and the two police officers who reached the scene ahead of the ambulance found no reason to believe otherwise.

The boy was completely lucid. He admitted that he had foolishly started to cross the street in the middle of a long block, then realized he could not make it. But instead of retreating to the curb, he stood on the side of the pavement waiting for a break in traffic. He didn't realize how hard it would be for drivers to see him in the rain.

"We can get in touch with you at Fort Bragg if we need you," the police officer said. "But you needn't worry. This thing doesn't reflect on you in any way. It's a wonder kids ever live to grow up, the careless things they do. That one's extremely lucky. Anyway, you're free to go."

"Is it all right if I stay around for a while," Broder inquired, "and maybe talk to the boy if they let him go?"

"They're going to keep him here over night just to make sure," the officer said. "He's got a couple of superficial cuts and a few bumps and bruises so he'll be a little sore in the morning. Anyway, his mother is here now, and sometimes it's better in cases like this, you know, not to talk to them. Parents are not always realistic when it comes to their own kids. She might want to blame you, no matter what we told her."

"I never thought of that," Broder said. "I appreciate the advice. To tell you the truth, though, I don't want to drive any more tonight. Is there a motel close?"

"About four blocks over. Are you sure you're okay? All this must have been pretty traumatic. I'll get somebody to take you over there if you'd like."

"Has it stopped raining?"

"Yes."

"I'll be okay then. But thanks anyway. I'm going to stay here for a while and dry out a little. And maybe see if I can get some hot coffee. I appreciate your concern, sir."

"Tell you what," the policeman said, "I'm going to feel out that mother a bit. Maybe she's one of the cooler heads. She at least needs to know how you feel, but if she shows any sign of wanting to rag on you I'll see that she doesn't get close. You don't need that. You wait here."

Broder had no desire to move. Thankful as he was that the accident had not been worse, all he could think of was how close he'd come to killing that child. Mere chance had decided the boy's fate and he might just as likely be mourning the boy's death at this minute. He began to shiver again. The firm composure he'd demonstrated at the accident scene dissolved and he was suddenly overwhelmed with anxiety. He was dreadfully tired. For the first time, he was aware of intense pain in his leg.

Why had he been so foolish as to come to Wilmington on little more than a wild goose chase? He wanted a room and a hot shower, a bed. He would not sleep, but if he could get some rest he'd be ready to go back to Fort Bragg tomorrow and report to his new unit. And grudgingly, face Captain Homer Oates.

"Mr. Broder, this is Mrs. Yeagle, the boy's mother." The officer walked toward him, a woman at his side. Broder did not notice her appearance, whether she was young or old, attractive or homely. She extended her hand and said, "I'm Joyce Yeagle. They told me the accident was not your fault, Mr. Broder."

"I'm so sorry, Mrs. Yeagle. I never saw him. He was invisible there in the rain, with lights coming toward me . . ."

"He says you took care of him after the accident, and got help fast. Some people run and hide after something like that, Mr. Broder. I'm very grateful to you for doing the right thing."

The police officer said he needed to go and excused himself, leaving Broder and the boy's mother standing outside the emergency room. Broder fumbled awkwardly for words.

What could he say to the mother of a child he had almost killed?

Joyce Yeagle put a hand on his arm. "They've taken him to his room," she said. "They want to keep him here over night, just to be sure. I think he'd like to see you, if you have time." They took an elevator to the third floor, where signs on the wall pointed the way to the room she'd been told her son would occupy. A nurse was there with the boy and apparently had just told him something funny so that he was laughing when Broder first saw his face.

The boy was pale-skinned, frail looking. There was something familiar about his appearance and in an instant Broder knew what it was. This was exactly the way he remembered young Hunter Saylor. The accident had been a terrible distraction, allowing him to forget for a time why he had come to Wilmington to begin with. Now he remembered.

∽

❧ JIMMIE DREADED going back to work at Mack Brown's car lot Monday morning. He dreaded to see Mack and he dreaded to hear Mack's probing questions. Mack would have recognized Donnie Shand and he would want to know who the others were. And what were they doing there on a Sunday afternoon parked on a street behind the car lot, and what was the problem that brought a police car to check them out?

Mack Brown would speak softly and show concern. He was there to talk if Jimmie had a problem he wanted to talk about, because Jimmie was his friend. But he would not let go. And then there'd be the gossip and innuendo, and well-intentioned advice, because Mack was Mack and that's the way he was.

Jimmie got to the car lot early. He hoped to get started on his chores before Mack arrived and then, with a little luck, there might be a customer to keep Mack busy and he could get through the morning without face-to-face contact.

He set about his initial chore, unwinding a long, heavy

rubber hose and sprinkling water on the dusty graveled area that made up the back of the lot. He worked earnestly to wet the gravel in a careful pattern and try to make it appear that this job was too intricate to be interrupted. He didn't see Mack Brown coming. Mack tapped him on the shoulder, and Jimmie looked into a face sterner than any his boss ever had worn before. Mack motioned for him to turn off the hose and said, "Come on up to the office and have some coffee, Jimbo. I'd like to ask you about a couple of things."

Jimmie trudged behind Mack Brown, dismayed at what was to come. Mack's usual friendly demeanor was lacking and he had no doubt that Mack was about to plunge right into his inquisition. Mack would be direct. He would want to know who was with Jimmie in the loaner Plymouth and he would imply that because it was his car he had a right to that information. And if Jimmie did not answer to his satis-faction, Mack would haul out his big weapon: The use of a loaner was a generous benefit, not an entitlement.

Jimmie could tell Mack Brown who his friends were. He hardly needed an excuse to be out on a Sunday afternoon with Colletta and Ray-Gene and Hunter, or to have met with Donnie Shand. All harmless enough. But he dreaded how Mack would remember the names, and call them up for days and weeks to come, and inquire about his friends and what they all were doing, and was Colletta his girlfriend, and who was Ray-Gene's family and were they all acquainted with Donnie Shand, too? Mack was nosy. Jimmie despised the prospect that his boss would use the names of his friends to snoop into his business.

Underlying his concern, of course, was the truth. No one, least of all Mack Brown, could know why they were meeting Donnie Shand.

Then Jimmie thought again about the police car and his outlook brightened. Neighborhood complaints about Mack's cars had prompted the policeman to stop and ask questions. This was information he could relay right up front, and it just possibly might distract Mack from further prying.

Mack waved him into a chair and pointed an invitation to the ubiquitous doughnuts. He poured each of them a cup of coffee. Jimmie sat back and waited.

"What I wanted to talk to you about," Mack began, "is whether you might have any ideas as to how we could improve things around here. Things like, you know, make the lot look better, do things more efficient, that kind of stuff. I figured you had been here long enough that maybe you'd come up with something I hadn't thought about."

Expecting Mack Brown to launch right into his probing questions about Sunday afternoon, Jimmie was caught off guard. He pretended to have a mouthful of doughnut so that it was impossible to speak and scrambled mentally to come up with an intelligent response.

"Take your time," Mack said. "We wouldn't want you to choke on a doughnut and get us all over the newspaper, even though we could use the free advertising."

Jimmie forced a slight laugh to prove that he appreciated Mack's little joke. He made a point to finish chewing, took a quick, careful sip of his hot coffee, and said yes, he actually had thought of a couple of things. Probably not too important, just notions that had struck him as he worked.

"I'd be more'n happy to hear them," Mack said.

"Well, I can just mention a couple off the top of my head, Mack. One is, I think we ought to have a row of cars down the side of the lot facing out, right up to the sidewalk over there," indicating the street that ran along the west side of the car lot. "I've noticed that a lot of people drive by on that side and if we had cars right up to the sidewalk somebody might notice something they liked and stop in to look at it. Do you see what I mean?"

"I sure do. It would give us a longer display, so to speak. Good idea, boy. Start picking out some of the nicer-looking stuff on the second and third rows that we could move over there. What else?"

"I don't pretend to know near as much as you about selling cars," Jimmie said. "You're as good at this business as anybody I ever saw."

"Just because I've been doing something a certain way doesn't necessarily mean it's the best way. Somebody new, like you, might see a way I hadn't thought of. I'd honestly appreciate any ideas you have, Jimmie."

"Well, I was thinking one day that we ought to move things around more and make it look like we're selling more cars. A lot of people drive by here every day, and if things look just the same it looks like nothing moves."

Mack Brown grinned broadly. He leaned toward Jimmie and clapped him on the knee with an open hand. "That's called rotating the stock, boy. Everybody in retail does it. I know we ought to do it, and you pointing it out just shows how lax I've been. I'll tell you what, skip the washing for the rest of the morning and move some cars. Back out two or three that've been up front the longest and switch 'em with the sharpest ones from the second and third rows. By golly, Jimmie, I'll make a car salesman out of you yet."

Jimmie gulped down the last of his coffee and hurried out of the sales office. He wanted to escape before Mack remembered to ask him about Sunday afternoon. Yes, there were questions that needed to be answered, but they were his own.

☙ THE PILLS DONNIE Shand delivered to Colletta were not the same as the ones she'd had before. These were different in color and size, and Colletta was upset. Donnie assured her they were the same substance, still prescription medicine, just like she would get at a drug store. "Medicine comes in brands, just like soap or toothpaste," he explained. "But this is the same stuff I brought you last time. You don't have to worry about it."

Colletta popped one of the new pills into her mouth and chewed it like candy. "I was only afraid because the other

147

pills worked so well," she said. "Just as long as they work the same, I don't care what they look like."

"I was wondering if it's normal for your arm to still hurt so bad after this long a time," Donnie said. "Are you sure you shouldn't go back to the doctor, Colletta? Maybe that break didn't heal right, or something."

Colletta was adamant: "No. All I need is pills to help the pain, and the doctor wouldn't give me any more. Momma called him about that."

"What'd he say?"

"He said she should give me aspirin or something. Daddy says doctors don't care how much pain you have, and they don't like to give you anything for it so you have to come to their office and they make more money."

"Does your mother know I'm bringing you pills?"

"She doesn't care."

"But does she know?"

"I never told her."

"I don't want to get you in trouble with your momma. And I don't want to get in trouble with her, myself."

"I won't tell her you brought me medicine, DJ, so don't worry about it."

"I didn't really mean it like that, but truth is, it's just as well we don't say too much to anybody. Don't you worry, either, Colletta, I'll get more medicine if you need it."

By the time Donnie Shand left the Saylor house, Colletta was euphoric. She declared the new pills even better than the old, pronounced herself pain-free and claimed to feel like her true self once again, thanks to Donnie.

He wouldn't tell Colletta, but Donnie had gone as far as he could. There would be no more free pills. Jaybo demanded his money up front and Donnie was nearly broke. He was still sympathetic and still wanted to help Colletta through her days of pain and still willing to push Jaybo as hard as he dared, but Colletta's money was all gone and Donnie needed cash.

There had been one constant in Donnie Shand's life, and this was that anything involving both him and Colletta also involved Ray-Gene and Jimmie. His next move was almost instinctive. He found Ray-Gene on the front porch, sulking after a quarrel with Grandma Freeman, and got straight to the point: "I took Colletta her medicine, but she's going to need more when it's gone. She thinks she will be well pretty soon, but right now she still has times when the pain is real bad."

"I know," Ray-Gene said. "She told us that yesterday."

"Well, here's the problem, Ray-Gene. I can't get any more free pills for Colletta. Jaybo sells those pills for eight dollars apiece, and I have to pay for mine, too. Not that much, but I don't make enough to be givin' them away."

"Nobody expects you to do that. You've already give her enough."

"I'd be willing to give her more, honestly. But the point is, I can't get them myself unless I pay Jaybo first."

"I understand that, DJ." Ray-Gene's irritation was beginning to show. "You want money, right?"

"I didn't mean it like that," Donnie Shand said. "I'm just warning you that I will need some help if we have to keep Colletta in pills very long, that's all."

They agreed that Jimmie should be brought in on things, and as soon as possible. He would do anything for Colletta, even if it meant getting pills from Jaybo and he would want to be involved. They found him walking home from work at Mack Brown's car lot, tired and dirty. He crawled into the back seat of Donnie Shand's Mercury, happy for a ride.

"Me and you may have to help pay for Colletta's pills," Ray-Gene told him. "DJ can't get them free any longer."

"She oughtn't to need any more," Jimmie said.

"She thinks she'll be all right pretty soon, but she may still need a few more pills for the days when the pain is real bad," Donnie explained, eyeing Jimmie in the mirror. "I told Ray-Gene I'd be glad to give her more medicine for free, except that I can't get it. I have to pay Jaybo up front."

"I'll help, Jimmie," Ray-Gene said. "I have some money saved and I get paid again Friday night. How about you?"

"Sure. I'll help. Whatever I have," Jimmie said. "Medicine costs more than I thought, DJ. If you weren't giving it to us at cost, we couldn't afford it."

AFTER HE HAD been dropped off at home and grabbed a quick lunch, Jimmie washed up superficially and headed for the Saylor house. He still was bothered by Colletta taking pills from Jaybo. How could she be sure that they were real medicine, no matter what Donnie Shand said? He knew that Donnie would not deliberately mislead Colletta, but to trust in Donnie's word required faith in Jaybo and faith in Jaybo was hard to come by.

Hunter met him at the door. They engaged in the routine banter Hunter had come to expect and apparently considered important. Jimmie made it a point to grant him a few minutes before inquiring about Colletta.

"She's layin' down," Hunter said.

"Is she sick?"

"I don't think so. She took a pill, and it made her dizzy. Want me to tell her you're here, Jimmie?"

"No, I don't want to bother her. We can go on talking. Maybe she'll be feeling better in a little while."

"Here she is, though," Hunter said, and Colletta emerged from her small, pink-walled bedroom.

Jimmie stepped to meet her in the middle of the room. They kissed lightly and hugged long and hard, eliciting giggles from Hunter, and stood for at arms' length, face-to-face, Jimmie's hands on Colletta's shoulders. She was plainly anxious and Jimmie wondered why. "I've been worried about you," he said softly.

Tears came to Colletta's eyes. "I love you, Jimmie," she said. "I want to be well for you. Summer will be gone and we'll wonder where it went. It feels like we're missing out on a whole year of our lives. Don't you feel that way?"

"Don't talk like that. You're going to be all right, Colletta. Your arm won't hurt for much longer, and there's nothing else wrong. Is there?"

"I don't know. I feel good one minute and just awful the next. But I know you're right. The pills DJ brought me this morning are really good for the pain in my arm. I don't think it will last much longer."

"Do you feel like getting out a little? I thought we could go for a walk or something."

Colletta brightened. She was tired of the house. Give her just a minute or two to get ready, and let Hunter get shoes on, and then they could walk anywhere Jimmie wanted to, but if he had no place in particular in mind she had an idea of her own. Could they walk to the old school, the one they went to when they were little — Hunter's school now? She wanted to play where they used to play, to lie on her back and slip down the tall, shiny metal slide, burning-hot in the bright sun, and sit in the old swings in the corner of the schoolyard with Jimmie at her side, twisting the steel chains like rubber bands until they were coiled tight and then let them unwind and whirl her round and round, kicking up dust with her feet, her head thrown back and her hair flying in the wind. She wanted them to be children again.

They did all of these things. They had a wonderful afternoon.

After the playground they decided to walk the long way back, slowly, reluctant to give up this day too soon. They stopped at the Barbecue Shack, where Sam told Colletta she had grown into a pretty young woman since he saw her last and took an instant liking to Hunter.

"Y'all should come around here more often," Sam said. "No better barbecue in the whole state of Carolina, guaranteed. Fact is, I'm so proud of it sometimes I give it away to stout young fellas like Hunter, here. How'd you like another one, Hunter, on the house?"

Hunter looked to Colletta, who said it was okay. Sam put the bottom half of a super-sized bun on a paper plate, piled it high with dripping slices of barbecued pork, put the top on it, brought it to the table, and set it before Hunter. He got another cup of ice and filled it with Coca Cola.

"You'll need something to wash that down with," he told Hunter, and put the drink beside the plate.

Hunter's "thank you" went unacknowledged.

Sam was looking toward the door. The affable face he had worn for Hunter went dark, became a scowl. "Damned well time you got by here," he said to someone coming up behind them. "You and me got some business to take care of, buddy."

Jaybo pushed by without noticing who was at the table. He and Sam went into the back. Their voices could be heard in the eating area, low at first but then rising with anger.

"Come on," Jimmie whispered, "we need to go."

❧14❧

APTAIN HOMER OATES'S headquarters was immaculately kept. Broder was well accustomed to the spit and polish gung ho military outfits thrive on, but no other unit he could think of measured up to this one in terms of pure surface luster. Oates liked to define himself as a soldiers' soldier. The enlisted men in the detachment described him in other ways.

After three days in the unit, Broder still was no closer than ever to finding out why he was there. Captain Oates had welcomed him perfunctorily at mid-morning on his first day, not to be seen again.

The detachment clerk, Specialist Jorge Ortiz, had tried diligently to get him squared away, but had not been alerted to his coming and had no better information than Broder did on the nature of his assignment. Captain Oates said, "Find him a desk," and Ortiz did. The captain said, "Pull the last ten years' safety reviews from the files," and Ortiz did. So Broder sat at a desk off to one side of the detachment headquarters outer office and pored over a decade of cryptic safety reviews, precisely as commanded by the enigmatic Captain Oates. "Study these," the captain said. Nothing more.

"Sergeant Broder, I still don't understand why I didn't get a copy of your orders," Ortiz was saying. "How do they expect me to pick you up if I don't know you're coming?"

"Don't worry about it, Ortiz," Broder told him. "I'm here, my old unit has dropped me, and the Army still has me under its great big thumb. I won't get lost."

Although he still was in the dark regarding the detachment as a whole, Broder had observed a few things about Ortiz. He was highly efficient, took his work very seriously, and knew all the in's and out's of Army administration. But more important, he was an extremely nice guy who seemed to have all the makings of a Puerto Rican Rondell Wilson. Broder hoped he would stay true to that image in the long haul, which was no small order.

"It looks like you're walking almost as good as new," Ortiz said. "How much longer on the crutch? Did they tell you yet?"

Broder groaned. "What I look like and what I feel like apparently are two very different things, Ortiz. It still hurts like hell sometimes. But I think they're going to let me throw away the crutch in a week or so, if I'm lucky."

"You a career man, Broder?"

"Hard to say."

"Meaning you're not sure?"

"I always thought I was, but things look different to me now."

"Because of the bad jump?"

"Not just the bad jump. No question I started thinking more about my future when they told me I might not jump again, but there's other stuff, too."

"Stuff you can talk about, or stuff that's none of my business?"

Broder laughed at that. Ortiz had a deceptively smooth way of inserting himself into the situation at hand, whether it was his business or not. Broder did not find it offensive.

"I'm really not sure I can explain it," he said. "I always thought my role was just to do what the Army told me, do it as well as I could, and not ask questions, right? But something happened that's got me thinking more about that."

"At the risk, again, of being told it's none of my business, what kind of 'something' are we talking about?"

"No secret about it. I hit a boy with my car. I didn't even

see him, and there was nothing I could do. He wasn't hurt bad, thankfully, but he could have been killed just as easy. I've been having nightmares about it."

"Yeah, I can see how you would."

"I woke up from one of those nightmares in a cold sweat, and right then I realized that if I went into combat I might be killing boys like him. No accident, just doing what I was told. I'd hate to have to live with that for the rest of my life. I've been thinking a lot about that. How about you? Career man?"

"Me? No way, man. I have a few weeks to go, then I'm a civilian."

"Then what?"

"Then I go back to Mayagüez and marry my sweet Elizabeth," Ortiz said, a proud smile spreading across his face.

"Elizabeth. A Puerto Rican girl?"

"She's Jamaican, actually, but she's lived in Puerto Rico since she was a little girl. We went to school together."

Broder felt a lump forming in his throat. He swallowed hard. "Sure," he said, "that must be very nice. I hope it all works out good for you."

He hardly needed something to remind him of Colletta, for rarely a moment passed that he didn't think about her, wonder where she was, what was happening in her life. He regretted giving up so easily on Wilmington, though he tried to reassure himself it was the only thing he could have done; he had no evidence that Colletta was there and no real chance of finding her if she was. Not only had Wilmington been a foolish dead end, but his accident could have led to a real tragedy. He was torn between bitter self-recrimination for having gone there to begin with and immense relief that things hadn't turned out even worse. The boy, after all, was still alive.

Broder tried hard to concentrate on the safety reports. Oates might be a sinister man, but he was not complex. His orders had been simple and direct: "Study these."

No questions, no excuses.

"You know anything about these reports?" Broder asked Ortiz.

"Alls I know is that one gets done every year, and stuck in the files. As far as I can tell, that's the end of it."

"Well, if I read through them one more time I ought to know them by heart. But I'm sure I will be rewarded in the end, no? The captain's going to pat me on the back and say 'Good job, Sergeant Broder.' And no doubt pin a medal on me!"

Ortiz laughed, but refused to be sucked into a conversation about Homer Oates. Broder had probed on four different occasions, hoping to draw Ortiz out on their commander, but all his efforts so far had fallen flat.

When he was not engaged in conversation with Ortiz, it was difficult for him to keep his mind off Colletta. He knew that he should read through the monotonous safety reports yet one more time and make doubly sure he was ready when he finally had to confront Oates. The reports might well be a sham, nothing more than something to keep him occupied, but he dared not count on this. He tried again to focus on the tedious pages and when Oates slammed through the door he barely had time to look up before the captain stopped at the end of his desk.

"Let's talk, Broder, in my office," Oates said brusquely, then turned and walked away.

Broder followed. The red door to the adjacent office bore the label "C. O.," painted in bold block letters, black with gold edging, to indicate that this was indeed the lair of the commanding officer. Under that, in the same lettering, was "Capt. H. Oates."

Broder stood at attention as the captain seated himself behind a cluttered desk.

"Forget that shit, sergeant," Oates snapped. "Pull up a seat and set down." He motioned toward a chair that was pushed well back, against the wall. Broder dragged it closer to Oates's desk and sat. "Let's get something straight right off the bat," Oates continued. "I don't like you, Broder. You are in my outfit for one reason. You've got a record that I can and will spread from here to Kingdom Come if you give me any trouble."

The captain paused, waiting for a response. Broder was silent.

"Okay, then. You're better off keeping your stupid trap shut, anyway. I have no use for soldiers who talk. My men listen, then they do. Are we clear on that?"

"Yes, sir." Broder's words dripped with contempt.

He had assumed that the phony, pretentious act Captain Oates had demonstrated earlier would continue and he was prepared to play along with it and act out the role of a good soldier, the way Colonel Hewlett had asked him to. His assumption, though, had proved wrong. If the good captain was going to play it straight, Broder had no qualms about doing the same.

"As you damn well know, sergeant, I'm safety officer for the division. Otherwise, you and I would never have crossed paths. That's a job nobody wants, but I'll take my turn at it just like everybody else. It takes too damned much of my time, investigating screw-ups like you. But once in a while I get lucky and find a screw-up I can put to good use. That would be you, Broder."

"Captain, you want to cut through all the crap and tell me what the hell you have for me to do?"

"You don't ask the questions in this outfit, sergeant, I do. You'll find out soon enough what I have in mind and if you've got half a brain you can use it to your own benefit. In the meantime, I'm making you detachment safety NCO. I want you out there inspecting things and you'd better make damned sure that none of the problems you've been reading about turn up again. You see a problem, you let me know. Now get the hell out of here!"

& *NO ONE WAS* permitted to say that Colletta was taking drugs. The pills Donnie Shand brought from Jaybo were medicine. She needed medicine. Without it the lingering pain of her broken arm was more than she could bear. From time to time she would brighten, and cheerfully pronounce her pain gone for good, only to be overcome an hour later with self-pitying pessimism that her arm had not healed right and she was doomed to a lifetime of suffering. The mood swings made Jimmie crazy.

"I wish I could make her stop taking that stuff," Jimmie told Ray-Gene. "I'm scared. Don't you think it's dangerous for her to take so many pills?"

Ray-Gene agreed. He was scared, too, but he tried to conceal that fact from Jimmie. He was afraid for Colletta and he was afraid that if something bad happened it would come back on Jaybo. And in the end, if Jaybo got caught up by the law, Grandma Freeman and his sisters would suffer as much as anybody.

Ray-Gene had risked more than Jimmie knew. He had confronted Jaybo directly, in a way he'd never dared before. He had agonized every minute of one long day over what to say and how to say it and then just blurted it out, in a desperate gamble: Would Jaybo please stop selling drugs to his friend, Donnie Shand? Jaybo laughed in his face. Ray-Gene came away unscathed by Jaybo's wrath, but disheartened nonetheless; he had been terribly naïve to hope that he could disrupt Colletta's drug supply.

"If she won't try to stop, there's not much we can do," Ray-Gene told Jimmie. "She's got to want to do it herself, don't you think?"

Jimmie shook his head. "She won't ever want to quit," he said. "We've got to do something before it's too late."

"Then the answer's pretty simple. Colletta doesn't have the money to pay for DJ's pills and DJ can't carry her for very long. If we stop kicking in she can't afford them, right?"

"That's what I've been thinking, Ray-Gene. I didn't want

158

her to run out of medicine if she really needed it, but she's way past that point and I'm going to tell her. She's got to stop."

Jimmie felt a sense of relief. If he and Ray-Gene stood firm, Colletta surely would come around. She would protest in the beginning, but in the end she would see things their way. If she actually had pain and needed medicine she should be taken care of by a doctor, who probably would give her something better than Jaybo's pills, anyway. He concentrated on this last thought and went to Colletta confident that they were doing the right thing.

Colletta did not respond the way Jimmie expected. She was compliant, said she was grateful to him and Ray-Gene for what they'd done and would always remember it, but she'd felt bad all along about taking their money and was relieved that they would not be spending any more on her. Besides, she was going to get a job and, "I'll pay my own way from now on. Momma already said I don't have to stay home with Hunter anymore."

Jimmie was ecstatic. "That'll be great, Colletta," he said. "It may take a while, but now that you're well you probably can get a good job like me and Ray-Gene did. You'll like having your own money."

Colletta glared at him contemptuously.

"Why do you think I'm well?" she demanded. "I still have a lot of pain, Jimmie. Why don't you believe that? DJ is the only one who trusts me anymore."

"I'm sorry, I just thought when you said you could get a job you meant—"

"I just meant I'd pay for my own medicine, that's all. I need the medicine, Jimmie, and I'll do whatever I have to to pay for it. DJ will help. I don't need you and Ray-Gene. I don't want any more of your money."

Jimmie was shaken by her outburst. This was not like Colletta, even the strange Colletta of recent weeks whose disposition he had seen change dramatically several times a day. He did not know how to reason with this Colletta. But he tried: "We thought you didn't really need the medicine anymore."

"I'm tired of you thinking I'm lying," Colletta said coldly. "Just go away and leave me alone."

"Don't act like that, Colletta. Me and Ray-Gene will help you. If you really need DJ's pills, we'll help pay for them. You know that."

"You keep saying if I really need them, like a question every time you say it. Or an accusation. You don't believe me and I don't care. I can take care of myself. I'm a girl, Jimmie. If I have to, I can whore on the street to pay for my pills."

Jimmie's resolve melted. The girl standing before him, defiant and determined, anger flashing in her eyes, struck him as more needy and helpless than he had ever seen her before. He hurt for her. This still was the girl he had loved from childhood, going back almost as far as he could remember. Right or wrong, he would not abandon her now.

❧ DONNIE SHAND had plenty of Colletta's medicine. A shoebox filled with little white envelopes, each containing ten pills, rested beside him on the front passenger seat of his car. He was parked on the street behind Mack Brown's car lot, screened by the cherry laurel. "Old Mack won't see us back here," he said, as Jimmie leaned his head through the car window. "Anyhow, this won't take much time."

"He's not paying any attention to me, long as he's got a customer," Jimmie answered.

"Well, I just wanted to let y'all know I'll have Colletta's stuff. Only problem is, Jaybo's upped the price by fifty cents a pill. He said his costs have gone up since he no longer works through Sam, and like any other good businessman he's got no choice but to pass along the increase. He said if I didn't want to pay it, I can go look for my own source. But don't worry, I got buyers for all this. I'll get my money back

160

and make a profit on it. Then I can get Colletta her medicine tomorrow."

"It's getting real expensive, DJ. I already thought it was pretty high, without an increase."

"I know, but if Colletta still needs it we don't have no other way to go. I know where to get it if I had the money to buy a lot, but when I can just buy a little at a time I have to get it from Jaybo."

"Colletta still needs it. I wish she didn't, but I don't think she could get along without it anymore."

"Is she good for now?"

"She's about out. But I guess she can make if for another day. Don't bring it by here, though. Meet me at Colletta's house at noon, okay?"

"I'll be there. Get as much cash together as you can."

Jimmie cringed as Donnie Shand gunned his Mercury and roared away with a squeal of tires. He looked toward both ends of the block, half expecting to see the police closing in. Nothing moved within sight of where he stood.

Donnie's carelessness had become a big concern for Jimmie. Donnie acted as if he didn't care if he was caught. Even though it was prescription medicine, not like cocaine or something, he was pretty sure that what Donnie was doing was criminal. It was stupid to burn off like that with a box of pills in the car, in plain sight. He was greatly relieved when the Mercury disappeared from view.

Jimmie pushed through the cherry laurel, back to Mack's car lot, and went back to work. Mack still hadn't mentioned that Sunday afternoon gathering on the street where Jimmie and Donnie Shand had just met and Jimmie wanted to believe he had forgotten. He knew that this was unlikely, though; Mack Brown had a memory like an elephant. He undoubtedly had seen the police car that day and was bound to be curious. It was only a matter of time before the subject came up.

But Jimmie had a more pressing problem for now, one he

couldn't put off any longer. Donnie Shand expected money tomorrow. Jimmie didn't have nearly enough and Ray-Gene wouldn't be paid for another week. He figured his best hope was Mack Brown and he was optimistic that his boss would advance him a week's pay. Mack had given him a loaner, after all, when no such benefit was promised at the time he applied for the job. A car to drive like his own, even an old jalopy, was of immense value in Jimmie's mind, worth at least as much as an extra day's pay every week. It would not occur to him that the loaner represented virtually no investment on the part of Mack Brown.

Mack stayed busy with a customer for the next hour, but the man left the car lot without closing a deal. Mack wore a somber expression when Jimmie approached him. "Did you see that sonofabitch who just left?" he grumbled. "He never had any intention of buying. I'll bet he doesn't even have a license. Just wasted my time."

Jimmie's optimism ebbed. He wished he could wait but he was out of time. He had to ask now. He would never do it for himself, but this was for Colletta. He screwed up his courage and, trying to sound nonchalant, said to his boss, "I was wantin' to ask you a favor, Mack. You think there's any chance you could pay me this week in advance? Tomorrow morning, instead of Saturday?"

Mack Brown looked surprised, but not angry. "I don't think I can do it," he said matter-of-factly. "All my business cash runs through the bank, son, and they write the checks on a set schedule. The schedule is for you to get paid on Saturday, and it would be a big hassle if I tried to mess that up."

Simple as that, and final. Mack's response left no room for appeal. Jimmie finished his morning's work without further conversation. If Mack wondered why he needed to be paid early, he didn't wonder enough to ask.

Jimmie did not visit Colletta in the afternoon. She would expect him, but if he went she would ask when Donnie

Shand was bringing her medicine. He would have to tell her about the money problem and that would make her worry, and maybe even try to do something foolish. He walked the streets instead, avoiding Colletta's block. He started walking in the direction of Grandma Freeman's house but changed his mind about seeing Ray-Gene, too.

Walking offered no escape. He could neither forget his problem nor think of a solution.

After an hour of haphazard circling in the oppressive mid-summer heat, he found himself at the edge of town and, with little thought to where he was going, tromped ahead, along the slough and through the live oak thicket to the creek bank where he had played as a boy. For a time he felt protected here, in the dense willows, distant from the pressing everyday world, safe from Colletta's distress and the demands of Donnie Shand and Jaybo and Mack's inquiries and policemen asking questions, in this place where he and Ray-Gene and DJ and Colletta had hunted frogs for something fun to do. But that was long, long ago, before Donnie Shand's mother smashed her husband's head with a brick and before Jimmie came to love Colletta not merely as a friend but as a girl. These things came back to him now. He could not hide in the willows and make them go away.

  COLLETTA'S HANDS trembled as she accepted the small packet of pills from Donnie Shand. "You got here just in time," she told him. "I needed these. My pain was bad this morning."

"I'm glad I can get your medicine, Colletta," Donnie said. "It makes me feel good to be able to help somebody who really needs it."

They sat in DJ's Mercury, parked just down the block from the Saylor house. Jimmie was in the back seat.

"I took fifteen dollars from Daddy's dresser this morning, while he was asleep," Colletta said. She handed two folded bills to Donnie. "That's all I could find. He probably won't even know it's gone, but if he misses it I'll tell him I had to spend it for medicine."

Donnie looked back at Jimmie. "How much you got?" he asked.

"Only twenty dollars, Donnie. That's all I have left, but I'll get paid Saturday."

"You think Ray-Gene's got any cash on him?"

"He already told me he wouldn't have until he gets paid again. I'm sorry, DJ, but Colletta's medicine costs almost as much as we make, especially now that the price has gone up. Can't you carry it until the end of the week?"

Colletta winced. "Nobody told me it was going up," she said, addressing neither of her two companions directly. "How come somebody didn't let me know?"

"It just now happened," Donnie said. "Jaybo only told me yesterday. Anyway, it doesn't make all that much difference, Colletta. It's just a few dollars more."

"You're not going to need the medicine much longer," Jimmie said. "We can pay the difference. Me and Ray-Gene will both get paid at the end of the week, then we can pay up." Then, to Donnie, "You said you would sell all the stuff you had yesterday and make a profit. You can carry the rest of this till the end of the week, right?"

In the mirror, Jimmie saw fear in Donnie Shand's eyes. "Only problem is, I already owe Jaybo," Donnie said. "If I don't pay what I owe, plus the price of these pills, he said he'd do something bad. I thought y'all would have more cash than this."

"What's Jaybo goin' to do, fire you and hire somebody else?" Colletta said. She feigned sarcasm, but alarm edged her voice and lined her face.

Jimmie tried to reassure her: "Jaybo won't do anything, Colletta. That's just big talk."

"No, it's not." She no longer pretended. "Jaybo's mean, Jimmie. If he said he'll do something bad, he probably meant it. I'm sorry for getting you in all this trouble, DJ. "

"It's not your fault," Donnie said. "I've been getting behind with Jaybo for a long time. Sometimes it takes me all week to sell the stuff I get and I don't make much profit. I had to buy this car and there have been some months I didn't even make enough to cover my payments. I know y'all think I make big money selling for Jaybo, but I swear I don't."

"How much you owe Jaybo?" Jimmie asked.

"I owe a lot. He said if I don't come up with at least four hundred dollars by the end of the week he'll break my arm." Tears welled up in Donnie's eyes. His distress was evident and compelling. This was the Donnie Shand who had earned the loyalty of companions in this fragile little fraternity, and Colletta and Jimmie were ready to bend to his will and help in any way he asked. But his will was shaken and uncertain.

Donnie Shand, who'd been their leader, was afraid.

"I don't know what I'm going to do," he said, voice wavering. "Jaybo don't threaten unless he means it."

"If I had the money I'd give it to you," Colletta said. "All of it. But I don't know any way to get hold of money like that."

"I do," Jimmie said. "I hate to, but this is an emergency. We've got to get Jaybo's money. We can go back and work the beach again, just like we did before."

❧15❧

THE IMAGES WERE both terrible and thrilling. The 82nd Airborne was at war and the war was brought into the detachment day room by television broadcast direct from the battlefield. Broder watched in fascination, along with a half-dozen others who had dropped all pretense of routine duty to witness the action in a place strange and far away. His old unit was there, somewhere, and who could imagine what dangers lay in store for friends and comrades he still felt close to? Except for his training accident, that single bad jump, Broder would be there with them.

"Holy Mother, look at that." Jorge Ortiz spoke in hushed tones, in awe of what they saw unfolding before their eyes.

"Kicking ass!"cheered a sergeant whose name Broder did not know.

"People are dying, Metcalf," Ortiz said. He still spoke softly, but his anger was plain. His response was met with silence.

Captain Homer Oates slipped quietly into the room. The men paid him no heed, ignoring the formalities of military courtesy to their commanding officer. All eyes stayed fixed on the television screen, on which American military might unparalleled in all the history of the world was on full and gaudy display.

Captain Oates stepped up close behind the group and watched along with them. When his sullen voice suddenly overrode sound from the television speakers, his stinging personal rebuke caught them all by surprise: "You ought to be there, Broder. The Army invested a shit-truck load of time and money training you for this, and you find a way to shirk your duty by pulling a phony jump accident. If I had my way you'd be in the stockade right now."

Broder was new, unknown to the men in the unit except Jorge Ortiz, merely a name, a recently assigned sergeant in this peculiar detachment where soldiers came and went virtually without regard. But they knew Captain Oates, the sinister commander who appeared to take pride in reprimanding his men to the point of humiliation, and the room emptied quickly. Broder was left to stand and face the CO alone.

"Captain, if you still have a problem with my accident, you need to take it up with higher headquarters," Broder said. "That investigation's been finished, and that investigation cleared me. But you know that."

"Cool it, Broder. I didn't come here to talk about your bad jump. I just hated to miss an opportunity to give those other assholes something to gossip about. Your name will be dragged though the mud by every man in this detachment now, and nobody's going to give you the time of day. So I'm the best friend you've got, sergeant, and your best hope now is to play on my team."

Broder was speechless. He still was at a complete loss as to what Oates had up his sleeve.

An expression of smug satisfaction spread across Oates's face, as if he knew that he now had Broder firmly under his heel. "I'll take your silence as affirmative," the captain said, "a sign that you're beginning to see things my way. That's good, Broder. Maybe now we can get on with it."

"You're the CO. I just follow orders." This time, Broder dropped the sarcasm.

"That's more like it. I've got a job for you, sergeant, and it's a job I wouldn't turn over to just anybody. You're tough enough to handle it or I wouldn't waste my time with you."

"Like I said, I just follow orders."

"Be at my office at six o'clock. You'll get your orders."

"Yes, sir."

Oates spun on his heel and was gone, leaving Broder to wonder what might happen next. The captain scared him. He wished there was someone in the unit he could confide in, that he knew Ortiz better, trusted him the way he would have trusted Rondell Wilson. His first impression of Ortiz had held up so far but there hadn't been enough time. Ortiz still might turn out to be the captain's confidante, the last person on earth he wanted to talk to. Whatever Oates was plotting, Broder faced it in isolation.

On the television screen behind him, Baghdad erupted under heavy nighttime attack by American bombs and missiles, shocking scenes played out through brilliant flashes of destruction. But the spectacle that had mesmerized him only moments earlier now seemed remote and not connected to here and now. Broder had his own war to fight.

Why had he ever agreed to an assignment to Homer Oates's detachment? Colonel Hewlett had offered him an out, made clear he would not be forced into something he wasn't willing to go along with. Why hadn't he grabbed that opportunity before it was too late? But on the other hand, Hewlett had promised to stand behind him. He wanted to trust Hewlett. And he'd come too far to back out now, which left him little choice except to play Captain Oates's game, whatever it was, through to the end.

An hour later, Broder stopped by the mess hall and picked lethargically at the supper he had no appetite for and lingered over coffee, talking to no one. After that he carried civilian clothes to the parking lot and hung them in the Mustang so that he would remember to get them to the dry cleaners another day. He sat in the car and listened to the radio, resting his gimpy leg, until it was nearly time for his appointment with the captain. At five minutes before six he walked into detachment headquarters.

A corporal whose nametag identified him as Grissom

was at the front desk, on charge-of-quarters duty. Otherwise the outer office was empty.

"You need something, sergeant?" the corporal inquired, barely looking up from his drug-store paperback.

"The captain's expecting me."

"If you say so, sergeant." Grissom motioned with a slight head gesture toward the door to Homer Oates's office.

The captain stood to one side of the room, his back to his desk, gazing out the window. His arms were folded behind him, criss-crossed at the belt, hands doubled into fists. The pose reminded Broder of a dramatic scene from a British war movie that had played a few months earlier in Fayetteville and he wondered if the captain might have seen it. Oates waited until Broder had stepped inside and closed the door, then turned slowly. "Thank you for being prompt," he said, in a tone surprisingly friendly.

"Sir, you said six o'clock."

"Let's get something straight, sergeant. I can do things for you," the captain said. "Things that work to your benefit if you've got the good sense to take advantage of them. If I didn't think you could do the job you wouldn't be in this outfit."

"Yes, sir. You made that clear before."

"Okay, then. If we understand each other let's get to it. For starters, have you thought about signing on for another tour of duty, now that you're cleared to jump again? Then we could get your assignment to the detachment frozen for a year or so and I can see pretty quick advancement for a savvy guy like you."

Broder was not prepared for this question. No one had told him he had been cleared for jumping.

Captain Oates raised his eyebrows, in mock surprise. "Oh, I forgot," he said. "You didn't get the word yet." He leaned over his desk and retrieved a sheet of paper. "You see, Broder, this just came in this morning. I wanted to give it to you in person, considering how important it is. Seems like the higherups have completed your medical evaluation and the bottom line is, after you have recovered from your injuries you'll be returned to paratroop duty. Colonel Hewlett personally signed off on it."

Broder stiffened. He had come to accept the likelihood of never making another jump, beginning with Oates's own sarcastic pronouncements back in the medical center. He would not give Homer Oates the satisfaction of seeing his surprise. He steeled himself to block any show of emotion and said, "Like you told me, captain, I'll always be Airborne, even if I never leave the ground again."

"So let's get back to my question," Oates replied. "How about your future in the Army? You in or out?"

"Oh, I think I have time to consider that before I have to make a decision. No reason to hurry it."

Now it was Oates who clearly struggled to maintain his equilibrium. Color crept up from his neck and streaked the lower part of his face, his irritation palpable. Broder feared for an instant that, through his own exaggerated coolness, he may have put himself at risk. This was not a level playing field; the captain not only owned the ball, but also wrote the rules of the game.

"Goddammit, Broder," the captain stormed, "don't get smart with me! I could ruin you in less time than it takes to spit."

"Sorry, sir. I meant no disrespect. I'd be the last man in the world to deny that the Army's been good for me. I'm proud to be Airborne. Nobody can ever take that away from me."

Captain Oates laughed. But there was no humor in his laughter, only contempt. "I don't give a piss-ant's hind legs what you think of the Army," he said, "or what the Army thinks of you, sergeant. From now on, it's what you can do for me. There's one hell of a big world out there besides the Army, and that's where the action is. If you haven't figured that out you're dumber than I thought."

"I'm sorry, captain," Broder began, "I thought you—"

"Stop thinking. We've got work to do. I'm about to send you on a job that'll tell me real quick whether you're worth the sweat off my ass. Do it right and your future suddenly is going to look pretty damned good. But you screw it up, Broder, and you'll wish you'd never heard my name."

⁂

❧ *RAY-GENE WAS* reluctant. He protested at first, but in the end succumbed to Jimmie's insistent pleas. They needed him. They were still a team, the four of them, the same team they'd always been, and he was still a crucial player. They couldn't do this without him. Ray-Gene might have held his ground, except for the fact that he felt terribly guilty. It was Jaybo who had dragged Donnie Shand into this mess in the first place and Ray-Gene could not escape the fact that Jaybo was family. Anyway, he wanted to be on the team, craved the completeness he felt when they all did things together, the purpose he never seemed to find apart from his friends.

And the team was still good. Colletta charmed and distracted visitors to sun-drenched Carolina beaches while her partners put nimble fingers to work then made their sly escape, concealed by innocent-looking running games in the sand. Her sweet and sincere conversation would be favorably remembered by victims who would never connect the pretty young girl with their misfortune.

Targets were plentiful; they'd stolen enough money by summers's end to pay off Jaybo many times over. They did it for Donnie Shand in the beginning, but once his debt was paid they stole for Colletta.

Every day, Colletta appeared to grow more dependent on Jaybo's pills. Donnie brought a handful of codeine tablets once when Jaybo wasn't able to get hydrocodone, but these made her sick. On another occasion he brought Demerol and assured Colletta this was prescription medicine, too, and would ease her pain. She insisted it wasn't as good as what he usually brought.

But hydrocodone was easy to get most of the time, in various brands that Donnie delivered in the familiar plain white envelope. And it was what Colletta wanted.

When Donnie boasted one day that Jaybo also could get her some "stronger stuff," Colletta screamed at him: "I don't want drugs, DJ! I just need my medicine!"

"It's not like I was using crack or smack or whatever they call it," she said angrily. "And I don't smoke marijuana or suck stuff up my nose or stick my arms with needles and I don't drink whisky and get falling-down drunk like my daddy and a lot of other fine people in Conway."

Jimmie took her hand and did his best to sooth her. "We know that, Colletta," he told her. "We all know you need the medicine. We know you're not doing drugs. Nobody thinks you're bad."

The flash of anger passed and Colletta began to cry. "I still have a lot of pain when my medicine runs out," she said between soft sobs. "Some days I don't have so much pain and I don't take the pills, and then I get sick and have awful sweats and chills all night. I know I'll get well when I get over the pain and I won't need medicine anymore and none of y'all will ever have to help me again. I'm sorry I've been so much trouble. I promise I'll get straightened out real soon. I will. I promise."

Such resistance as the boys might have harbored dried up faster than Colletta's tears. Colletta needed them. They saw her as the victim of an entrancing monster she could neither control nor get free of and they would stand by her, culpable but willing accomplices. They would break any law and run any risk to help support her habit.

Pangs of conscience were rationalized away quickly, before they had time to take root and ripen: Colletta was in pain; Mr. Saylor was a drunk, and left nothing to pay for Colletta's medicine; Jaybo was family; Jimmie loved Colletta, and felt responsible for her; life wasn't always pretty — Donnie Shand's mother had crunched his daddy's head with a brick. They were a team. When one was down the three others were there to lift and support and sustain.

The infusion of beach cash made life easy. Jimmie and Ray-Gene paid for Colletta's pills and still managed to save much of what they earned at Mack Brown's car lot and the IGA store. Donnie Shand met Jaybo's quotas without getting into debt again. When Colletta started work in early July, cashiering a few hours a week at a Walgreens store, the boys insisted that none of her pay would go for medicine. Her money was needed more at home, they argued, and she reluctantly agreed to hand her earnings over to her mother every payday to help with the family's bills.

Caught up in their fools' paradise, they were not ready for the two-pronged crisis brought on by the end of summer. Their easy-money source dried up almost overnight when the crowded Grand Strand beaches suddenly turned to long, empty stretches of sand and three members of the team found themselves back in school so that even the hours they could work for honest pay were severely curtailed. The boys pooled funds, Ray-Gene and Jimmie surreptitiously withdrawing money from savings accounts, and managed to scrape together enough to pay for Colletta's pills for a few weeks. By early November, though, the situation was bleak.

"I don't know how we can do it any longer," Ray-Gene told DJ. "Me and Jimmie have spent all the money we've got saved and we don't make enough to get by any longer. You think Jaybo might carry us for a little while, till Colletta gets well? He knows we'd pay him back, however long it takes."

"Jaybo won't do it," Donnie replied. "He just refuses to work that way, even for us. He won't trust anybody when it comes to money."

"I don't know what we're going to do," Ray-Gene said. "We've got to keep Colletta in medicine. We'll graduate school this year, DJ, and if she got sick and had to go in the hospital or something she'd probably not make it."

"I want to keep her in school as much as anybody, Ray-Gene. I wish I hadn't dropped out myself, but it's kind of late to be worryin' about that now."

"Colletta would be heart-broken if she had to drop out," Jimmie told them. "She promised her momma she would graduate high school, no matter what. Me and Ray-Gene are supposed to graduate, too, but if I have to I'll give up school and get a full-time job if that's what it takes."

"Popeye Broder would kill you before he'd let you do that," Ray-Gene said. "Or if he didn't, your momma would."

Jimmie's eyes filled with tears. "I love Colletta more than anything, and y'all know it," he said. "Nobody can stop me from doing what I have to, to take care of her."

"We love her too," Ray-Gene said. "Not like you, but me and DJ love Colletta more than family. No four people in the world have ever been closer than us. Don't you think so, DJ?"

Donnie Shand looked at the ground and nudged bits of rock with the toe of his shoe. "I'm going to find some way to make this work," he said. "Trust me. We're going to get Colletta through the year."

& MACK BROWN was suspicious. Or maybe he simply was being nosey, Jimmie couldn't be sure. The loaner Jimmie had driven the last two weekends, a cherry-red Dodge Shadow two-door, was still on the lot, hadn't had as much as a look from a potential buyer since Mack took it in trade. But now Mack acted as if it was one of his hottest properties, likely to sell at any minute, and he was reluctant to let it go unless Jimmie really needed it for something important.

"It's not so much that I mind you taking a car in the middle of the week," Mack said, "it's just that I don't understand what you need it for. And that's a nice little Dodge, just the kind of car somebody's going to be looking for."

Jimmie felt squeezed by Mack's sudden curiosity. He wanted to unload on his boss and demand that Mack just tell him yes or no, could he have the loaner or not? Why did Mack always have to play games? He was afraid to show his irritation, though, because Mack didn't like for him to talk back and might complain about his attitude and maybe even deny him the car. "It doesn't have to be the Dodge," he said, and knew immediately that he had given Mack Brown an unintended opening.

Mack jumped on it: "Thing is, if I knew what you planned to do, I might have something more suitable. How 'bout something roomier, like that silver Buick on the back row? It seems to me like if you're going to be hauling a bunch of kids around town or something, the Buick would give you more space."

"Sure, Mack, the Buick would be fine. It doesn't matter."

"Tell you what, Jimmie. Go ahead and take the Dodge. It runs real good and has low miles on it, considering its age."

Jimmie breathed easier. The Buick had been a ruse, Mack's not-too-subtle ploy to try and lead him to open up about his plans. When he didn't fall for it, Mack capitulated, no doubt to lie in wait tomorrow, ready to try again. But there would be time to think up a good story before Jimmie came to work tomorrow after school, something to satisfy Mack's curiosity, maybe even give him something to gossip about.

Getting a loaner was critical. Jaybo had conditioned their big break on the use of some car other than Donnie Shand's Mercury. Jaybo didn't like his pick-up men to be seen too often in the same place by the same people and the risk extended to their automobiles. Ray-Gene had been the first to suggest that a loaner from Mack Brown's car lot, if Jimmie could pull it off, would be the perfect solution.

After work, Jimmie rushed through dinner and said he needed to take Colletta somewhere. His mother was reminding him not to be out too late as he flew out the door. He picked up Ray-Gene first, then drove toward Donnie Shand's house. Donnie ran down the block to meet them, let Ray-Gene climb out onto the sidewalk so that he could fold down the seat-back and squirm into the cramped back seat of the Dodge.

"Couldn't you get something bigger?" he complained.

"Mack played games with me," Jimmie said. "I felt lucky to get anything at all. I think he may be a little bit suspicious about what's going on."

"Mack Brown's just a silly old fool," DJ said. "He don't know what's going on up his own ass."

"He still worries me. You know where we're going?"

"Yeah, head down to Pawleys Island. I'll give you more direction when we get there. Just make sure we get there by seven."

Jimmie drove south out of Red Hill on Route 544, crossed the Intracoastal Waterway, turned right on 707 at Socastee. He was nervous, careful not to drive too fast and risk getting stopped for speeding or to attract attention by driving too slow. He kept a wary eye on the rear-view mirror, half expecting to see flashing lights at any minute, finally relaxing when he picked up U.S. 17 just north of Murrells Inlet. The Pawleys Island turnoff was only minutes ahead.

"Do I just keep on going, right to the island?" he asked Donnie.

"Just keep going until I tell you to stop. There's a signal I've got to watch for. I'll tell you when I see it."

Ray-Gene had been quiet. That meant he was nervous, too, and when he spoke his voice was tense: "I wish I knew what we were getting into, DJ. You think what we're doing is dangerous?"

"Of course it's not dangerous," Donnie Shand said. "We just pick up Jaybo's stuff and drive back to Conway. What could be dangerous about that?"

"What kind of stuff?"

"Just stuff. We don't need to know what it is. Jaybo's not paying us to check it out, just to pick it up and bring it to him. Couldn't be more simple than that."

"But you know it's something illegal, right?" Ray-Gene

persisted. "And if we got caught we'd be in big trouble."

"Who's goin' to catch us, Ray-Gene?" DJ's voice rose in exasperation. "You worry too damn much about problems that don't exist. We'll make good money tonight, and this is just the beginning. Jaybo said he could use us regular if we do this run and prove to him that he can trust us. It couldn't be easier."

Jimmie eased the Dodge slowly along a narrow road that ran directly behind a row of weathered, closely bunched beach houses. He remembered a salt-marsh flat off to the right, but the night was too dark to see anything outside the beam of the car's headlights. Flashing lights some distance ahead drew his attention and he slowed even more, careful not to come up too fast behind a car stopped on the edge of the road. A man stood at the back of the car, with the trunk lid raised, pointing a flashlight toward a rear wheel.

"Stop here, Jimmie," Donnie called from the rear seat. "Pull right up behind him, like we've stopped to help."

Jimmie did as he was told. The man stood awkwardly in the glare of the headlights. He might have been any local beach habitue, dressed in faded jeans and short tan jacket with a fisherman's hat slouched low on his head. He raised a hand to shade his eyes, almost in a military salute, and lifted the flashlight in a gesture of friendly greeting.

"Get out, Ray-Gene," Donnie directed firmly. "Let me out to talk to him."

The man said nothing until Donnie was out of the car, and spoke first. "Have a problem, sir?" Donnie said. "Jaybo sent us down to help."

"It's about damned time," the man growled. "Half the people in South Carolina have come by here offering to help me change my tire. You're twenty minutes late. Tell Jaybo he'd better get somebody here on time next time, or he can take his business somewhere else."

"I'm sorry, sir," Donnie said meekly. "This is just our first trip, and I guess — "

"Just shut up and get this done before some yahoo who's been by here before comes back again and gets suspicious."

The man leaned into the trunk of his car and opened a tackle box. He lifted a top tray filled with lures and other fishing paraphernalia and took out a package, slightly bigger than a normal-sized brick and wrapped in newspaper and tied with white cotton string. He handed the package to Donnie without looking up and slammed shut the lid of the trunk.

"Now get moving," the man said. His tone was angry and threatening.

Ray-Gene scrambled into the back seat so that Donnie could get in the car faster, and Jimmie backed up a few feet and then drove forward, around the other vehicle, as fast as he dared. The road dead-ended at the beach only a few hundred yards farther on. Jimmie turned around quickly and started back the way they'd just come.

Tail lights ahead told him the driver of the other car had found a closer place to turn and was in front of them now as they drove toward the highway leading away from the island. He wanted to drive fast, to get back to Conway and distance himself from all that had just taken place, but he was afraid to get close to the other automobile.

"That was easy," Donnie said. "We can make some good money driving for Jaybo, if that's all there is to it."

"That's not all there is to it if we get caught," Ray-Gene said, echoing Jimmie's thoughts. "If something went wrong and we got stopped by the police we'd be in a ton of trouble, DJ. You don't even know what's in that package, right?"

"I don't know, and I don't want to know, Ray-Gene."

Jimmie turned back north, toward Conway. He could not shake an overwhelming sensation that something bad was about to happen. How had he ever let himself be talked into this in the first place?

But he knew the answer to his own question, knew there was no blame he could place elsewhere. He had vowed to do anything necessary to take care of Colletta. Ray-Gene and DJ had followed his lead.

"Drive careful," Ray-Gene warned. "This is not the time to get stopped by one of them big-bellied sheriffs with a gold badge on his chest. And he'd probably have on big sunglasses, even in the dark."

Jimmie and Donnie Shand did not laugh.

☙16☙

BRODER FOLLOWED Captain Homer Oates's instructions to the letter. The timing had to be precise, the captain insisted, and Broder rehearsed it again in his mind. Nothing could be put in writing. Know where you are supposed to be and when you are supposed to be there, the captain said. Then do what you are supposed to do. Like it's a military operation.

He went back to his quarters and put on civilian clothes. He usually changed at the end of the day, so this was not peculiar. He'd waited longer today because he assumed he ought to be in uniform when he reported to Captain Oates, but then the captain said get out of military clothes, dress like you're just going out for a beer. And drive your own car. Sure, Oates had noticed the Mustang. Used to drive one himself and admired the sergeant's.

Now Broder drove north on I-95, staying squarely on the speed limit, and tried to figure out what he was involved in. Traffic was heavy. A continuous caravan of automobiles and heavy trucks zipped by in the passing lane. I-95 always lived up to its reputation as a speedway.

His calculated equation of speed and distance proved accurate; at precisely nine o'clock he saw the specified exit sign, slowed, and left the Interstate.

A gasoline station and adjacent convenience store were there, exactly as the captain had described them, on a large and open and brightly lit site that stood like a tranquil oasis beside the busy highway. Little activity was apparent. The

181

driver of a long black Mercedes sedan with darkly tinted windows and Maryland license plates pumped gasoline at one of several pump islands and Broder noticed a luxurious motor home with a yellow, open-topped Jeep Wrangler in tow parked off to one side, parallel to a white wood-plank fence that bordered the property.

He stopped at a pump close to the convenience store and got out of the car and went inside the store and walked about, as if stretching his legs from a long drive. The only other person in the store was a cashier, a pretty red-haired woman about the age of his mother. She smiled pleasantly when Broder approached the counter with a candy bar and handed her a five-dollar bill.

"You didn't get gas?" she asked. It was a simple query, not a complaint. She didn't seem to care whether he bought gasoline or not.

But her question bothered Broder. It had occurred to him that it might look funny, stopping at the pumps but not putting gasoline in his tank. That was the captain's orders: Leave the Mustang at a pump island and go inside, but do not pump gasoline. He assumed someone was supposed to see all this, but he'd hoped no attendant would notice.

He had prepared an answer, just in case. "No, I just filled up a little ways back," he said. "I don't have much farther to go."

"You're from around here, then?" the woman said, still smiling pleasantly.

"Just visiting," Broder told her. He did not want to engage the woman in conversation and have her inquire about where he was visiting, how long he planned to stay, all the questions he knew she'd want to ask. He took his change quickly, thanked her, and hurried out the door.

"How's the captain?"

The query was voiced from somewhere to his left, near a dark corner of the building. Broder turned. An old man came out of the shadows and walked toward him. The man was slightly built and somewhat stooped, with wild, stand-up white hair that made him look something like Albert Einstein without the moustache. His dress was nondescript except for a large silver belt buckle that glinted in the over-overhead lights.

"The captain sends his best regards," Broder said, and the old man nodded knowingly.

"Come over here to my house-on-wheels, lad. I've got some Florida trinkets for the captain," he said.

The old man was surprisingly agile, given his frail ap-pearance, and Broder had to walk fast to keep up. They went inside the motor home, which was luxuriously furnished, and the old man motioned Broder into a chair, then stepped into the kitchen area and took two glasses from an overhead cabinet. "First off," he said, "you must join me in a drink. Specialty of this house is rum and Coke."

Broder wanted to decline, but felt compelled by circum-stance to accept the old man's hospitality. He took the drink. The old man had made it strong, with too much rum for Broder's taste, but the feel of the glass in his hand was some-how comforting and for a moment he might have forgotten where he was and who he was drinking with.

"Like I said," the old man told him, "I've got something for the captain."

"I expected you would."

"Drove up from Miami with it, as you probably know."

"No, I don't know. I don't want to know. Don't tell me anything else. Just get whatever it is I'm supposed to take to the captain and I'll be on my way."

"Okay, okay. Just hold your horses. Thought you might like to relax a bit and have a drink with me, is all."

"Sure. But we've had the drink. I need to get going."

The old man took their empty glasses to the sink, rinsed them hurriedly with plain tap water, and stood them upside down on a dish rack. He pushed open a pocket door that had kept the back part of the motor home closed off from where they sat and disappeared from view for a full five minutes. When he returned he carried a badly faded denim laundry bag that looked to be stuffed with clothing.

"Here it is," he said, thrusting the bag toward Broder. "You'd best be gettin' on back down the road. You wouldn't want to keep the captain waiting, and I wouldn't drive too fast if I were you."

Broder took the laundry bag and pushed open the door, glad to be on his way.

"Be careful of that step," the old man said, "and give the captain my regards."

Broder stowed the bag in the trunk of the Mustang and pulled back onto I-95, this time southbound. It was all he could do to stop himself from turning off the Interstate at the first exit, finding some deserted street or road where he could park and pull the bag out of the trunk, dig into it and see what mysterious merchandise he was hauling back to Captain Oates. But he figured it was sealed, maybe in an invisible way that would betray his tampering without him even knowing it.

He needed to gain the captain's trust. Poking through the laundry bag was not the way to do it.

There was no question in his mind that he was carrying something that could bring him a world of hurt if he got caught. If that happened, would Colonel Hewlett come to his rescue, or had Oates set him up beyond Hewlett's reach, to take a fall that ended with hard time in Leavenworth?

This was too risky. When Colonel Hewlett asked him to go to work for Oates, did he know what perils Broder might face? Don't worry, the colonel had told him, I'll know what's going on. That meeting in the colonel's office was as clear in Broder's mind as if it had been yesterday, and the colonel's promise: Nobody's going to abandon you. Yeah, right. He was sorry he'd ever met Lieutenant Colonel Eldon Hewlett or Captain Homer Oates, sorry he'd let himself be dragged into this absurd mess.

He could almost hear the words of his mother, as he'd heard them a hundred times, "Sorry's like a warm sun that comes out in the morning, after the frost has already killed the tomatoes. It's nice, but it won't change things." How he wished he'd had Allou Broder's wisdom when it might have done him some good!

The night was pitch black when Broder arrived back at the headquarters detachment parking lot. Such light as the nearby street lamps offered was smothered by the tall and dense Carolina pine trees that surrounded the area, shining through in only a few scattered patterns that made the darkness more eerie. He took the laundry bag from the trunk of the Mustang and slung it over his shoulder, then picked his way step-by-step along the narrow asphalt walkway that led through the trees to a brightly illuminated area in front of the unit HQ.

Corporal Grissom was asleep on a cot beside the front-office reception desk, snoring loudly. Broder kicked gently at a metal leg of the cot and when that didn't work grasped the toe of Grissom's boot and shook his foot. Grissom roused himself reluctantly. "What the hell you want, sergeant?" he demanded.

"Open the door to the captain's office," Broder said.

"Like hell I will. Ain't nobody authorized to get into the captain's office."

"I am. Now get me the key."

"The CO never told me to let you in, or anybody else," Grissom said. "What in the hell would you be supposed to get in there for, this time of night?"

"I have to leave this for the captain," Broder said evenly. "He needs it first thing in the morning."

"His laundry?" Grissom stared at the denim bag Broder carried, and pulled himself up from the cot to a standing position for the first time since his diffident awakening.

Broder set the bag on the end of the desk.

"Be cool, Grissom," he said. "All I need is for you to open

185

Robert Hays

the door and let me put this in the captain's office. Like I said, he needs it first thing in the morning. You watch me put it in there, then you lock the door again. Okay?"

Grissom was still hesitant: "Last thing I need is to get in trouble with Oates. You're being square with me, right?"

"Yes, I'm being square with you. This is exactly what the good captain ordered me to do. Neither one of us wants to get in trouble."

Grissom stretched his arms over his head, then moved around the desk and slid out the top drawer. He took a key from a small plastic box and turned to the door to the CO's office, fumbled with the lock for a minute, and pushed open the door. Broder entered. He set the laundry bag in Captain Homer Oates's desk chair, then left the room and pulled the door shut behind him.

"Lock it back," he told the corporal. "And thanks. Sorry I had to interrupt your sleep."

"Forget it," Grissom said. "Sorry I gave you a hard time. Just doing my job."

Broder walked out into the clear, cool night, wondering what he'd just deposited in the captain's chair.

He was dead tired. He went to his quarters and lay on his bunk in the darkness, on top of the covers and still fully dressed. Dawn would come soon and he needed to sleep. He need not tell himself that during the last few hours he had passed a point of no return in this ridiculous drama he had become a part of. He had not so much as a hint of what might lie ahead, and in the meantime all he could do was cower in the darkness like a wild animal hiding in the black of night deep in the pine woods. And like that wild animal, Broder felt hunted.

There was something explicitly familiar in the fear that gripped him, a sense that he'd been in this spot before. He knew it for what it was, understood that it was real and true and he could not make it go away. He feared being power-less, unable to alter circumstances when terrible things were

186

about to happen. In his mind's eye he saw Wilma Shand smashing her husband's head with a brick, and then there was an image of Ray-Gene, gasping for breath and bleeding from the mouth.

And there was another vision. This one was Colletta, her face bruised and swollen, crying, and helpless and afraid. He thought for a long time about Colletta and longed to see her, to take her hand in his and hear her sweet voice and have her tell him everything would be all right. They would be safe, together, and walk in the sunlight again.

☙

☙ FEW THINGS GAVE Jacob Saylor the strength and determination he needed to forego the bottle, which had become his crutch and his constant companion. His worry about Colletta proved to be one of those things. He had been sober for less than twenty-four hours, but that was long enough to validate his worst fears: Something was seriously wrong with his daughter and she needed help.

It was difficult enough for him that the little girl who had been the center of his universe was all grown up. He had watched her mature, year after year, through the haze of alcohol-clouded perception, poignantly aware of the wondrous transformation that was taking place before his eyes.

Had he the power he would have made her stay forever an innocent child, his own flesh and blood embodied in that wisp of an angel who clung to him and needed him (and who might be more forgiving of his own shortcomings, though he never would have admitted to such reasoning). But like all fathers he had learned to accept the inevitable. He was proud of the beautiful young woman Colletta had become and humbled by the fact that a merciful God, somehow, had permitted him to sire such splendid progeny.

Whatever was going on now was new and different. He had tried to ignore it for a long while, hoping every day to see an end to it or to see some sign that he was imagining problems that didn't exist. Getting sober had been his last best hope, and he could no longer deny the obvious; Colletta was moody and anxious, became emotional at the drop of a hat, and had bouts of nausea and vomiting that she was not able to hide. She often flew into a rage when he asked about all this, surprising and uncharacteristic behavior for this compassionate girl who meant more to him than his own life.

Mr. Saylor was desperate to discuss his misgivings with someone. But who? Colletta's mother was always at work and had no time to talk. Probably just as well, because she'd twist things around and find a way to blame him, not only for Colletta's problems but also for any difficulties that beset the rest of the family. This was a discussion he didn't need because deep down he already assumed that he was somehow at fault. He tried to bring the subject up with Hunter, but it was clear that the boy had no notion what was going on with his sister.

Jimmie Broder would know. Jimmie was like a member of the family. Except for that time when the Broders sent over charity at Christmas, Mr. Saylor had never felt insulted by Jimmie or had reason to accuse him of being judgmental. He liked and trusted Jimmie Broder and he had known for years that Jimmie would do just about anything for Colletta.

Jimmie surely would come today. Mr. Saylor sat on the front steps, nervously folding and unfolding his trembling hands, and waited for him to make an appearance. The boy was predictable; he showed up within the hour.

"Hey, Jimmie," Mr. Saylor said. "I haven't seen you in a while. Mack Brown been keeping you busy?"

"I've been around," Jimmie answered, his surprise evident. "You weren't here the last couple of times I came, or maybe asleep."

"How've you been?"

"I'm good, Mr. Saylor. You doin' okay?"

"I'm okay. Just old and tired. Your momma and daddy well?"

"Yes, sir. How's Colletta today?"

Jacob Saylor was relieved. Jimmie was the first to bring up the topic he most urgently wanted to discuss. He had spent the last half-hour going over in his mind possible ways to approach the subject of Colletta's health and well-being, and still wrestled with the question right up to the instant Jimmie mentioned Colletta's name. "She's . . . she's not real good," he stammered. "I'm worried about her."

"Is she sick?"

"I don't know what's wrong with her. She won't confess up to being sick, but she's been puking a lot and she looks awful. But it's more than that. She just ain't herself. Haven't you seen it, Jimmie?"

"Yes, sir, I have. I know what you're talking about."

"You mean you know what's wrong with her?"

"No, sir," Jimmie said, "I just meant I've noticed it, too. That she's not herself sometimes."

The door opened quietly behind them. Colletta peered out, a wan smile lighting her hollow-eyed face. Mr. Saylor slipped into the house, desperate for a drink, loathing himself because he hadn't the strength to stay sober even for another hour, much less the time it would take to pursue and rid the world of whatever demons might be causing his little girl's affliction. How could God grant him this beautiful child but deny him the courage to help when she needed him most?

Clenching his bottle, though, he rationalized that if Jimmie had noticed Colletta's problem the girl probably was in good hands. She and Jimmie most likely had started to talk about her trouble already, now that it had been brought out into the open. He'd met his obligation as a father after all, and got help for Colletta, and nobody could blame him for what happened from here on out.

❧ COLLETTA WELCOMED Jimmie with her prettiest smile. "Hey, Jimmie," she said sweetly. "I was hoping you would come."

"I can't go a day without seeing you, Colletta. I hate the weekends when I don't see you in school, and then I have to work and sometimes you do. But you probably knew I would come today."

"Come inside," she said, taking his hand.

Her father had disappeared into the back of the house and the dingy little living room was deserted. Jimmie started toward the sofa, but Colletta tugged gently on his arm and pulled him toward her bedroom door. "This way, Jimmie," she whispered, and pushed open the door and led him into her room. "I want you to lie down with me, just for a little while."

"Are you still sick?"

"No. I'm not sick anymore. Did Daddy tell you I was?"

"No. He just said you hadn't been yourself. I just thought maybe—"

"I am not lying down because I'm sick. I'm lying down because I want you to lie down with me and hold me. I want you, Jimmie, real bad."

Jimmie sat on the edge of the bed and watched in fascination as Colletta slowly undressed. The sight of her unclothed body left him breathless.

"Take your clothes off, silly," Colletta taunted. "I get to watch you, too."

He undressed as quickly as he could, embarrassed, trying to hide his nakedness. Colletta stretched out on the bed, on top of the bedclothes, and watched.

"Now come here," she said. "You have to lay beside me and hold me for a little while and tell me you love me."

Jimmie lay beside her, and Colletta lay her head on his chest and drew her body tight against him. "I do love you, Colletta," he said. "I've loved you for as long as I can remember. You know that."

"Yes, but you have to tell me. I love you too, Jimmie. I probably loved you the first time I ever saw you."

"We were just little kids."

"I know. But I loved you when we were little kids."

"Me too."

"Jimmie, I'm sorry I've been sick so much and caused so much trouble. If I hadn't broke my arm and had so much pain—"

"Don't talk about that now. You couldn't help it. You're going to be all right soon. We've got a lot to look forward to."

"But every time I try to convince myself of that I have a problem again. I don't think I'm ever going to get well. The pain always comes back when my pills wear off. And then I get sick again. I'm sick now, and I shouldn't need another pill for an hour."

"Just lie still and be calm. You'll feel better in a minute. Can I kiss you?"

Colletta never had a chance to answer. Her nausea hit hard, in sudden convulsions. She vomited violently, all over herself, all over Jimmie, all over the bed.

❧ IT WAS COLD for early March, unexpected, and tiny ice crystals floated in the air and sparkled in the beams of the headlights like miniature diamonds as Jimmie drove west toward Florence. Jaybo had set this one up on short notice, so that Ray-Gene had to come by Mack Brown's car lot and catch Jimmie at work and see if he could get a loaner on a couple of hours' notice. That turned out to be easy enough; Jimmie had learned to concoct a pretty good story, just in case Mack was curious as to why he needed a car mid-week.

The long bridge at Galivants Ferry showed patches of ice. Jimmie slowed the old Ford to a timid crawl, facing an icy highway for the first time.

"Exactly where are we supposed to stop?" he asked Donnie Shand.

"A little further, I think," Donnie said. "Up there on the second span somewhere. I don't guess it makes too much difference, though. They'll find us."

"Just tell me when."

"Right up there, another hundred yards or so."

Jimmie stopped the car and put on the emergency flash-ers. Donnie took the key and got out. He opened the trunk, then stood shivering at the back of the car, waiting expect-antly.

"What is he going to say if somebody else stops?" Ray-Gene said to Jimmie. "You think he's figured that out yet?"

"I hope so. You know how DJ is. I tried to feel him out on that, and all he'd say is, 'Don't worry about it.' I just hope nobody else comes along before the delivery man does."

"Are you scared, Jimmie?"

"Of course I am, Ray-Gene. How many of these have we done? Our luck's going to run out one of these days and we're going to get in serious trouble. It's too big a risk."

"But how else can we pay for Colletta's medicine?"

"Colletta's got to get off that stuff. She keeps saying she won't need Jaybo's pills much longer, but I don't see her getting any better. I'm about to go crazy trying to figure out what to do."

"Maybe just a few more pick-ups for Jaybo, and we'll have enough money to get her through till summer. Don't you think?"

"Somebody's stopping. Set quiet, Ray-Gene. Let DJ han-dle it, like he says. I just hope this is whoever we're waiting for."

It was. No more than a couple of minutes later, Donnie Shand slammed shut the trunk lid of Jimmie's loaner Ford and climbed back into the car with a whoop of exhilaration. "We're good at this, guys," he bragged. "Easy as pie. I can't believe Jaybo is paying us big bucks for this."

"You got the stuff?"

"It's in the trunk."

Jimmie waited until the pickup truck driven by their contact was out of sight, then pulled back onto the roadway and drove ahead. Bright headlights from a car coming up close behind were reflected back into his face by the rear-view mirror. He flipped the mirror into its night-driving position to get the lights out of his eyes. Even though he slowed perceptibly, the car behind them refused to pass.

"How come you're going so slow?" Ray-Gene asked. "It don't look slick along here."

"It's not. I'm trying to get that fool behind us to come on by."

"Why not just take off and leave him, if he won't come around? Probably some old guy who's afraid to get over fifty. He's not going to pass. How much further are you going before you turn around and head back to Conway, anyhow?"

"I'll turn around the first place I come to, if I can just get this guy off our ass."

"Punch this rattle-trap up to seventy and get us home," Donnie Shand said from the rear seat. "I told Jaybo I'd get the stuff to him straight off. We ain't got time for some old fool who's goin' to ride your bumper all night."

The loaner Ford responded easily when Jimmie stepped harder on the gas pedal. They pulled away from the car that was following, but it immediately speeded up, too. In less than a minute it was once again close on their rear. Jimmie slowed again but the other driver refused to pass.

"This is scaring me, DJ," Jimmie said over his shoulder. "That could be the police!"

"Just get on the speed limit and hold it there," Donnie directed. "You were already speeding, so if it was police looking to write a ticket they would have stopped us before now. This junk-heap got taillights and stuff?"

"I didn't check it that close."

"Don't look back," Ray-Gene whispered. "If they see us acting scared, they'll get suspicious."

"Why are you whispering?" Donnie demanded. "They can't hear you!"

"I don't like this at all, DJ," Ray-Gene said. "You know

what kind of trouble we could be in if we got caught with Jaybo's stuff. You don't even know what you're packing."

"We're not goin' to get caught, Ray-Gene. You're worrying about some old fool driver that just likes to follow too close. Even if it was the police, like I said, they would have stopped us already if they was going to. Jimmie's driving careful. They wouldn't have any reason to stop us."

Jimmie's palms were sweating on the steering wheel. He couldn't take his eyes off the mirror. Whoever was behind them was staying right on his bumper, in an obviously deliberate pattern. This was no careless driver simply unaware of the danger of following too closely. But he tried not to let his nervousness show when he asked Donnie, "What do you want me to do?"

"Okay," Donnie said. "Cut off toward Marion. If this guy follows us, we'll go in there and find some lighted place. He'll probably go on toward Florence, but we have to get turned around someplace anyway."

The Route 41 intersection and Marion spur were just ahead. Jimmie slowed and signaled his intention to turn. The vehicle behind them dropped back, then made the same turn, although it did not close the space between them and resume the tight tailing position it had held for the last several miles. Jimmie watched the mirror intently, hoping for a sign that their pursuer's interests lay elsewhere.

"Turn in here," Ray-Gene said, indicating a lighted gravel parking lot that served a dilapidated roadside produce stand. "See if they follow us."

Jimmie made a quick turn into the empty parking lot, without a signal, and cut sharply to the right, so that the loaner Ford was pointed back the way they had come. When the dark-colored sedan that had caused all their anxiety passed without slowing, he hurried back onto the highway and headed toward Conway.

"I told y'all there wasn't anything to worry about," Donnie said.

"But just the same," Ray-Gene answered, "I'll be glad to get this done with. We still don't know but what that was somebody following us. You get a good look at the car?"

"Just a car, Ray-Gene. No police markings, no whip antennas or nothing. Relax and enjoy the ride home. And think about the easy cash we picked up tonight."

"The easy cash ain't worth this risk, DJ. I don't think I want to do this anymore. How 'bout you, Jimmie?"

Ray-Gene's question was the one Jimmie had not wanted to face. He'd never been more afraid in his life than he had during the last half-hour. His palms were still sweaty and he could still feel his heart pounding in his chest.

From the beginning, Jimmie had been fully aware that what they were doing was both wrong and dangerous. He'd rationalized for a time that because they didn't know what they were picking up for Jaybo they were somehow less culpable. And he supposed it could be prescription medicine like Donnie was getting for Colletta. But then he got a good look at the package Donnie took from the man on Pawleys Island; it was too small to be anything other than hard drugs. This was insanity.

"I agree, Ray-Gene," he said. "DJ, we can't do this anymore. This is my last trip."

"You'd better think twice about what you're saying," Donnie Shand responded coolly. "How else you figure to pay for Colletta's medicine?"

❧17❧

THE YOUNG television reporter's tone of voice was appropriately earnest. She said commanders of the 82nd Airborne Division had begun the process of returning control of one Iraqi city to its citizens: "In Samawah, little more than a hundred miles south of Baghdad, a U.S. Army colonel began the transition from Army occupation to Iraqi self-rule." He said the action stood in stark contrast to the heavy fighting when American troops entered the city with bombs, artillery shells, and machine-gun fire and went on to report that two American soldiers and perhaps as many as six Iraqi civilians had been killed in Baghdad overnight.

Broder felt guilty. This was supposed to be his war. He should be there with his division. He had friends there, some of them already wounded and possibly crippled for life and some destined not to survive.

He also felt confused and uncertain, even though he had tried hard to maintain a public show of unwavering patriotism and support for the action his division was involved in. He was Airborne, a trained killer, prepared to carry out his mission whenever ordered to do so and so long as actual combat had been only a remote possibility he'd given little thought to the moral imperative at work in all this.

But war looked different on television and in the newspapers. Dramatic scenes of sophisticated, high-tech American weapons raining death and destruction on Iraqi soldiers and civilians had given him another perspective. How many innocent children had the American bombs killed? Were the Iraqi soldiers young men like him, young men looking for better lives, young men who had followed blindly and without question? Were they in uniform of their own free will, or had they been given no choice?

There should always be a clear purpose for going to war and he was confused as to the reasons for this one. He was commencing to see murky images in varying shades of gray where once the gung ho military precepts, sharply focused in black and white, had gone unchallenged in his thinking. And no one should follow blindly and without question, not when they had a choice.

Broder's misgivings about the war added to a general and growing sense of apprehension he felt every day. He was a reluctant player in an unsavory game, being used by both Captain Oates and Colonel Hewlett, and even though he still wanted to trust the colonel it was hard to predict an acceptable outcome.

In the beginning, he might have justified this perverse situation to himself as a price he was willing to pay simply to hold his place in line. To jump again had been his overriding goal and if this assignment was an obstruction he had to get past to regain his paratrooper harness, so be it. Now he was starting to second-guess his commitment to that goal, and his life had become infinitely more complicated.

"Somebody's over at HQ looking for you, Broder," Ortiz called through the open day room door, offering a welcome respite from his tormented self-analysis.

"Who is it?" Broder asked.

"Didn't say. I told him you'd be in the day room catching up on the war and I'd fetch you for him."

"Give me a hint, Ortiz. Military or civilian? Does he look friendly, or should I be worried?"

"You'd only be worried if you had something to worry about, Broder," Ortiz said. "Like if your conscience was bothering you about something, right? All I can tell you is that he's a good-looking black dude in uniform who looks friendly enough, but big enough to hurt you if you've done him wrong."

Rondell Wilson was waiting, standing awkwardly in the hot sunshine in front of detachment headquarters.

"This all you got to do over here, Broder, sit around and watch television all day?" Wilson chided. "You might as well have stayed in the hospital!"

Broder responded in kind, clasping Wilson's huge hand: "How come they let you get away? No invalid patients to torture today?"

"Hey, even I get a day off now and then. So how is the gimpy leg?"

"Doing good. Don't need the crutch anymore."

"Fantastic," Wilson said. Then, his voice lowered, "Can we get out of here and go somewhere where we can talk?"

Broder motioned with his head, toward the shade of the tall pines that surrounded the parking lot where he kept the Mustang. "Let's get out of the sun," he said. "Are you on a tight schedule, or would you like to take a ride?"

"Like I said, I'm off for the day. But are you free to come and go like that, no checking out or anything?"

"I'm Safety NCO, Wilson. A job it looks like Oates created just for me. Supposed to be out inspecting. I only report to the good captain himself, and he's off the post today."

"No kidding? And that's what he wanted you so bad for? Safety NCO?"

"Forget about Oates," Broder said. "Things are working out okay for me over here. But how about you? Everything going good?"

"Same old same old. The Army keeps finding ways to hurt guys, especially jumpers, and we keep patching 'em up. Looks like you still have time to shine the Mustang every once in a while."

"It turns out Oates is a Mustang admirer. Encourages me to find time to keep it clean. Seriously, do you want to get out of here — get off-post for a beer or something?"

"Yeah," Wilson said, "I'd be real happy to. Any place you choose."

&- THE MEXICANA was nearly empty. The waitress brought cold bottles of Corona Extra, and Broder sat back in his chair and looked Wilson straight in the eyes. Wilson had clearly indicated a need to talk but he'd said little during the drive across Fayetteville. Broder sensed that he was holding back, that whatever was on his mind was something he was reluctant to bring into the open. And he was surprised that Wilson hadn't mentioned Colletta.

"I didn't say it well enough up front, man," Broder said, "but it's damned good to see you. I was planning to get back over to the medical center as soon as I could and check up on you."

"Guess I beat you to it," Wilson said. "I've been worried about you. That whole thing with Captain Oatmeal was too weird for me, man. To tell you the truth, I've been scared for you. You telling me straight? Everything's okay?"

"Absolutely. Oates is nothing more than another asshole captain who thinks he ought to be a general. Likes authority way too much. I guess they just stick him in a place where he can't do too much damage. But hey, I've got some good news: I've been cleared to jump again, just as soon as I get back in shape. Colonel Hewlett himself signed off on it."

Wilson looked surprised. "Are you serious? That's great," he said. "But I have to tell you, I never expected it to happen. I've never seen a guy as smashed up as you were put back in the silk. You're sure about this?"

"Sure as the sun comes up early in the morning. Oates delivered the news to me personally. Wants me to get on with re-upping. Said he'd keep me in the unit and take good care of me until I'm ready to start hard training again."

"I'm really happy for you, man. I know that's what you want."

"I don't know. I'm not as sure about things as I used to be, you know? I mean, this war and all. There's nothing in the world I'd rather do than jump and it's still hard to see any life but Airborne, but some things just don't seem as clear-cut as they used to. Know what I mean?"

"I hear you."

Their waitress brought new Coronas and the two men stopped talking to savor long drafts. Broder was disappointed not to see Maria. He wanted to tell Rondell Wilson that Maria was a friend of Colletta's, if only as an excuse to say Colletta's name. He wanted to tell him that this was where Colletta used to work. He wanted to hear Wilson ask about her, say again how pretty she was, talk about the times she had come to see Broder in the hospital. He wanted to hear again how lucky he was to have a woman like Colletta in his life and pretend, just for now, that it was true.

But Wilson spoke first: "I'm holding something for you, Broder. I can't hold this back any longer. She said it's important." He took a small, square envelope from his pocket and handed it across the table. "She said you'll understand."

"What is this?"

"She came to the hospital yesterday, knowing you'd be gone. I told her I would direct her over to your new place, take her over there myself if she wanted me to. She said it would be best if she didn't see you and would I please make sure you got this. And then she was gone, just like that. I'm sorry, Broder."

Broder held the pastel yellow envelope Wilson had given him and struggled for the courage to open it. It was addressed simply to "Jimmie," in Colletta's delicate handwriting. The flap was sealed only at the tip and he passed fingers across the sealed spot softly, conscious that it may have been touched by Colletta's lips.

"You can tell me anything you want to," Rondell Wilson said. "I'm a good listener. You know that. And if you don't want to tell me anything, I'll understand that, too."

Broder slid a thumbnail under the edge of the flap and opened the envelope. On a single sheet of yellow note paper, Colletta had written:

> Dear Jimmie,
>   I'm sorry I couldn't tell you goodbye in person, but I just couldn't face you. If we were together, Jimmie, somewhere deep down you'd always blame me for the things that happened. You deserve so much better. I loved seeing you again, but I know now it was wrong for me to try to come back into your life. Have a good life, Jimmie, think of me sometimes and know I'll always love you. Please don't try to find me. And don't blame Wilson. He's one of the good guys.
>
> Forever,
Colletta.

& *JAYBO'S REACTION* was not what Donnie Shand expected. Instead, Jaybo responded amiably and, it seemed to Donnie, showed at least some degree of sympathy and understanding. Ray-Gene and Jimmie probably were right to be uneasy about their role as couriers, Jaybo said, because they were inexperienced amateurs who could easily make a mistake. He'd worried some, himself, about the danger they could be in and he had no objections if they decided to quit without making another pick-up run.

"You know the story: A horse steps on a nail and the king gets his head chopped off, or whatever shit they did to kings back then," Jaybo said. "Well, I'm the king in this operation, Donnie. And you're one of my main men—let's say a duke or something. We don't need any horses steppin' on nails and bringing us down. You understand?"

"I understand, Jaybo. But how come you let Jimmie and Ray-Gene do your pick-up work to begin with if you were worried about them?"

"Simple. To help you out. I take care of my people."

"I appreciate it, Jaybo," Donnie said. "You've helped me a lot."

"You got in too deep giving away pills to that girl. You can't give stuff away free, Donnie, no matter who it is. We gotta pay, you know, all the way up the line. Anybody don't pay, it catches up."

"I understand that. I knew better, but I just thought they would come up with the money, Jimmie and Ray-Gene. And that wasn't the only reason I got behind."

"It was the main reason," Jaybo said. "And I was too soft because Ray-Gene's family and I know them other kids are friends of his. So I'm partly to blame for this, too."

If not the longest conversation Donnie Shand ever had had with Jaybo, this undoubtedly was the most personal. Jaybo seldom commented on matters not strictly business, never mentioned names, and tended to maintain a cool detachment that Donnie found both comforting and frustrating. He was afraid of Jaybo, but had come to consider him something of a mentor and, deep down, yearned for him to be more open. He had served Jaybo well and in Donnie's opinion that entitled him to know more about Jaybo's view of things.

"Tell you what," Jaybo said, "out of the goodness of my heart I'm gonna be generous to all y'all and kick in enough pills to take care of Colletta for a couple a weeks, free of charge. Okay?"

Donnie was astonished. Jaybo did not hand out free merchandise. But he tried to act not surprised. "Sure, Jaybo," he said, casually as he could make it, "that would be real generous of you. We'd all appreciate that a lot."

"Just one thing you gotta do in return."

"Name it," Donnie said.

"While she's doin' the free stuff, I want you to make her try something different. She can get good stuff cheaper than that prescription trash."

"Good stuff? Like what? Colletta has been really firm about only taking prescription medicine."

Jaybo's irritation was apparent. "Get real!" he said, his voice rising. "That little girl sure ain't having pain from a broken arm after all this time, like she says. She's hung up on that high-priced stuff and she can't afford it. You want to do something for her, get her off them expensive pills."

"I don't know if I can, Jaybo."

"Look. That's some good stuff you brought in last night, and I'll hold some out for her. You get it to her. And make her try it. You hear what I'm saying?"

"Sure, Jaybo. Whatever you say."

"But don't think I'm gonna make a habit of giving stuff away. I'm in this business to make a profit, just like everybody else. There's no profit in giving stuff away, especially stuff that costs hard cash up front."

"I understand. And I'm working for profit, too."

"You're coming along real good, little man. You've got good potential," Jaybo said, calm again. "I count on you to help me move my stuff, okay? And I expect we can work something out before long on the pick-up end, you know, so you can do it on your own, without messing with nobody else. I pay my pick-up men good."

"That'd be good, Jaybo. Only thing is, where would I get different cars to drive?"

"Don't worry about it. Like I said, I expect we can work something out. Now I gotta get moving. You come by in the morning to get your stuff, I'll have the pills for Colletta."

Donnie Shand felt as if a great weight had been lifted from his shoulders. Jaybo was right; Colletta could no longer pay for the prescription medicine now that Ray-Gene and Jimmie had been scared away from the pick-up jobs. Jaybo was doing them all a favor by pointing the way to something else, and all Donnie had to do was see that Colletta gave it a chance. He wanted to find Jimmie and Ray-Gene and let them know the good news. Maybe they could all go together and tell Colletta. Things were going to work out after all and he was proud of his role in making this happen.

→ *MACK BROWN* apparently was bothered about something, but Jimmie had no idea what. Mack had worked at a frenzied pace all afternoon, realigning the cars in new rows and then moving them again, changing the price signs on windshields, stalking up and down the sidewalk on the opposite side of the street to view the car lot from different angles.

Jimmie was afraid to ask if there was a problem because Mack preferred to initiate discussions like that on his own timetable. He busied himself as best he could, working at the far end of the lot from Mack as much as possible. He raked and shoveled gravel wherever he could find a spot that wasn't level, polished cars he'd polished only days earlier, and dragged the heavy rubber hose all around the lot and sprayed water to keep the dust down.

Business had been slow during the winter months and Jimmie had worried for a time that Mack couldn't afford to keep him on the payroll. But Mack Brown had promised that his job was safe.

"There's always work to do around here," Mack had assured him. "We have to be ready for the next customer, even in the cold. Make sure the cars all start, keep 'em clean and ready to go. We may go a bit without a sale, then you get a nice sunny afternoon and a half-dozen buyers show up all at once. You got to be ready for them."

Now that spring was at hand, Mack seemed confident that sales were about to pick up substantially.

His decision not to make any more pick-up runs for Jaybo had made things at work much simpler for Jimmie. He would not need a loaner during the week now, and wouldn't have to worry about coming up with an explanation for Mack Brown as to why he wanted one. Lying to Mack had been hard.

Unfortunately, the relief he felt over no longer having to con his boss to get a loaner was offset by a greater anxiety. Without the money from Jaybo's courier runs, he had no idea how they could afford Colletta's medicine. He felt responsible for it. He had promised that he would find a way to meet Colletta's needs, to do anything necessary to take care of her. Was he a coward for being afraid to risk another pick-up run? Where would he turn now?

"Come on up and have some coffee with me, Jimbo," Mack Brown called. "Got something I want to talk about."

Jimmie went with Mack to the sales office, where Mack poured coffee for both of them and waived him to a chair. "I've been thinking a lot about this business over the last couple of weeks," Mack said, "and I've pretty much come to a conclusion. We need to expand. Just not enough room here for the stock you have to have in today's market. So what I'm thinking is, since there's no room to expand here there's one of two ways we can go. We can either get a bigger lot somewhere and move everything over to it, or we can add a second lot and keep this one pretty much like it is. What do you think?"

"I don't know what to say, Mack," Jimmie replied. "You sure know this business better than anybody. Whatever you decide is apt to be the right thing."

Mack Brown looked pleased. "The two of us get along pretty good, Jimmie," he said. "I'd want you to be involved in all this, is why I'm discussing it with you."

"I'm honored, Mack. That means a lot to me."

"So here's what I'm thinking," Mack went on, shifting into the rapid-fire delivery that always betrayed his excitement. "You'll be graduating from school in a few weeks, and you could go to work full-time, right?"

"Sure, Mack, if you want me."

"What have I been saying, boy? I'd need you to help run the bigger operation, which is why I'm throwing all this out at you. Maybe it's sudden-like, and I should have give you a little more heads-up in advance or something, but like I just said, I'd want you to be involved. Otherwise I couldn't do it"

"That's good. Sure, I'd like that, Mack."

"Then it's all settled," Mack Brown declared. "I'll start looking for new space tomorrow. We'll be all set for a big opening in the summer. If we end up in two lots you probably would manage this one, or if we go to just one bigger place we'll have a huge inventory-reduction sale—loads of advertising—and get our stock down some so we don't have to move so many cars. Either way, we've got a ton of work to do."

"I'll work hard."

"One more thing," Mack said. "Given your new status, it's time you have a full-time car. It ought to be a nice one, too, so as to reflect good on the company. There's a dealers' auction in Charlotte this weekend. I'll go pick up something for you."

Mack Brown kept on talking, excited, laying out high expectations for the business, but Jimmie heard little more of what he said. His mind was racing ahead. He would have a full-time job, and for the first time in his life he actually had a promising view of the future. *Me and Colletta can get married, and live like a real family. I can take care of her.* He wanted to run straight to the Saylor house and tell Colletta, run home and tell his mother, find Ray-Gene and DJ.

Mack kept him in the sales office for the rest of the afternoon, tossing out random ideas about how the two of them would run the new business, enthusiastic about their prospects, pledging grand rewards. Mack had made good money over the years; together, by expanding their volume, they could make small fortunes. It all seemed to be set in stone.

Jimmie's head was in the clouds when he walked away from the car lot. He hurried to Colletta's house, oblivious to a cold night wind that knifed through his lightweight jacket. Swirling gusts blew gutter dirt into his face as he waited on the steps while Hunter fumbled with the door latch.

"Hey, Jimmie," Hunter greeted him. "I thought that was you. You can come in. Did you come to see Colletta?"

"Yeah, but I wanted to see you, too. Is Colletta here?"

"No. She went to meet my momma at work, and help carry home some groceries. I think it'll probably be about an hour before they get home. Want to stay and talk?"

"I'd like to, Hunter," Jimmie said. "You and me haven't had a lot of time to visit lately. But my mom and dad are expecting me at home. I'm late already." He hated to leave Hunter standing there alone, hated the disappointment that showed in the boy's eyes. Hunter's life was full of disappointment under the best of circumstances, and Jimmie tried hard not to add to it. "You know what, Hunter," he said impulsively, "let's you and me get together one of these days and spend some time just talking and stuff. Okay?"

Hunter's face brightened. "You bet," he said. "Any day you want to, Jimmie. I'll see you again soon." He stood in the open door and watched as Jimmie hurried away, waving a hand and smiling.

With his enthusiasm dampened by not catching Colletta, Jimmie became conscious of the cold night air for the first time. He ran to keep warm, ran because he was excited, ran because he wanted to tell somebody his news. He arrived home out of breath, his face flushed from exertion. Popeye Broder was slumped in a shabby easy chair in the living room reading his newspaper. He looked up sharply when his son rushed in: "You in a big hurry to get home tonight?"

"I was running to keep warm," Jimmie said.

"Couldn't Mack Brown have let you drive something home?"

"He probably would have if I'd asked, but I didn't know it was gettin' so cold."

"You and Mack seem to be getting along pretty good. I had my doubts about him when you started working over there, but I guess he's been fair enough."

"I'm glad you think so," Jimmie said, "because I've got

208

some real good news about me and Mack."

"Your momma just about has supper on the table. Let's go tell her."

While Jimmie hung up his jacket, Popeye Broder put his newspaper down, stood, and stretched his arms above his head. Although his youthful muscle-building efforts were years in the past, his huge arms still bulged tightly under his shirt-sleeves. He put a rough hand on his son's shoulder as if to guide him toward the kitchen.

Jimmie's mother already had the food on the table. Three dinner plates were set, and she was putting out spoons and forks. "I thought you were goin' to be late," she said, over her shoulder to Jimmie. "You know we don't wait supper anymore."

"He's got something to tell us," Popeye Broder advised. "Sounds like it might be important."

Allou Broder put down the flatware. She turned her full attention to the boy and asked, "What is it?"

"Well, Mack Brown has this big plan," Jimmie told them, his eyes lit with excitement. "He's going to expand his car lot, get another place or maybe run two lots, depending on how things work out, and he wants me to come to work full-time when I finish school. It'll be almost like a partnership. If we get two lots, he says I'll manage the one where we are now."

He paused and waited for some sign of approval. Neither of his parents spoke. He looked first to his mother, then his father, then asked of both, "Don't you think that's great? Mack thinks we'll make a lot of money."

There was an uncomfortably long silence, but finally his father said, "Well, sure, I guess it could be a good opportunity. At least you'd know you had a job when you get through school. That's worth something."

Allou Broder stood facing away, looking out through the kitchen window into the darkness. "I think you can do better than being just a used-car salesman," she said quietly. "Did

Mack talk about an actual salary? What about benefits, like health insurance? Benefits are just about as important as salary these days."

"We didn't get that far," Jimmie said. "But he sounded like I'd be almost a partner. Mack Brown's made tons of money selling cars, Mom. Look at that Cadillac he drives. I'll get a car too, pretty soon now."

"There are other things in life more important than the car you drive," his mother said. "You're talking about your future, Jimmie. The decisions you make now could make a big difference down the road."

"I know that, Momma. I'm thinking about my future. If I get set up in business with Mack, me and Colletta can get married and probably even buy us a house some day. That's what I want. I think about the future a lot."

The sound his mother made was something between a sigh and a sob, a low moan, a sound he never had heard before, a sound evincing pain. "Jimmie, Jimmie," she said huskily, "you're too young to be talking about marriage. Colletta's too young. There's a whole world out there you haven't seen, outside of Conway, outside of South Carolina."

Jimmie was stunned by their reaction. He looked at his father, who looked away. He turned back to his mother. "I love Colletta, Momma," he said. "I don't care about the rest of the world. I wish for once you could see things my way."

ஃ18௸

CAPTAIN HOMER OATES was blunt, as usual. He handed Broder an unlined white index card with an address penciled on it, shoved a package across his desk and said, "Deliver this today." The package was small, not much bigger than an average-sized shoe box, wrapped in plain brown paper and sealed with transparent tape. The only marking on the wrapper was the number 287, in inconspicuous numerals hand-printed in black ink in an upper corner of one end.

"When you get to Wilmington, go straight to the address on the card and give the package to whoever comes to the door," Oates said. "Under no circumstances leave until you have delivered it, and under no circumstances deliver it without putting it directly into somebody's hands. Understood?"

"I understand, captain," Broder said. "Does this mean I'm expected?"

"You're expected. Now get moving."

Broder took the package from Oates's desk and left the room, and stalked through the outer HQ office without so much as a nod to the assistant detachment clerk who had shown him in only minutes earlier. From there he stopped by his quarters briefly to check and make certain everything was secure, then went straight to the parking lot. He locked the package in the trunk of the Mustang, held open the the driver's side door for a moment to let the interior heat dissipate, and seated himself wearily behind the wheel.

His head throbbed from too much drink. His stomach churned with nausea. His crippled leg ached from a long night of pacing, without rest, because he could not sleep.

Colletta's note had hit Broder hard. Sure, he should have been ready for it. Hadn't Maria told him Colletta was agitated when she left Fayetteville, and might not be coming back? But once past the guilt trip he'd suffered after talking with Maria that day at the Mexicana, he had persuaded himself that Colletta would return. Seeing him again would have called up bad memories for her, of course, but surely she would think back on the happy times, too, and know there was a place for him in her life.

Colletta's message, with its air of finality, might very well have dragged him into even deeper anguish except for the embrace of Rondell Wilson. Broder had handed Wilson the note, without any word of explanation, and Wilson had read it somberly and then read it through twice more. He was obviously surprised and puzzled and didn't know what to say.

"It's a long story, Wilson," Broder told him. "No need for me to try and explain it."

"Tell me as much or as little as you want," Wilson said. "I'm sorry, Broder. I know it hurts."

"I'll tell you the whole thing one of these days, sometime when I feel up to it. I promise."

After another beer at the Mexicana, they'd gone to an old hangout of Wilson's and Broder had had too much to drink. Wilson had played the stalwart comrade, let him despair at will over tequila sours, then drove him back to the base and walked him to his quarters. Although Wilson had left him sprawled on his bunk, he'd soon been up pacing the floor. A long, cold shower at dawn and a quart of black coffee in the mess hall were all that stood between that hard night and Broder's appearance in Captain Oates's office a half-hour ago.

He drove instinctively, barely aware of his surroundings. Once off base he worked his way through the usual heavy morning traffic in Fayetteville, crossed I-95, and headed toward the coast on Route 87. Oates had set no timetable. He had no desire to be in Wilmington before noon and no reason to hurry. Whatever sinister mission he had been sent on, he'd play by his own rules until he reached his appointed destination.

He slipped past the hamlet of Dublin and was considering whether to by-pass Elizabethtown or drive into the city and look for a coffee shop when he first saw the unmarked police car coming up close behind him. It was unmistakable, complete with whip antennae and clearly visible emergency lights inside the windshield. He could see the two occupants of the front seat, men in dark glasses, sinister in appearance.

Haunted by old fears, Broder felt a sense of near-panic. He turned on Route 41, toward town, hoping his pursuers would not follow. The trailing vehicle turned with him and stayed close behind. These men were making no effort to go unnoticed.

Broder turned off the highway at his first opportunity, a dingy roadside diner, went inside and climbed onto a stool at the counter and asked for coffee. The police car parked alongside the Mustang and the two men, one tall and one short and both neatly dressed in dark-blue suits, entered the diner. They took the stools next to him, one on each side.

"Are you Broder?" the tall man asked.

"Yes, sir."

The lone waiter behind the counter, an old man, somewhat scruffy, apparently made a quick decision that he was needed elsewhere. He ducked through a curtained doorway and disappeared into the kitchen.

"FBI, Broder."

The tall man flashed identification, but put it away before Broder had time to see it closely. "We'd like to talk to you outside."

Broder slipped off the stool. The short man grasped him firmly by the elbow and guided him toward the door: "Let's talk in the car, sergeant. This way, if you don't mind."

Broder had an urge to break and run. Federal authorities represented his worst fear. Whatever he was delivering for Captain Oates surely was illegal and if these men searched his car they would find the package. Would he be subject to military justice or the civilian courts? Neither option ap- appealed to him. But escape was out of the question, and he let himself be led docilely to the black Ford Crown Victoria sedan parked beside the Mustang and crawled into the back seat as directed. The short man got in beside him, while the other slipped behind the wheel.

"I'm Agent Schuler," said the tall man in the front seat. "My partner is Agent Hines. We've been watching you for some time, Sergeant Broder. Can you guess why?"

"No, sir," Broder told him. "I haven't a clue."

"We're not after you, Broder," said the man beside him. "We know what you're doing, and we know you're not in- volved. We know you took this assignment at the request of Colonel Hewlett and we've been working with the good colonel for some time. As you've probably figured out by now, Captain Oates is our target."

"I don't know anything about what Oates is doing. I just follow orders."

"The fact that you don't know what you're hauling won't save your ass, Broder," Schuler said. "If we search your car and find what we expect to find, you're looking at hard time. You clear on that?"

"Yes sir, I understand. But I'm telling you the truth."

Hines took off his dark glasses. He looked much less severe, and Broder perceived a slight hint of sympathy in the agent's eyes. "We need your cooperation, sergeant," Hines said, the harshness gone from his tone. "Colonel Hewlett told us you took on this job to help him nail Oates, okay? We're the hammer you're looking for."

"I need to see your ID's again, maybe a little closer this time. Where's your base?"

214

"You're right to be cautious," Schuler said, reaching into the breast pocket of his suit-coat and slipping out a compact leather folder that held his identification. Hines produced his as well and Broder studied them carefully, matching photos to the faces of the two men. "We work out of the Carolina field office," Schuler told him, "but I can tell you this goes higher. Since it involves the military, it goes to the top."

"Okay," Broder said, handing back their respective documents, "what do I do now?"

"First off, we need to see what's in that package you're hauling in the trunk of the Mustang. And you probably have an address to deliver it to, which we need to see."

The index card Oates had given him was in Broder's shirt pocket. He gave it to Hines, who studied it closely and then handed it to Schuler. Agent Schuler copied the information from the card into a small field notebook and gave it back to Broder. Neither man commented on the name and address, leaving Broder to assume this might be information they already had.

"How about that package?" Schuler said. "Can we take a look at it now?"

"Could I refuse if I wanted to?"

"You could, but you'd be in deep water, Broder, paddling upstream," Agent Schuler responded. "Let's move this show around back, where some local in the diner won't be watching us out the window and asking funny questions."

Broder backed the Mustang behind the building, next to a fenceline overgrown with lush mimosa, and popped open the trunk. The package had slid forward, so that he had to bend low to retrieve it. Hines took it from him, turned it slowly in his hands and studied it intently. "Let's see what's in here," he said, and carefully slit the wrapper with a sharp pen knife.

As Agent Hines opened the box, pushed aside packing material and carefully undid folds of clear plastic wrapping and sheets of white tissue paper, Broder got his first look at the merchandise he was about to deliver for Captain Homer Oates. It was not what he expected. Nestled in the box was a six-inch dagger, chiseled from hard brown flint, with an intricately carved wooden handle of approximately the same length. Agent Schuler, who meanwhile had pulled on rubber gloves, carefully lifted the stone knife from the box into the sunlight.

"Magnificent!" Schuler said, almost in a whisper. "Absolutely magnificent!"

Broder could see that the handle depicted a crouching human-like figure with a slack-jawed, gaping mouth and closed eyes. This was topped by a fanged serpent head. The handle had been exquisitely sculpted from what looked like brown teak wood and smoothly polished. The dagger blade was thick and stubby, with sharp edges and slightly blunted point, manifestly the result of tedious chipping from a block of hard stone.

"What do you make it to be?" Hines asked his partner.

"Mexican Aztec," Schuler said. "Probably fourteenth century. This baby could go for anywhere from thirty to fifty grand! And I'll bet you both a steak dinner it's on somebody's list of pre-Columbian art that was stolen from some Latin American museum. And most likely smuggled into the States through Central America."

The FBI men retrieved a camera from their car and proceeded to take a number of closeup photographs of the dagger. When they had finished, they put the open box back in the trunk of the Mustang and took more pictures, including some from angles that would show the license plate. Finally, they asked Broder to hold the open box so that the artifact was visible, then took his picture.

"Evidence," Schuler explained. "We need a paper trail on this one and your delivery is part of it. We need a closeup of the name and address card Oates gave you, also."

The agents' processing went on for another half-hour,

though it seemed much longer to Broder. He stood by idly, desperate for them to finish their work and tell him what to do next. As a final step they marked the inside of the box in some cryptic manner, carefully resealed the package, and returned it to the trunk of the Mustang.

"What are your instructions, once you get to Wilmington?" Hines asked.

"I'm just supposed to deliver the package to that address you have and give it to whoever answers the door."

"That's it? No payment, no proof of delivery?"

"That's it. Just hand them the package and leave."

"Okay, Sergeant Broder, we want you to do exactly as you were told. Leave the package and get back to Fort Bragg, just like you would have if you'd never seen us. Don't worry about what happens next. We'll be in touch."

Agent Schuler smiled for the first time during the entire encounter and extended his hand. "And thank you for your help, sergeant," he said. "We'll tell Colonel Hewlett you did good."

∾

⅌ COLLETTA WAS euphoric over Jimmie's news. A near-partnership with Mack Brown was more than they could have hoped for, would give them more money than they ever had imagined. They could get married right after they finished school, get their own apartment, and they'd have a nice car — maybe a Cadillac like Mack's, didn't Jimmie say?

If he wouldn't mind her working after they were married, she wanted to keep her part-time job at Walgreens. She still would have time enough to make a proper home, she was a good housekeeper and knew how to cook some, and one day they could start a family, and after that maybe she wouldn't work, would that be okay? She wanted a family. Hadn't he said he wanted a family too?

She talked and talked, bright and animated.

Jimmie could not remember seeing her more happy. "I'm glad you like it," he said, when she finally ran out of words.

"I feel real lucky that Mack's giving me this chance. Giving *us* this chance, Colletta."

"Do Ray-Gene and DJ know about it yet?"

"I didn't tell anybody else except my mom and dad. I ran over here last night to tell you first, but you weren't here."

"I know. Hunter told me."

Colletta's mother was still asleep and Mr. Saylor hadn't been seen for two days. Hunter already had left for school. Jimmie and Colletta stood face-to-face in the middle of the living room, close, holding hands, giddy with excitement.

"I guess we need to get to school," Jimmie said. "I'll tell you the truth, though, thinking about our future and stuff, it'll be real hard to keep my mind on classes the rest of the way. School doesn't seem very important now."

"I wish we could get married today, and had our own place to live. Do you think we could start looking at places to live before too long, Jimmie?"

"Sure we can. But right now we have to go."

Colletta retrieved her books, bundled in white plastic grocery bags marked with gaudy red IGA imprints, and pulled the door shut behind them. The first rays of sunshine had easily overridden last night's chill and the day was beginning warm and pleasant.

For the last three weeks, Colletta had monitored azaleas along the path of their long hike to school, hopefully counting the days until the first buds opened into full blossom. She said it was something important to watch for because this year's azalea season would mark a momentous passage in their lives. When the flowers faded, they would be almost done with school, like little birds leaving their nests. Until now, that had meant facing a less-certain world. But Mack's generous offer suddenly had made the challenge much less daunting.

She cocked her head, listening. "I love the mockingbirds, don't you?" she said. "They're happy this morning!"

"Mockingbirds are always happy."

"I think they're especially happy this morning, like they know our story. They're singing just for us."

"You get silly sometimes, Colletta."

She stopped short and whirled to face him, her dark eyes livid with indignation. "Why do you always think I'm silly when I get sentimental?" she demanded. "Why can't I just be allowed to think pretty thoughts sometimes?"

"I'm sorry. I didn't mean anything. Just forget I said that, okay?"

Colletta burst into tears. Jimmie dropped their books on the sidewalk and took her hand, then pulled her to him in a gentle embrace. "Let's not go to school today," he said. "Let's go someplace else, where nobody will know where we are all day. Someplace where there'll just be the two of us. Don't you want to do that?"

"Yes. I want to."

She stood and waited expectantly.

"Do you want to take your books home first?" he asked. "I can carry them with us, if that's better."

"Yes, please carry them. I don't want to go back. Where are we going? I don't feel like walking a hundred miles, Jimmie. But I don't care where we go. I just want to get away someplace where nobody will see us and hide all day, away from the rest of the world. Can we do that?"

Jimmie knew where to go. The dense stands of willow along the creek offered a hiding place he'd used in his own times of distress. A place of solitude for one would protect two as well, shield them on this clement day from the world Colletta yearned to escape. In that place where they had played as children, hunting frogs with Donnie Shand and Ray-Gene, he could comfort her, hear her troubles, listen to her laugh and cry, help renew her spirit.

Colletta stood aside as a signal for him to lead the way. He thought they should circumvent the Saylor house and she understood why. This was not a time to be confronted by Wanda Saylor, who would question why her daughter was not in school, nor to meet Mr. Saylor as he stumbled home looking for a place to sleep.

The old footpath along the slough and through the live oak thicket to the banks of the creek was still dimly visible.

"There aren't many kids in the neighborhood anymore," Jimmie declared. "Only a few more years and this trail will disappear."

"Do you ever think about that day we came from the creek and saw DJ's daddy get killed?" Colletta asked.

"Not really. Not unless Mack Brown mentions it or something."

"That was an awful thing to see. I had nightmares about it forever. I think about it sometimes when I get depressed and I try to persuade myself I'm better off than DJ and think what that must have been like for him. It doesn't really help me, though."

Jimmie walked in front, clearing the way, pushing back weeds and branches that overgrew the track. The distance was greater than he remembered. He slowed to let Colletta catch up. Her face was lightly flushed from the brisk pace and her breathing was becoming labored. "Maybe this was not a very good idea," he said. "I didn't think it was this far."

"I want to go on," she said. "We're almost there. We can find a log to sit on, or grass, and nobody will bother us."

Before they came to the actual creek-bank, they slipped into a small ravine where a thicket of scrub pines and live oaks was overgrown by honeysuckle. The tangle of green, fragrant vines created a beautiful labyrinth, a complex maze of ceilinged caves and tunnels and live-walled rooms open to the clear blue sky. In this glorious place they could hide like hunted criminals, confident of their concealment and unafraid of discovery.

"It's beautiful!" Colletta exclaimed. "I don't remember this, Jimmie. Was it always here like this?"

"I guess it's grown more."

Colletta lay back on a lush cushion of greenery. Jimmie put down their books and stretched out beside her. Vines shielded them on all sides and afforded a partial canopy that protected them from the bright sun. Although less than a mile from town, they might have been on another continent.

Colletta yawned. And laughed. "There's a happy feelng here, Jimmie, away from everyone," she said. "I'm glad we didn't go to school."

"We can stay here all day if we want to."

"You'll get hungry!"

"So will you."

"Thirsty, maybe. But I don't ever get hungry anymore."

"You need to eat, though."

"I'm sick so much. Most days I don't feel like eating."

"I worry about that, Colletta. You oughtn't to be sick so much. Do you think it's all those pills you take?"

Her demeanor changed abruptly, from happy contentment to discernible irritation. She threw up a hand, almost as if to strike him, and clapped it against her own forehead. "Don't start on that again!" she commanded. "Don't start on my medicine. You always bring it up, and I'm sick of it!"

"If you can't even talk about your medicine, there's something really wrong," Jimmie said, suddenly angry, though his words were spoken more harshly than he intended. "You keep saying you won't need Jaybo's pills much longer, Colletta, but it never changes. Be mad at me if you want to, but I'm sick of this, too. I don't think you've even tried to stop taking those damned pills."

His angry response surprised her. She started to reply, then fell silent. They lay together without speaking, side by side, looking up through the green vines to the cloudless blue sky, enveloped by a rising symphony of mockingbird music.

❧ DONNIE SHAND caught up with Ray-Gene at school at the end of the day, but they looked in vain for Jimmie and

221

Colletta. Donnie was eager to divulge his good news about Jaybo's generous offer. He had hoped to tell Ray-Gene and Jimmie at the same time, and Colletta too, if she happened to be there, but he couldn't keep it to himself any longer. He reported the whole account to Ray-Gene, including Jaybo's demand that Colletta be persuaded to try something new. "And Jaybo's right," he said, "she's taking that expensive prescription medicine that we can't afford. But he's willing to give her enough free pills in the meantime to keep her going."

"Jaybo's lyin'," Ray-Gene said. "I know him too well, DJ. He'd beat you up for a few dollars. He's not giving his stuff away like that."

"He already did, Ray-Gene. I've got Colletta's medicine right here in the car. Two weeks' worth. Jaybo gave it to me this morning, just like he said."

Ray-Gene couldn't argue with the obvious, but remained skeptical of Jaybo's motives. Even if no ulterior purpose was apparent, there had to be something in this for Jaybo, something worth a lot more than the price of a two-week supply of pills.

Conceding that they had missed Jimmie and Colletta at school, Donnie drove slowly along the streets those two would take on their walk home. The search was fruitless. He parked on the street across from the Saylor house.

"I guess we ought to go to the door and see if they're home yet," he said. "Else we can set here awhile and see if they come."

"Go to the door if you want," Ray-Gene said. "I still don't go around that house. Old man Saylor's probably in there drunk, and he don't like me coming around."

Donnie Shand agreed that discretion might be the better part of valor in this instance, especially given that he also was uncertain of Jacob Saylor's stability — drunk or sober. They waited another half-hour. When Jimmie and Colletta still hadn't appeared Ray-Gene suggested they go by Mack

Brown's car lot and see if Jimmie might be at work.

Mack Brown was with a customer. Ray-Gene and DJ strolled about the lot, casually, checking out Mack's stock and discussing the kind of car they hoped to own. Mack finished with the time-waster, as he would define the man later, and waved them over. "Hey, guys," he greeted them. "See anything you like?"

"Seen a few," Ray-Gene said, "but you wouldn't be interested in our offer. Has Jimmie been here today?"

"I don't believe he's scheduled to work till Thursday," Mack said. "Has he told you about our new business plan?"

They told him no, and Mack Brown proceeded to relate his scheme, laying out in detail his promise to bring Jimmie into the enterprise, his desire to find a new business site, his grand expectations for expansion. It would not occur to him that, next to telling Colletta, reporting his great opportunity to DJ and Ray-Gene was the thing Jimmie looked forward to most of all. That reward was lost to Jimmie now; Mack had stolen his thunder.

So far as Donnie Shand and Ray-Gene were concerned, Mack Brown's disclosure left them wide-eyed and envious. They left Mack's car lot with a greatly exaggerated view of Jimmie's new prospects for success.

Donnie's own news about Jaybo's generosity was overshadowed by Mack's revelation, but he was determined to make the best showing he could. He needed to deliver Colletta's medicine, for she would be almost out of pills by now and growing more agitated by the hour. Much as he cared for Colletta, he'd grown weary of her emotional highs and lows and, especially, her juvenile temper tantrums. He had no desire to face another of her flareups, expected or not.

Donnie had decided not to spring everything on Colletta at once. He'd tell her about the free medicine first, with no strings attached, and then, a few days later, he could work more cautiously into the demand that she try a different product of Jaybo's. Her resistance would put a damper on the good news if he tossed it all out up front, and in any case he needed time to figure out how to entice her into trying something new. He would not dare to face Jaybo without having made an all-out effort.

Ray-Gene chose not to go back to Colletta's. DJ dropped him off at home and got back to the Saylor house at twilight. A dark figure prowled the sidewalk, alternately watching the door and looking away, pacing a few yards in one direction and then reversing course, stepping gingerly as if walking barefoot on hot pebbles. Donnie could not make out the man's face, hidden in the shadow of a decrepit, wide-brimmed black hat. But he knew it was Jacob Saylor.

"Hey, Mr. Saylor," he said quietly, moving closer.

Mr. Saylor stopped short, startled, looked surprised to see another human being. He stared at Donnie, showed a flash of recognition, but plainly could not attach a name to the young man's face. "Who are you?" he demanded.

"It's Donnie Shand, Mr. Saylor. I brought Colletta's medicine. Do know if she's home?"

"Ah yes, Colletta's medicine. You're a good boy, Donnie Shand. Colletta needs her medicine

"Is she home?"

"I don't know. I've not been inside. You ought to go on in, though, and take Colletta her medicine. She's been sick a long time, you may know. Jimmie Broder was going to help her but I don't think he can. I don't think anybody can. She's all grown up now. She used to be so little . . ."

"Her medicine helps, Mr. Saylor."

"Yes, I think it might. Go on in and take Colletta her medicine. Tell her mother I was here. Could you do that?"

"Sure, Mr. Saylor. Is there anything else?"

Jacob Saylor did not answer. He looked at Donnie Shand blankly and turned and walked away.

ᖰ19ᖳ

BRODER HAD no trouble finding the address Captain Oates had scrawled on the index card. It was in one of Wilmington's most desirable residential areas, a grand old mansion on a quiet, tree-lined street with several blocks of comparable homes separated by generous, handsomely landscaped and immaculately kept lawns. He almost expected a formally attired butler to answer the door, but was greeted instead by a pleasant, grandmotherly woman who wore a faded house dress and was barefoot.

"I suppose this would be something Harmon is expecting, though goodness knows what it is," the woman said, her accent marked by a sweet coastal inflection largely lost in the younger generation. "I guess you would like me to sign something?"

Broder told her no, she needed only to confirm that he had the correct address and check the parcel to make sure it was not damaged. She looked the package over carefully, thanked him politely, and bid him good day.

It was well past noon. He decided to stop somewhere for lunch before starting back to Fayetteville. He drove past a couple of busy franchised restaurants and sought out a local café that looked to be uncrowded. More than anything, he wanted a tranquil setting in which he could feel far removed from the events of the morning. His contact with the federal agents had unnerved him but, paradoxically, given him a sense of relief at the same time.

He seated himself at a small table next to a window. The

sole waitress was busy delivering an order nearer the back. "I'll be with you in a minute, hon," she called in his general direction, and he waved his hand in casual acknowledgement.

Although he had been given no orders as to reporting back, he already had determined how he would complete his assignment. He had delivered the package precisely as Oates had instructed and wanted to convey that fact directly to the captain. The sooner the better. He would go straight to HQ once back on the post and report in, and assure the captain that his mission had been carried out. And he would take immense satisfaction in knowing secretly that Captain Homer Oates's goose was cooked.

Broder thought about agents Hines and Schuler, worried about his own forced role in some future prosecution. God, how he hated the notion of having to testify in court about delivering Oates's contraband. I'd have bet a right arm it was drugs, he thought. Who would have figured the good captain to be dealing in sophisticated art objects?

"Sorry to be so slow, hon," said the waitress, plumping a glass of water on the table in front of him. "I've been busy as a one-armed paperhanger today. You doin' okay?"

"I'm fine, thanks."

"You like a menu, hon, or want to hear today's specials?"

Broder elected to order from her verbal inventory. The "specials," he assumed, were most likely to be ready in the kitchen without a long wait. The waitress mumbled the first dish too fast for him to understand, but her next suggestion was crab-stuffed flounder. This sounded good so he ordered it. She was back in no time with his food.

"I'll bet you're a soldier," she said, recklessly placing his order on the table. "Least ways, you look like one. Am I right?"

"Yes, ma'am, I am. How can you tell?"

"Just your look. You know, clean-cut and all. And you look confident, like you know what you're about."

"I'll take that as a compliment," Broder said, "but there's lots of guys around who'd take issue with that last part."

"You stationed at Fort Bragg, hon?"

"Yes, ma'am."

"Airborne?"

"Eighty-second."

"I thought so. What d'ya think about this war going on in Iraq?"

"Mostly, I worry about friends who are over there in combat. I know some of them won't be coming back."

"Yeah, war's nasty business," the waitress said. "Just be glad you're not over there in the middle of it, yourself."

Left to his own thoughts again, he wished that she had not brought up the war. He wanted not to think about it, but there it was again. No way he could escape.

The war had caused him no small amount of personal soul-searching and forced him to face questions he had not considered before. He still was immensely proud to be a U.S. Army paratrooper and still had full confidence in his own abilities and training, injuries suffered in his hard landing notwithstanding. The thing that was missing now was his faith in the system. Soldiers had to follow orders without question, and deep down he was afraid that he might never be able to do that again.

&* JORGE ORTIZ grinned from ear to ear when he showed up at detachment headquarters and motioned with his head, silently, for him to come close. "The captain was just asking about you," he whispered.

"Is he in there?"

"Sure 'nough. Go on in. His door's open."

Oates answered his light knock without looking up. His "Come in" was surprising in tone, almost pleasant.

"Mission accomplished, sir," Broder reported, standing at attention before the CO's desk.

"Drop the phony dramatics, sergeant," Oates demanded.

"Did you get the package there?"

"Yes, sir."

"No trouble?"

"No trouble, captain."

"And put it in the hands of the man of the house?"

"No, sir. A woman came to the door. My instructions —"

"I know what your instructions were, Broder," the captain interrupted. "And you put the package directly in the hands of the woman who answered the door?"

"That's right, captain. She checked the address, looked the package over, and thanked me. She said it was undoubtedly something Harmon was expecting."

"No names!"

"Sorry, sir. No names."

"You did good, sergeant. Now I want you to take a couple of days off, then check back in. I'll have something else for you to do."

"And my duties as safety NCO . . .?"

"Dammit, I said take some time off. I don't want to see your sorry ass around the detachment. Come back in three days. Understood?"

"I understand," Broder said, and turned his back casually, like a civilian, and left the office.

Common sense said he ought to go straight to his quarters and get to bed. He was still physically exhausted from too many hours without sleep and, although the day had included an element of excitement given his intersection with the federal agents, the drive to and from Wilmington had not been particularly stimulating.

Sleep would have come easily. But for the first time since that day when Homer Oates showed up at the medical center asking questions about his bad jump, Broder felt totally free of the sinister captain. His future was no longer in this vile man's hands and he wanted to celebrate his newfound freedom. He wanted company.

He drove to the hospital, went straight to the orthopedic

ward, and caught Rondell Wilson just as Wilson was about to go off duty. Wilson greeted him with enthusiasm: "Man, I'm glad to see you. And you're back among the living, yet!"

"Yeah, well, you can't keep a good man down, they say."

"You truly were in sorry shape last night. Did you manage to get any rest?"

"Can't say that I did. Are you hungry? I'd like to buy you dinner and start all over again tonight. And this time I'll still be in condition to drive us home. Promise. You interested?"

"Let me get into my civvies first?"

"Take as much time as you want."

They went to Wilson's quarters, where Broder carried out a mock inspection while Wilson changed out of uniform. Wilson missed a belt-loop in his haste and Broder told him, "Take your time, man. It's not like someone's expecting us."

"I just hate to keep people waiting," Wilson replied. "We drinkin' to anything in particular tonight?"

"Nothing in particular. Everything in general. Take your pick. But no more tequila sours for me. Not tonight. Only beer and conversation. I might go easy on the beer, even."

"That means you want to talk."

"Like I said, conversation. There's a difference."

"Oh, yeah? Explain it to me."

"Conversation means no agenda. Anything that comes up. Talk means I've got problems, or you've got problems, and somebody damned well needs to listen to us whine."

"Okay, then. We'll eat, and then it's beer and conversation, just like you said."

Conversation — aimless, free-wheeling, go-where-it-may conversation — was exactly what Broder had in mind. Conversation would reflect his mood, the sense of exhilaration that came from escaping the hold of Captain Homer Oates. Empty conversation was what he planned, needed, yearned for. But any possibility of a night of hollow, happy exchange promptly disappeared when he made a fateful turn toward the Mexicana.

Broder himself did not understand why he drove in that direction. It was not what he intended. Although he'd been to the Mexicana only a few times, it was as if he drove there by rote, unaware of his action until it was too late.

They had entered the Mexicana parking lot before Wilson noticed where they were, and then he turned to Broder with an expression of disbelief. "Conversation, my ass!" he exclaimed. "We gotta talk, Broder, just like I said."

Wilson sternly pointed the hostess to a table on the opposite side of the restaurant from where they had sat the night before, when he had delivered Colletta's note. It was a small difference, perhaps, but anything that might call up less pain might be worth the chance.

"Okay, I suppose this is all about your burning desire to get back in the harness," Wilson said, once they were seated.

Broder ignored his sarcasm. "I'm all mixed up on that," he said. "I can't see ever being ready to go to war again, but there's nothing like jumping, nothing else I'd rather do."

A waiter, short and heavy with hair too long and a tiny gold hoop earring in one ear, recommended steak tampiqueno. He said it was a specialty of the Mexicana and the chef on duty was the one who made it best. Wilson said he was famished; the steak tampiqueno sounded good, just so long as it was fast. Broder took the easiest out and ordered the same.

"Okay," Wilson said, "you want to jump, but you're no longer gung ho Airborne. I guess it's just a matter of what price you're willing to pay."

"I don't care anymore."

"Look, my friend, it's not a question of jumping or not jumping that's eating you up. It's that note I gave you last night. It's Colletta, man. You've got to talk to me about her."

"I told you before, it's a long story."

"Yeah, right. And you said you'd tell it to me sometime. This is the time, Broder. You can't bury it. If you didn't want to talk about Colletta we wouldn't be here."

Broder gave in, easily this time, willing. He poured out his story, leaving few gaps for Wilson to question. He talked about Ray-Gene and Donnie Shand and Jaybo; he talked about Jacob Saylor and Mack Brown; he told how his life had revolved around Colletta and how he thought she was out of it forever, and how everything had changed after his bad jump, when Colletta suddenly reappeared as if from nowhere.

"And you've never seen the boy?" Wilson asked, softly.

"I didn't know about him until after she was gone. I only heard after we'd gone our separate ways."

"You've got to find her, man. Whatever the future holds, you'll never feel complete until you've made your peace over this woman. She's got too much of a hold on you."

Wilson paused and looked up, and Broder felt a gentle hand on his shoulder. Maria stood at his side.

"Jimmie Broder," Maria said, "come here early Saturday and wait. Colletta will have to come some time during the morning and pick up her last paycheck."

*

&- THEY WOULD make one more pick-up run for Jaybo. It was a last recourse, not something Jimmie and Ray-Gene wanted to do but the only way they could keep Colletta in medicine until the end of school when Jimmie's new high-paid job with Mack Brown kicked in. Jimmie had calculated the days carefully; a single courier run would do. Barely. The two free weeks, courtesy of Jaybo, had helped. They tried hard to push aside their doubts about Jaybo's motives and look on the positive side. Jaybo's unexpected generosity had given them precious time and Colletta's outlook was infinitely brighter. For two weeks, she needn't face her usual uncertainty and the terrible fear it generated. And when Colletta was happy, the boys were happy.

Donnie Shand had been apprehensive about going back to Jaybo with their request for another assignment. Jaybo was still angry because Donnie had botched his scheme to get Colletta to try something new. Donnie had done his best, but Colletta was still unshakable; she needed medicine, not drugs. Jaybo said he wouldn't give up, and Donnie needed to keep after her, wear her down.

"She's nothing but a weak little pussy," Jaybo had exploded finally. "What kind of man can't make a weak little pussy do what he wants? You got no future in this business, little man. You ain't tough enough."

And then there was Jaybo's earlier complaint that Jimmie and Ray-Gene posed risks as couriers. That would have deterred Donnie Shand at the time, but after giving it more thought he'd convinced himself that Jaybo was lying, trying to save face because they wanted to quit. And Jaybo had held out good prospects for Donnie himself to continue to make his pick-up runs so Donnie used that as an opening. Jaybo went along with it. Jaybo was menacing, but sometimes quite transparent.

"Jaybo said he'd give y'all another chance, out of the goodness of his heart," Donnie told Jimmie and Ray-Gene.

"But this will be the last one, for sure," Ray-Gene proclaimed. "Does Jaybo understand that, DJ?"

"I didn't push that," Donnie Shand answered. "He didn't complain that y'all quit before, but he's not forgot it. Seemed best not to get too far into it."

"Just as long as we all agree on it," Ray-Gene said.

"Jaybo already told me I could keep on working pick-up runs. It's not a job that takes us all. Next time he needs us, I'll handle it by myself."

"Don't you think that'd be dangerous?" Jimmie asked.

"Of course not. Anyway, if something happened, what difference would it make if you and Ray-Gene were there? I mean, it's not like y'all were armed bodyguards."

Jimmie made the others promise him they would not tell Colletta what was going on. She felt bad enough not paying for her own medicine and he'd led her to believe that he had plenty of cash to take care of her when the free pills ran out.

Colletta was confident that she wouldn't need the medicine much longer, and anyway they would be married soon and it would be proper then for him to pay her way.

"She keeps saying she won't need those pills much longer," Ray-Gene said. "Do you really believe that, Jimmie?"

"I don't know. I keep hoping she won't. But you don't have any responsibility for Colletta, Ray-Gene. You don't have to be involved in this stuff with Jaybo, either. It's not your problem."

Ray-Gene's hurt was apparent. "I thought we were all in it together, like we've always been," he said. "We're still a team, right? Nothing's changed. You and DJ and Colletta are like family to me, Jimmie. I'm doing this because I want to. I thought you understood that. If I was the one needed help, you'd do it for me, right?"

Jimmie wished he could take back his words. He wanted to recall the tone he'd taken with Ray-Gene, the edge he'd let creep in in an instant of exasperation. Ray-Gene, the sweet-tempered, loyal, forgiving friend who had been at his side from as far back as he could remember, was not at the root of his resentment. He gripped Ray-Gene's hand and said, "I'm sorry, Ray-Gene. I didn't mean that. We're still a team. We're still family."

Donnie Shand stood between, arms over their shoulders like a mother goose gathering in her hatchlings. He pulled them together, huddled them as he'd often done when they were children. Donnie was still their leader.

"Jaybo said go ahead and get a good car lined up from Mack Brown because he may need us on short notice," the leader said, making things normal again.

"We'll be ready," Ray-Gene said. "This team's ready for anything, right?"

Jimmie agreed. And he was encouraged about the future, in which he could see himself and Colletta together forever.

More immediately, he was confident that he would not have to face the worry that went with getting a loaner from

Mack Brown. Mack was going to be handing over the keys to Jimmie's personal company car any day now. Mack said there was no need to wait; school would be ending in less than a month and Jimmie's starting date as a full-time sales manager was just around the corner.

In his own mind, Jimmie already was a partner in the operation. He had been going to the car lot every day after school even though he was paid for only three afternoons a week. Popeye Broder had suggested sarcastically that his son might want to put a cot in the sales office and move in, just in case a potential buyer happened by in the middle of the night.

Mack Brown was pleased with his new associate's enthusiasm — so pleased that he decided to speed up presentation of Jimmie's new company car and had it on the lot the next afternoon. He had kept the vehicle under wraps at home, after picking it up at the Charlotte auction, and made a show of awarding Jimmie the keys.

Mack explained that the two-year-old Buick LeSabre, red as a ruby and showing every bit as much glitter, had been in service with a rental agency. It must have been in the hands of only the least-demanding of drivers, according to Mack, because it was unblemished as a new-born baby. He claimed that he'd looked at every vehicle in the wholesalers' inventory and when he spied this one he knew right away it was superior to anything else they had.

All this mattered little to Jimmie. The Buick was his, to drive as his own, and he could not have been prouder had it been a jewel-encrusted Rolls Royce outfitted for the queen.

❦ DONNIE SHAND'S prophecy proved correct. Jaybo had a critical pick-up in two days, down the coast maybe as far as Charleston, and if Donnie's team was up to the job it was theirs. They would haul more merchandise this time, Jaybo said, and that meant a bigger reward when it was delivered. This could be a payday to remember.

Two days meant Sunday. There would be no school and no work at Mack Brown's to interfere and Ray-Gene contrived a quick schedule change at the IGA by promising to pull a double shift on a later weekend.

Jaybo waited until the last minute to spell out the particulars.

"He just give me the details an hour ago," Donnie Shand told Jimmie, surveying the interior of the Buick. "I'll fill y'all in after we pick up Ray-Gene. Mack did you good. Leather seats, even!"

Ray-Gene waited at the curb, and was in a good mood. "This'll be a good chance to try out your new car, Jimmie," he said. "We probably would have done this anyway, if we'd all had the day off. You would have wanted to take us on a nice Sunday drive, right?"

"Sure I would," Jimmie told him. "But Colletta would be with us."

"What kind of excuse did you make for not seeing her this afternoon? I mean, in case we get asked."

"Told her I had to work. She probably won't ask more than that. If she does, I'll say I had to drive over to Myrtle Beach to look at some cars or something."

"We didn't see you, then?" Donnie asked.

"Right. But like I said, she won't ask."

The rear of the Buick swayed almost imperceptibly as they swept around a wide curve. A low rumble became a bumping thud. "Get over, Jimmie," Ray-Gene yelled from the back seat. "I think we've got a flat tire or something!"

Ray-Gene's guess was right and changing a tire alongside the road was a challenge, especially given that none of the three had done it before. Jimmie had changed tires a few times on the car lot and knew what to do, but the shoulder of the highway was narrow and slanted. Passing traffic rushed by dangerously close. They were relieved when the job was finished without incident, but Donnie Shand worried over the lost time.

"We're already half an hour late," Donnie warned. He was nervous, and it showed. "Can you make it up, Jimmie?"

"It didn't take that long. We're no more than ten or fifteen minutes behind. Anyway, we got a little leeway, right? You said get there by four o'clock and we'd aimed at fifteen or twenty minutes early, just in case."

"We absolutely have to be there by four o'clock. These guys don't wait."

"I think we'll make it," Jimmie said. "But I have to be careful not to drive too fast on that little spare tire."

"We're not picking up anything heavy, are we?" Ray-Gene asked. "I mean, with that little spare we don't want to put a load on it."

"It's not going to be anything heavy," Donnie answered, obviously determined to demonstrate that he was unruffled. "When Jaybo says more merchandise, he probably means two or three of them little packages instead of just one. But it sure won't be anything heavy enough to hurt that tire."

"Speaking of little packages," Jimmie said, "what's in them, anyway? I think you know, DJ, and me and Ray-Gene have a right to know too. We're involved. Are we hauling drugs for Jaybo?"

Donnie stared out the window, refusing to face Jimmie, and said nothing.

"Come on, DJ," Ray-Gene said, "we got a right to know, like Jimmie says. What is that stuff? You know what it is."

Donnie Shand swiveled in his seat so that he could see them both, more or less face-to-face. "All right," he said, "so I know what it is. Of course I do—me and Jaybo work close together. But you guys don't need to know."

Ray-Gene started to speak, but stopped short when Donnie signaled with a raised hand. "Listen to me," Donnie said firmly. "Here's the story, and this is the way it has got to be. Neither of you knows anything about what we are picking up for Jaybo. Absolutely nothing! I asked y'all to go down to Mt. Pleasant to buy some sweetgrass baskets and Jimmie wanted to drive his new car. If I happen to pick up something else, it's a complete surprise to y'all. That's the story I'll tell, and that's your story too."

Now it was Ray-Gene who was slow to respond. "What you're saying," he said finally, "is like what would happen if we got caught or something."

"You got it, Ray-Gene."

"But you've always said there was no danger we'd get caught, right?"

"Look, Ray-Gene. I don't expect to get caught, okay? All I'm saying is, if something went wrong, I'm the one responsible for Jaybo's stuff. You and Jimmie had nothing to do with it. I'm trying to protect you, is all. You could honestly tell anybody that you didn't know what we were hauling. Doesn't that make sense?"

Ray-Gene and Jimmie accepted Donnie's position without argument, but the discussion had brought them back to harsh reality. This was not the pleasant Sunday afternoon outing of Ray-Gene's earlier fancy. Rather, it was a treacherous journey that could reward them handsomely if things went according to plan or land them in jail if things went wrong. They had had good reason to quit the pick-up runs before, and good reason to make this one their last. Jaybo's business in the light of day was no more savory, and no safer, than Jaybo's business in the dark of night.

Their contact instructions were simple. They were to drive slowly along Route 17 toward Mt. Pleasant and watch the roadside stands where local families sold the handmade sweetgrass baskets the area was famous for. At one of these, they should see a black and silver-gray Chevrolet pickup truck towing an empty boat trailer. The driver of the truck was their contact.

"You start watching along the other side of the road, Ray-Gene," Donnie directed. "I'll watch this side. Let Jimmie know as soon as you see anything."

Traffic was not heavy. They passed two stands where no

one was visible except three or four basket-weavers working patiently in the shade of bright-fabric awnings stretched between poles. A tan Dodge minivan they had followed for the last few miles turned off at a third stand, and was the only vehicle there. It was almost four o'clock.

When Ray-Gene spotted the truck and trailer at the next stand, half hidden by a gray Volvo station wagon, it was too late for Jimmie to get stopped.

"Get turned around fast," Donnie demanded. "We don't have much time."

A siding a few hundred yards further on let them turn and go back. Jimmie eased the Buick off the highway at the basket stand. He parked beside the empty boat trailer, behind the station wagon. Donnie instructed his companions to look at baskets while he took care of business.

A man and two women were ahead of them, surveying the exquisite handiwork of the basket-weavers. Jimmie and Ray-Gene stuck close together and picked up an intricately crafted basket and pretended to study it closely. Ray-Gene turned it slowly, admiring the pattern and colors. Jimmie ran his fingers over the remarkably strong weave, intrigued by the texture of the grasses.

Donnie Shand strolled about the stand for a minute or so and gradually worked his way back to the side next to the parking area. "Looks like somebody lost their boat," he said loudly.

The woman turned to look at Donnie, lowered darkly shaded glasses as if to see him better. "I just sold my boat to a fisherman," she said. "Do you happen to know where I could get a good deal on another?"

Donnie turned and walked to her.

A brief interval of friendly conversation. The woman had left-over boat accessories to sell. Where were they? She said they were conveniently stowed in the toolbox on her truck. Sure, Donnie was interested. Could he see them?

Yes, of course.

The phony transaction was quickly completed. A banker's box that held four smaller, newspaper-wrapped packages tied with string was transferred from the pickup to the trunk of the red Buick. Now all that stood in the way of a successful finish to Ray-Gene's and Jimmie's final courier run for Jaybo was an eighty-five-mile drive back to Conway.

They were barely ten miles from home when the flashing lights appeared in the rear-view mirror.

❧20❧

LIEUTENANT COLONEL Eldon Hewlett was more animated than usual. He welcomed Broder cordially and dropped the formalities of rank. He was pleased with events as they had played out so far and he was grateful to Broder for letting himself be used to help expose the shady dealings of Captain Homer Oates. He'd called Broder to his office to tell him so.

Gratitude was not what Broder had come to hear. He wanted the colonel to say that his stint in Oates's outfit was finished and his transfer back to a combat training unit was in the works. All the uncertainties about his long-term future notwithstanding, he wanted to jump again.

After more time to think about his situation, Broder was troubled. Why had he ever been confident that his single contact with the federal agents spelled emancipation? Surely they needed more on Captain Homer Oates than a single stolen artifact. Anyway, Colonel Hewlett had never mentioned a time-frame for this assignment nor made promises as to what might come next. For all he knew, the colonel simply might plan to abandon him once they had Oates, and leave him to the normal vagaries of Army administration.

His old unit was in Iraq and he'd never catch up to it. What if some special orders clerk in personnel decided that Sergeant Jimmie Broder, smash-legged Airborne, was a perfect candidate for an opening for an Infantry drill sergeant at Fort Jackson? He wanted his decision about the future to be based on better choices.

But these concerns would have to wait until the colonel got past the fervid pleasures of springing the trap on Oates, a full accounting of which Hewlett barely was getting warmed up to. "I've always admired the French culture," the colonel was saying, "even if the French aren't with us in the war. The French have a saying, *'Si vous ne voulez pas être trompé par les marionettes, vous* devez *obtenir à l'intérieur la tente* — If you don't want to be deceived by the puppets, you must get inside the tent.' Do you see what I'm saying, Broder?"

"I'm not sure I know what you mean, sir."

"Simple, sergeant. In the case of Captain Oates, we needed somebody inside his operation — inside the tent, so to speak. Somebody we could watch, but also somebody we could trust. In other words, somebody like you. We knew the captain would get you involved in his operation one way or another. You had an agent following you every time you left the unit."

"I had no idea," Broder said.

"Of course you didn't. You weren't supposed to. We wanted you to do exactly what Oates told you to do and we'd be watching, just like I told you in the beginning. We were always ready to come in and bail you out if we needed to, or let you lead us to the evidence. And that's exactly what happened."

"Sounds like you were coordinating this whole operation, then. Right from the start, when you asked me to play along when the captain started recruiting me."

The colonel stood and stretched, which Broder took as a sign their meeting was over. He stood, too, ready to leave. The colonel motioned him back into his chair.

"Stay, sergeant," he said. "We have more to talk about. No, I wasn't coordinating anything, and I'm sorry if I made it sound like I had an important role in it. I don't mean to take credit for any of this thing. I got into all this just like you did. I was asked by someone higher up."

"How high does it go, then?"

"That's a conversation we don't need to have."

"Sorry, sir."

"No need to be. The truth is, I couldn't tell you if I knew. I'm sure you understand."

"I understand," Broder said.

"There is something else I wanted to ask you about, sergeant. As you say, Captain Oates did recruit you. A real hard sell. But he seemed to believe you were particularly susceptible, for some reason. Do you know why?"

"Yes, sir. Somehow, he knew about some trouble in my background, when I was just a kid in high school."

"Serious trouble, Broder?" the colonel asked.

"Serious enough. But not a criminal record."

"How did he know, then?"

"I have no clue, sir."

"Tell me more about the trouble, sergeant. We need to find out how the captain could have come by that kind of information."

Reluctantly, Broder told Colonel Hewlett details about his past that he had never expected to disclose. There was no way to sugar-coat the story. Captain Oates's apparent assumptions that he used drugs and had a criminal record in South Carolina, even though they were wrong, were too close for comfort. Oates might be off target, but he clearly knew too much.

"I've got contacts at the Provost Marshal's office," Colonel Hewlett said. "I'm going to run this down. Maybe I'll ask the feds about it, as well."

"Thank you, sir. I appreciate it."

Broder, to his own surprise, felt a sense of relief. The thought of Captain Homer Oates snooping into his background had bothered him more than he cared to admit. He wanted out of Oates's unit, and now that he'd finished the job Colonel Hewlett sent him there to do he saw no reason why he shouldn't be reassigned immediately.

The colonel might have read his mind: "You probably

have important questions of your own, sergeant. Where does all this leave you, right?"

"Yes, sir, I'd hoped we could talk about that."

"I assume you have no great interest in staying in the headquarters detachment as, what is it, safety NCO? What would your preference be, then?"

"Colonel, I just want to get back into a combat training unit, so I can jump again. Nothing else."

The colonel's countenance, an obvious look of surprise, should have forewarned Broder but it puzzled him instead. Surely Colonel Hewlett, Airborne to the core, would expect a jumper to be eager to get back into the harness. From those very first hours in the medical center, going back to the colonel's earliest visit, Broder had made his wishes clear: He wanted to jump again.

"I'm sorry, Sergeant Broder, I thought you understood." The colonel softened his tone and lowered his voice, as if pained by what he was about to say. "With the injuries you got in that training accident, you'll most likely never be allowed another jump."

"But I don't get it, colonel. My medical report cleared me to jump. You signed off on it."

Colonel Hewlett tilted his head far back, stared momentarily at the ceiling, and sucked in a long, slow breath. He placed his elbows on the desk, forearms extended upward, and lowered his head until his face was buried in his open hands.

"I'm sorry, sir," Broder persisted, "had you forgotten?"

The colonel uncovered his face, but still looked away. "Sergeant Broder," he said, "I owe you an apology, and I do sincerely apologize. The medical evaluation was faked. We had to make Captain Oates think you'd be around for a long time, otherwise he probably wouldn't get you involved at a level that would do us much good. That meant getting you to reenlist and I was afraid you wouldn't do that if you were told you couldn't jump again. I am truly sorry."

Colonel Hewlett's pronouncement left Broder speechless. The colonel waited for his response, but he said nothing. This was the man in whom he had placed his highest hopes, and his hopes had just been dashed. The deception was ugly and hateful.

The colonel appeared to be uncomfortable with the sergeant's silence. He made an effort to salvage his own dignity: "A commander sometimes has to do things he doesn't like to do, sergeant. He has to make a quick decision and run with it, let the chips fall where they may."

"A good commander earns the loyalty of his men," Broder replied, unconcerned that he might be treading dangerous ground. "How do lies and deceit accomplish that?"

The colonel stiffened. "Don't forget where you are, Sergeant Broder. I may not look too good to you right now, but I won't tolerate insolence."

"No, sir. I wouldn't expect that you would."

Broder had said too much, and knew it. Colonel Hewlett dismissed him on this sarcastic note and he walked back to his quarters as dispirited as a man just condemned to the gallows. Not only was he disillusioned with the colonel, but he was furious at himself. Only days ago, well after Captain Oates had delivered Hewlett's phony medical evaluation that cleared him to jump, he'd all but made up his mind that he wanted no future in the military. What had changed? Sure, he wanted to jump again, but like Wilson said, at what price? He was no longer fit for combat, either physically or mentally. This was the secret understanding he'd come to, a hard but certain truth he had been reluctant to accept.

If only he had had the courage of this conviction, been willing to admit to this bitter but valid conclusion, the phony medical evaluation would have meant nothing. The difficult scene he had just played out with Colonel Eldon Hewlett might have been avoided.

Broder felt as if his life was unraveling. With no future in Airborne, where would he turn? What else could he do?

From the instant Colletta walked into the medical center and softly whispered his name, he had been powerless to escape his most difficult and painful realities. His past was like a tuft of grass growing through asphalt pavement in a parking lot, deep-rooted and persistent, not to be kept down.

Broder had never been particularly religious, but he had a strong moral sense that verged on superstition: There always is a price to pay, in one form or another, if you do wrong. This was his mother's teaching and it was what he believed. You have a choice between right and wrong, Allou Broder claimed, and your conscience knows which is which. Mack Brown had told him once that only those who believe in God are afraid to commit sins in secret, when no one will ever know. Maybe so. But stealing money from tourists on sunny summer beaches, running drugs for Jaybo on dark, forbidding nights — these acts were not done in secret. These acts had brought pain to others, and these acts gnawed at his conscience.

He had done these things for Donnie Shand in the beginning, and then for Colletta. Donnie, Ray-Gene, Colletta — how different the world had looked then, in their company, when one member of the team could always entice another, when collectively they could explain and defend any act as essential to the well-being and survival of their little band. Wouldn't a merciful God forgive such acts of selflessness?

Broder wasn't too sure about God but he never would forget what he'd learned from his mother. He had done too many wrongs, and now he surely was being punished.

§

THE PATROLMAN was polite but blunt. There were no preliminary courtesies. He had followed the red Buick for the last ten or fifteen miles and witnessed enough incidents of erratic and unsteady driving to raise concern. He had watched Jimmie drift across the center line of the highway more than once, come dangerously close to the edge of the pavement another time and in general drive too fast on that undersized, temporary tire. This latter act alone constituted recklessness.

The officer studied Jimmie's driver's license closely, then said firmly, but without antagonism, "Better step out of the car."

Jimmie opened the door and pulled himself out, trying to rush without looking nervous, terrified at the prospect of being caught with Jaybo's drugs. He did not believe he had driven erratically and he had been extremely cautious about speed limits. No matter. He would be polite, cooperative, promise to be more careful. Anything, so long as he did not give the officer reason to search the car.

"Have you been drinking?" the officer asked.

"No, sir. I don't drink."

"Are you doing drugs?" A routine, straightforward question. The officer was not friendly, but—so far, at least—not openly hostile.

"No, sir. I don't do drugs, either."

"You go to school?"

"Yes, sir. I'll be graduating high school pretty soon."

"You got a job?"

"Yes, sir. I'm going to be a partner with Mack Brown, in his car business."

"Really?" For the first time, the policeman's demeanor appeared to soften. "How did you come to get hooked up with old Mack?"

"I've been working for Mack a long time," Jimmie replied. "He set up a plan to expand his business when I finish school and me and him are going to be partners, more or less."

"I bought my first car from Mack Brown, way back," the officer said, and smiled. "And Mack helps us out sometimes when we're tracking stolen vehicles. You think Mack would vouch for you?"

"Yes, sir. I know he would."

The questions became less formal. The officer asked who

was in the car with Jimmie and where they had been. He beamed a flashlight inside the Buick to view Ray-Gene and Donnie Shand, who apparently passed his inspection without further questions. He advised Jimmie to get to a tire shop soon as possible and not risk driving too far on the undersized spare; it was intended only for emergency use. He hoped the original tire could be repaired because a new one would be pretty expensive.

Jimmie's outright fright had subsided somewhat, but he still was terribly apprehensive. He tried to hide his shaking hands.

"Well, I really hate to spoil your night any more than I already have," the policeman said, "but I called it in before I made the stop and the rules say I have to write you a ticket for careless driving. My sergeant checks up on these things, so I don't really have any choice."

"Yes, sir, I understand," Jimmie told him.

"I believe I can save y'all a court appearance, though. I can take you before a local judge tonight, and I believe he may waive the ticket and let you get on your way. He'll talk stern, but he's pretty easy-going, deep down. He lives right down the road a piece. We can get this taken care of right now."

He directed Jimmie to follow the police car, unmarked, the portable flashing light that had been displayed inside the windshield now stuffed under the driver's seat. They would be at the judge's house in no more than ten minutes. And, yes, he'd radio ahead so the judge would be ready for them.

Ray-Gene and Donnie, who could hear none of this from inside the car, were frantic to know what was going on. They peppered Jimmie with questions, both speaking at once.

"Wait a minute," Jimmie demanded. "I'll explain it all, but you have to give me a chance."

He quickly told them the situation, emphasizing the fact that the policeman had not suggested anything more serious than careless driving. "I think it was just that little spare tire that got his attention," he said. "But he's going to get my ticket fixed by the judge and we can be on our way."

"And there's no way they're going to say they need to do a search?" Donnie asked.

"I don't see how they could, now. The man didn't say anything about looking in the trunk or anything like that. It's just a driving ticket, DJ."

Donnie Shand showed his relief, but was still cautious. "Just in case something else did happen," he said, "remember what I told y'all before. You didn't know what was in that box. If anybody takes a fall on this it's going to be me, okay? We were going to look for sweetgrass baskets and that's all you know."

"Then how come we didn't get any baskets?" Ray-Gene asked.

"I should have thought of that, and bought one. Just say they were too expensive, or you didn't find one you liked or something. Damn, I should have thought of that."

"We didn't expect to need one," Jimmie said flatly. "We didn't expect to get caught. There wasn't any reason to get one."

A series of winding streets through an affluent residential area eventually brought them to a large and impressive red-brick house, set far back from the street among tall pine trees, dogwood, azaleas, and crape myrtle. Jimmie stopped in the driveway behind the police car, some distance from the house. The officer motioned the three forward with a wave of his hand.

The man who opened the door was middle-aged, short and heavy but distinguished in appearance, with rather long gray hair and thick gray moustache. His dress was casual. He said nothing, simply turned and walked down a hallway and into a wood-paneled room that held a sofa and chairs upholstered in red leather and a large walnut desk, and had built-in, floor-to-ceiling bookcases along two walls.

The man took a chair behind the desk, still not speaking,

and waited for the patrolman to say something.

"Judge, I stopped these boys for careless driving, coming back from a trip down to the Mt. Pleasant area looking for sweetgrass baskets," the officer reported. Then, turning back to Jimmie, Ray-Gene, and Donnie, "This is Judge Jim Pillory. You're lucky. He's the fairest judge in Horry County."

"Don't let my name scare you," the judge said pleasantly. "We haven't pilloried anybody in these parts for a century, far as I know." When the laugh he apparently had hoped for didn't materialize, he proceeded more seriously, "Okay, then, let's see what we've got here. What are your names?"

"Donnie Shand, sir."

"Ray-Gene Kepley, sir."

"Jimmie Broder, sir."

Judge Pillory surveyed them sternly. "Which one of you was driving?"

Jimmie stepped forward: "I was, sir."

"Is what Officer Demotte tells me true, young man?"

"Yes, sir. I wasn't bein' as careful as I should have been. I'm normally a good driver, but I guess I got a little careless, and I forgot about that little temporary spare tire."

"And you're Broder? What's your daddy's name?"

"Popeye Broder, sir."

"I don't know your daddy, son. Do you think he would be embarrassed to know you were standing here in front of a judge right now?"

"Yes, sir, he would be."

"How about you other boys? Did you notice his driving was getting careless? How come y'all didn't caution him on it?"

Donnie Shand took a short step forward. "Sir," he said, "I think it is mostly my fault. I was talking too much, and I probably got Jimmie distracted."

Ray-Gene stepped up beside Donnie. "I was talking, too," he told the judge firmly. "He's a real careful driver. It probably wasn't his fault as much as it was mine."

The judge turned to Officer Demotte. "It looks like we've got some young men here who have the courage to take responsibility for their actions," he said. "Do you think that ought to influence my decision some?"

"That's for you to decide, judge," the officer said. "But they didn't give me any trouble, if that helps."

"Yessir, that does help some."

"And young Broder here is about to go into partnership with Mack Brown, which I think must say something about him. He's been working with Mack a while, now."

"I believe we might be able to straighten these boys out and make productive citizens out of them," the judge said. "Do you go along with that, Officer Demotte?"

"Whatever you say, judge."

Judge Jim Pillory suddenly pushed his chair back from the desk — an action that was almost violent — and stood, pulling himself up to the best height he could manage. He slapped the desk hard with the flat of his hand and glared at the three young men standing before him.

"Goddammit, we are through playing games here," he roared. "What would you have said if Officer Demotte had asked if he could search your automobile? What if we decided to search it right now? Do you young jackasses think you're dealing with nincompoops here? Do you really think Officer Demotte would drag your sorry butts before a judge on a routine traffic ticket? Do you? Sweetgrass baskets, my ass!"

The judge's sudden outburst took the boys by complete surprise. Jimmie felt all the blood drain from his face. He quickly put his hands behind his back, out of the judge's view, afraid they might begin to tremble again. Ray-Gene's shoulders slumped and his chin dropped, so that he stared at the floor. Only Donnie Shand was without visible signs of being shaken by the startling turn in Judge Jim Pillory's attitude.

"I could get the three you on my docket and have you in

court before the end of next week,"the judge said hotly. "We could find enough evidence in your car to get a conviction in ten minutes. Do you think we don't have enough professional drug runners around here? Or maybe you think we have so many that amateurs like you can get away with it? Do you take us for complete fools? Speak to me!"

"No, sir," Donnie Shand said stoutly.

"That's good, son, because I've still a good mind to send the three of you to prison for twenty years. If any one of you had been in trouble before, I swear I'd do it. We got all the cocaine and marijuana and heroine in the world coming up from Florida and all the illegal prescription drugs coming down from New Jersey and Pennsylvania and New York, like Interstate 95 over yonder was a big pipeline. It used to pass us by, until some local hoodlums got involved. And the last thing we need is a bunch of empty-headed juveniles like y'all deciding to get into the drug trade."

The judge paused, and stood glaring at the three boys as if to let them agonize over what he might say next and give his message full impact.

"I don't want to see any more people ruined in this," he went on at last, "and that's the only reason you're walking out of here instead of going straight to jail. But I'll tell you this, and y'all damned well better remember it: We know who you are, and where you're at right now is like crappin' in an outhouse. You may be relieved, but there's still stink. Now get them to hell out of here, Demotte, before I change my mind."

Officer Demotte herded his stunned charges from the judge's house and led them briskly back to the cars out front. They waited obediently for him to tell them what came next.

"You may be the luckiest boys in South Carolina right now," Demotte said. "You're lucky I didn't look for a reason to search your vehicle and you're lucky Judge Pillory knows Mack Brown has been a good friend to area law enforcement. But you had better hear this well, all three of you: We know what's going on. Somebody's going down real soon. Get out of it now, or the next time neither I nor the good judge in there will bail you out. In fact, if I catch you again I'll make sure you're hung out to dry. Do you understand what I'm saying?"

"Yes, sir," they mumbled in unison.

"One other thing. There's a lot of surveillance going on. If I were you, and I happened to be hauling something I didn't have the good sense to dispose of on the way over here, I'd take a back way home and dump it all somewhere in the Waccamaw River."

• *HIGH SCHOOL* graduation was a big event. Popeye and Allou Broder went early so they could get seats close to the front of the school auditorium and have a good view as Jimmie crossed the stage to receive his diploma. Ray-Gene entered with Grandma Freeman and Ravonelle. Most of the parents would be there, and Mack Brown slipped quietly into a back row corner, slightly embarrassed to be seen but proud as any father. The mood was light and happy, celebratory, charged with optimism.

Colletta was nowhere to be found.

"Did you see her come in?" Jimmie whispered.

Ray-Gene said no, he hadn't seen her.

The stress of their surreal appearance before Judge Pillory had made for a difficult week for Jimmie and Ray-Gene. They also worried about Donnie Shand. Given the advice they'd received from Officer Demotte, they had dumped the banker's box, which meant that Donnie had to report to Jaybo empty-handed. Donnie had outlined a careful story. First, he would tell Jaybo that, in the end, he alone had made the courier run; Jimmie and Ray-Gene had backed out at the last minute and knew nothing of what went on. And second, he went to the right place at the appointed time but the contact didn't show. He never received Jaybo's merchandise.

"But he'll know better, DJ," Ray-Gene had protested. "If

he hasn't paid those people, they'll come looking for their money. And if he paid them and complains, they'll tell him you did get his stuff. These are all real bad people, DJ. You can't get away with it."

"But it will take time for Jaybo to catch on," Donnie had argued. "Soon as I've talked to him, I'll take off for Florida or somewhere where he can't find me. Maybe Miami. There's a lot of rich people in Miami and they need somebody to pick up their trash and stuff like that. I'll get by. Jaybo's going to get caught sooner or later and go to jail. Then I can come home."

Those were the last words they had heard from Donnie Shand.

Colletta had run out of medicine early in the week. The days since had been marked by a series of pitched battles, highs and lows, anger and compassion, Colletta at her best and Colletta at her worst. She insisted that Donnie had her pills and was holding out on her. At least once every day she proclaimed herself well and said she didn't need Jaybo's medicine anyway. Hunter told Jimmie that Colletta was too hard to live with; he wished he could divorce his sister and his daddy, both, and live with his mother on the beach. Mr. Saylor had become alarmed over Colletta's sickliness, again, and stayed closer to the house, though he hadn't been fully sober in more than three weeks.

Jimmie heard little of the rambling, pretentious speeches. His mind was awash in worries about all these other things. Where was Donnie Shand? How would they ever know if they truly were safe from Judge Pillory? And most of all, how could Colletta have missed graduation?

He stood when others stood, sat when they sat. There was a song and a final word of inspiration and then when everyone else lined up and walked across the stage to be graduated, he lined up and walked with them in his allotted slot. Someone handed him something, someone else shook his hand. Everyone smiled. And so he finished school.

He should be excited. Maybe Donnie Shand's scheme would work, and that business with Judge Pillory couldn't hang over them forever. He had a bright future as Mack Brown's partner and being married to Colletta, if she could only get herself straight. Yet the only point at which he felt any gratification came as he paraded toward the back of the auditorium in the recessional and, looking to the side, into a sea of faces, saw the happy smile his mother wore and the pride in Popeye Broder's eyes.

The scramble outside the auditorium after the ceremony was frenzied. Jubilant mothers and fathers looked for sons and daughters, new graduates looked for their parents and sought out friends for last-minute goodbyes.

Jimmie found Ray-Gene and said, urgently, "I've got to go see what happened to Colletta. Want to come?"

Ray-Gene declined. He thought he ought to walk home with Ravonelle and Grandma Freeman. But let him know if something was wrong. He'd worried about Colletta, too. She must be sick, because she had been looking forward to graduation for weeks and only two days ago she'd complained that her mother would not be able to get off work to be there and see her walk across the stage and get her diploma. Ray-Gene didn't think she'd miss the event herself unless she felt real bad.

"Nobody probably expected her old drunk father to be here," Jimmie said, "but I know that she planned to come and bring Hunter."

Jimmie pushed through the crowd and found his mother and father and told them he needed to go check on Colletta. They said they understood, but he could tell they were disappointed.

"I hope she's all right," his mother said.

She said more, but her words trailed off as Jimmie turned and ran down the street, toward the Saylor house. Ray-Gene was right. Colletta would not miss graduation, even if she had to crawl to the auditorium on hands and knees. Even with her problems, there had been only a few days when she was physically ill to that extent and when Jimmie last saw her, only hours earlier, she'd seemed to be feeling better than usual.

Hunter met him at the door. There was no smile this time, no friendly greeting. Instead, Hunter took him by the arm, without speaking, and steered him to Colletta's room. Mr. Saylor followed, unnoticed, and stood beside the door, back against the wall. His face was reddened by drink and his eyes teared and bleary, and his pain was apparent.

Colletta lay face-down across her bed, crying hard, her small body shaking. She turned her face to him when Jimmie got close and he was horrified by what he saw. Her face was a mass of bruises, one eye swollen almost shut. Her nose had been bleeding. There were scratches on her neck.

"My god, Colletta," Jimmie cried, "what happened to you?"

She barely managed, between sobs: "Jaybo."

"What did Jaybo do, Colletta? You've got to tell me!"

Colletta clung to him and sobbed violently.

"Please, Colletta," he urged, "tell me what happened."

"I went to see Jaybo . . . to see if I could get my medicine," she told him, still sobbing. "He was mad, Jimmie . . . He started hitting me and wouldn't stop. . . . And then . . . he forced me, Jimmie . . . Jaybo . . . Jaybo raped me."

Jacob Saylor slipped from the room as quietly as he had entered. He went to his room and took his old pistol and a handful of shells from their hiding place among the socks and underwear in a dresser drawer. He left the house by way of the back door, but no one heard him go.

ॐ21ॐ

BRODER STILL was a stranger in headquarters detachment. He'd become superficially acquainted with Jorge Ortiz, but was close to no one, which was exactly the way he wanted it; he was only passing through. He recognized that the unit was seriously lacking in esprit de corps, not surprising given that it was commanded by Captain Homer Oates, but gossip went through detachment ranks as rapidly as it might have in any of his earlier outfits. Today, the gossip was about the good captain himself, who had left HQ in the company of two sinister-looking fellows judged by Corporal Grissom to be gamblers, mobsters, or government agents.

"Grissom is certain that the captain left under duress," Ortiz confided. "He said one man walked on each side of Oates, elbow to elbow, like he was all but handcuffed. What do you make of it, Broder — *bueno o malo?*"

"Who knows? Maybe the good captain is involved in organized crime or something."

"Yeah, right. Biggest crime I know of is keeping that man in the good ole U.S. of A. Army, much less giving him any kind of command."

"Oates must have his supporters somewhere along the line," Broder said, "though he does strike me as pretty old to still be a captain. Know anything about his background?"

"Some. He was in the reserves in South Carolina, a cop or something, and got called to active duty. In the Gulf War, maybe. Anyway, he worked some kind of deal to stay active."

257

"How do you know all this shit, Ortiz?"

"I've seen inside his jacket."

"You saw his file? How did that happen?"

"I've got a friend in the post personnel office. What you glory-hogging jumpers don't realize, Broder, is that while you are out there playing soldier the Army is being run by administrative geniuses like me and my amigo in personnel. Want to know something, ask us."

"So it would have been easy for Oates to see my file, I mean before I was transferred into his unit?"

"Sure. Any time he wanted."

"And he could have found out where I was from, stuff like that?"

"Routine, Broder. Why?"

"Nothing. Maybe explains something I had been wondering about, is all. So what's going on with you? Your getting-out date, I mean."

"Right around the corner," Ortiz said.

"And you'll be heading back to, where, San Juan?"

"Mayagüez."

"And back to Elizabeth, right?"

"Fantastic, Broder. How'd you remember her name?"

"It's a pretty name. You're a lucky guy, Ortiz."

Their conversation was interrupted by the ringing of the detachment phone. Ortiz had mentioned earlier that there were few incoming calls, and most of these were personal calls for Captain Oates. He knew they were personal because when a call related to detachment business it always came back to him for action. And if the captain's door was open he always got up and shut it before he talked.

This time, though, the call was for Broder. It was Agent Schuler.

"We need to get together with you, Sergeant Broder," Schuler told him. "Can you meet Agent Hines and me later today? Say, around two o'clock?"

"Where?" Broder asked.

"We can't come there, for obvious reasons. Can you get off the post?"

"Yes. Anywhere you need me."

"There's a convenience store north on I-95, at Exit . . ."

Broder knew the location. He'd been there before. It was the place where he'd picked up Oates's contraband from the old man in the motor home.

"I'll be there at two," he promised, and put the phone down.

Ortiz looked on with poorly concealed curiosity, but said nothing.

"We were talking about your Elizabeth," Broder reminded him. "Tell me about her. I think I know exactly what she looks like — tall, willowy, blonde, blue-eyed, very beautiful, right?"

"I told you, she's Jamaican. She's brown-skinned."

"A blonde and blue-eyed brown woman? Sounds rare, Ortiz. I'm beginning to think you just made up this beautiful Elizabeth, created her only in your own simple mind."

Ortiz grinned. "Damn it, Broder," he said, "you're going to piss me off one of these days and I'm going to wake up in the stockade and realize you were only jerking me around, but it will be way too late because I've already done something really bad."

"I don't know what you're talking about. Unfortunately, I don't have time to stop and figure it out because they need me at the Pentagon. Somebody's got to tell them how to get us out of this stupid war."

Broder left HQ with Jorge Ortiz's laughter in his ears, on his way to meet agents Schuler and Hines. What he wanted very much to hear from them was not laughter, but a firm declaration that his involvement in Captain Homer Oates's mess was finished. And why would they choose that place to meet him? If he'd been followed, as Colonel Hewlett said, the agents surely must know about the clandestine meeting at which he picked up merchandise for Captain Oates. Of course they did. And it wouldn't matter, because the Oates affair was over and done with. Homer Oates was on his way to prison.

Broder considered how close he'd come to opening the laundry bag that night and checking its contents. Would it have mattered? Would the agents have swarmed in on him and made an arrest? They wanted to keep him in the dark, all along, and if he'd come to know too much he may very well have put himself in jeopardy. Would Colonel Hewlett have come to his rescue, or would he have ended up facing serious charges and been left hung out to dry? He wondered, too, if the bag contained the ancient Mexican-Aztec dagger he'd delivered to Wilmington.

Simply considering what might have been made Broder angry. He would trust no one. Not Colonel Hewlett, and not the agents he was on his way to meet.

SCHULER AND HINES had arrived at the Interstate oasis ahead of him. Broder saw their unmarked but obvious black Ford parked near the white picket fence, in very nearly the same spot where the motor home had been when he picked up Oates's goods. He went inside the convenience store and spotted them immediately, strolling an aisle like two casual travelers shopping for souvenirs. They were ludicrously conspicuous, neatly groomed and packaged in their standard dark-blue suits. To make the picture complete, Hines still wore his dark glasses.

Broder could not be sure if they would recognize him, and didn't wait to find out. He walked straight to them and extended his greetings: "Good afternoon, secret agent men. Nice to see you again."

Agent Hines laughed. "Ah, yes," he said, "It's our friend, Sergeant Broder. Isn't this a nice surprise."

Now Broder was on the defensive, unsure whether Hines was joking or, somehow, confused. Agent Schuler came to his rescue, extending a hand to him in greeting and offering a friendly smile. "It's good to see you again, sergeant," he said. "Thanks for coming."

"Sure. But this would not have been my first choice of places to meet."

"Understood," Schuler said. "You'll understand why we asked you to come here, in good time."

Agent Hines had gone to the front of the store, where he leaned on the checkout counter and waved for Broder and the other agent to join him. The woman behind the counter was familiar. Broder recognized her as the same person who had been there the night he made the pick-up for Captain Oates.

"Let's go join Agent Hines, shall we?" Schuler said, stepping aside and extending an arm in invitation for Broder to go first. Schuler followed close behind as Broder went to the front of the store.

"Is this the man we talked about earlier?" Hines asked the woman.

"Yes, sir. That's him," the woman said.

"You're certain?"

"I'm certain. He stopped his car at a gas pump but didn't pump any gas. That's peculiar, and that's why I remember it."

"Did the two of you have a conversation?" Agent Schuler asked her.

"I don't know that you'd call it a conversation. I tried to be friendly, but he didn't seem to want to talk. I remember he said he didn't need gas because he didn't have far to go."

"Are you positive this is the same man?" Hines asked.

"Yes, sir. Like I said, I'm certain it's him."

Agent Hines thanked the woman for her cooperation and steered Broder toward the door. As they walked past, the woman looked at Broder with an expression of contempt, like he had just been identified as Jack the Ripper. Schuler guided him to the agents' car, opened a rear door and directed him to sit inside.

"What the hell is going on here?" Broder demanded.

"Just be cool, sergeant," Schuler urged. "We just wanted you to be clear as to what we could do if we felt a need. As you well know, we've got a mountain of evidence linking you to the piece you delivered to Wilmington. You also might be interested to learn that the old man you picked that item up from, the hospitable fellow in the motor home, was arrested right after you left here. He could identify you, but he's a criminal. Now we have that nice woman behind the counter, who can place you here that night if we needed her testimony."

Broder felt icy shivers run up his spine. He'd been set up. He was in deep trouble, with nothing in his defense except his own word. And it would be his word against that of the colonel and the two federal agents. He was screwed.

"Now, before you get too panicked over this, sergeant," Agent Hines said, "you need to understand that we have no intent to charge you with anything. It's just that we play the game by our own rules, and our rules are designed to give us the biggest edge we can get."

"Oh, I understand," Broder said angrily. "You've got me in a spot where I have no choice except to jump through whatever hoops you guys set up. If I don't play it your way, you'll have me behind bars before sundown, right?"

"You seem to have it figured out pretty well," Hines told him. "Like I said, it's our rules."

"I give up." Broder spoke like a man broken, a man who saw his last ray of hope fading quickly. "Just tell me what you want me to do now."

"Nothing, Sergeant Broder," Schuler said. "The truth is, we want you to do absolutely nothing. It's just that we like to operate with a high degree of control, and to the extent we can, in secret. That means we can't afford to have guys like you running around telling stories about us. That's not too difficult to understand, is it?"

"Whatever you say."

"What we say, Broder, is keep your mouth shut. Nobody hears any of this from you, ever," Hines said menacingly. "Never forget what we can do to you if we hear that you've been telling tales about us. Are we pretty clear here?"

"We're clear. Your game, your rules. Lopsided score in your favor."

The agents dismissed him and stood and watched as he left the parking area. As he drove south toward Fayetteville, Broder seethed with anger and frustration. What kind of men operated this way? He was furious with Hines and Schuler, furious with Colonel Hewlett, furious with himself for blindly falling into their trap. He was bound to silence when he wanted very much to shout to the whole world how these men behaved.

♧

☙ WHOEVER WAS pounding on the Saylors' front door was persistent. Hunter, scrunched forlornly in a corner of the sofa hoping that Jimmie would come and tell him Colletta was all right, was afraid to answer. When he finally comprehended that the visitor would not go away, he unlatched the door and timidly squinted out through the slightest crack to see who was creating such a stir. It was Ravonelle.

"Get Jimmie Broder to come with me quick," Ravonelle pleaded, "something awful's happened. Hurry, Hunter!"

Hunter rushed to Colletta's room and tugged at Jimmie's arm. "It's Ray-Gene's sister," he said, visibly shaken, "and she's all scared about something. She wants you to come."

Jimmie sat hunched on the edge of Colletta's bed. "Tell her I can't come," he directed Hunter. "Tell her it will have to wait. Colletta needs me here."

Hunter returned to deliver this message, but Ravonelle, when she saw that he was alone, pushed him aside and ran to Colletta's room. "You've got to help us," she screamed at Jimmie. "He's hurt bad. For god's sake, come help."

Colletta raised her head and stared coldly at Ravonelle, who seemed oblivious to her presence in the room. "Go on,

Jimmie, and do whatever it is she wants," she said quietly.

"I won't leave you," he answered, "not like this."

"Go. I don't want you here. There's nothing you can do."

Ravonelle had turned to leave, but stopped at the door and looked back. "Please, Jimmie," she begged. "You've got to help us. You've got to come now or it will be too late."

Reluctantly, as much stung by Colletta's rejection as he was alarmed by Ravonelle's desperation, Jimmie followed Ravonelle outside. She urged him to drive her back to Grandma Freeman's house and please, please hurry. "Mr. Saylor shot him, Jimmie," she cried. "He's hurt really bad."

No emergency vehicles were in sight when they reached the scene of Ravonelle's terror, only Jaybo's ancient Oldsmobile parked at the curb a few yards down the block. The beam of the Buick's headlights fell on a dark form sprawled motionless on the sidewalk. Jacob Saylor sat placidly on the curb nearby.

Ravonelle was out of the car before it came to a complete stop, and fell to her knees beside the prone figure. Jimmie saw the victim lying on the dirty gray concrete, gasping for breath, a trickle of blood leaking from one corner of his mouth. Only his neck and the lower part of his face were visible through the open car door, and a slender hand that clutched at his throat. In the yellow glow of the car's interior lights, Ray-Gene looked like a stage actor in the radiance of tempered footlights, playing the role of a dying hero.

When he was out of the car and closer, Jimmie could see the extent of the bleeding. Blood had pooled beneath Ray-Gene's back, flattened against the sidewalk, and begun to run in a little rivulet to the curb, and already had commenced a new and widening pool in the filthy gutter. They struggled to lift Ray-Gene into the car, trying to lower him onto the seat gently. Jimmie ran to the driver's side and flung himself behind the wheel while Ravonelle crawled into the back seat. "Hold on, Ray-Gene," Jimmie pleaded. "We'll get you help as fast as we can."

"I'm sorry, Jimmie," Ray-Gene whispered hoarsely. "Tell DJ . . . tell him and Colletta . . . tell them I'm sorry to break up the team."

"You're not going to break up the team, Ray-Gene. I'm not going to let you. You're going to be okay. We'll have you in the emergency room in no time and they'll fix you up. Just hang in there, Ray-Gene, like DJ would want you to."

During the long few minutes it took to race to the hospital, Jimmie prayed, and implored God to spare this good and innocent human being, this life-long friend who was the most sincere and trustworthy person he ever had known. Ravonelle reached over the back of the seat and cradled Ray-Gene's head in her arms, weeping, begging her brother to stay alive just a little longer.

"We love you, Ray-Gene," she sobbed. "You've got to get all right for Grandma Freeman. You know you've always been her favorite. She'd just die if anything happened to you."

Then they were at the emergency room. A madding flurry of action. Doctors. Nurses. Technicians. All the wonders of medicine were here, but the two who loved Ray-Gene best were afraid in their hearts that these would not be enough.

"Who did this to him?" someone demanded to know.

"I don't know," Jimmie said numbly. His response was mechanical. He had no thoughts of his own. His pain was too deep, his mind paralyzed by the shock of watching helplessly as Ray-Gene gasped for life.

They waited in a cramped anteroom, sitting motionless, hand-in-hand, hoping desperately for word that things were not as bad as they looked. Time was good, wasn't it? The doctors would stop Ray-Gene's bleeding, they'd find that his wound wasn't nearly as serious as they had feared, they'd have him stabilized. He would be in surgery soon, or maybe there was no need for surgery. Bullet wounds always were scary; maybe Ray-Gene's was only superficial. They said all these things, but they did not believe.

"I was inside when Mr. Saylor came," Ravonelle said quietly. "We had just got home from graduation, and Ray-Gene went back to the store for Grandma Freeman. I think he was just coming home when Mr. Saylor met him. I heard the shooting, and when I got outside Ray-Gene was already down. He told me to get you, Jimmie, and that's what I did."

"I just can't figure out why Mr. Saylor would do it," Jimmie told her. "He had an old grudge of some kind, but nobody ever thought he'd do something like that."

"Jaybo's to blame, Jimmie, as much as if he had pulled the trigger himself."

"I don't know what you mean."

"Don't you understand?" Ravonelle asked, apparently surprised. "Mr. Saylor didn't intend to shoot Ray-Gene. He thought it was Jaybo. It was because of the terrible thing Jaybo did to Colletta."

"I didn't think anyone knew about that except me."

"Mr. Saylor had to know, and I knew. I was there, Jimmie." Tears welled up again in Ravonelle's eyes, and her lip trembled. "I heard something going on, and I saw what Jaybo was doing to Colletta. I couldn't stop him. I tried, God help me I tried, but when Jaybo gets mad, nobody can stop him. I couldn't be more sorry, Jimmie, and more ashamed that Jaybo's family."

"It's not your fault, Ravonelle," Jimmie whispered. "You would have stopped it if you could. You didn't choose Jaybo to be your uncle."

An emergency room doctor eased into the anteroom, his face telling them the dreadful words even before he spoke. "I'm very sorry," he said, "but the bullet just did too much damage and he'd lost too much blood. We did all we could." Ray-Gene was dead.

  THE AUTHORITIES took less than a week to close their file on the Kepley homicide. They simply wrote it off as "drug related." Never mind that Jacob Saylor, who sat quietly after the shooting and waited for the law, was well known for his drunken binges but never had been suspected of using drugs. They figured that on this night he needed something more than his bottle. And never mind that it was Jaybo, and not Ray-Gene, that they had marked as a dealer. It was all in the family.

Police had always expected Jaybo to be eliminated one day, by either a competitor or a disgruntled customer. It seemed to them a logical jump that if young Kepley lived in the same household he no doubt was involved in drugs, as well. There was no evidence that Mr. Saylor was either a customer or a competitor, but he readily confessed to the shooting and that was all they needed. And they would be moving in on Jaybo soon enough.

Jacob Saylor would never talk. He would go to his grave without ever telling what Jaybo had done to his daughter. Investigators had not talked to Colletta, interviewed her mother only superficially, and of course had no reason to question Jimmie. He had told no one what happened to Colletta, nor had Ravonelle.

Mack Brown told Jimmie to take as much time as he needed away from the car lot. Mack didn't realize how close Jimmie had been to Ray-Gene, how great and difficult his loss. He understood that Jimmie and Colletta were in love and planned to be married soon, a situation Mack wholeheartedly approved of, and he understood that Colletta was ill and now her daddy was in all this trouble and that was reason enough to give Jimmie time off. "We've got the rest of our lives to sell cars, Jimbo," Mack said. "A few days off right now won't make much difference."

Jimmie missed Donnie Shand. Donnie would understand what he was going through and be a pillar of strength. The old team leader would mourn the loss of Ray-Gene too, of course, and Jimmie wished he could send word of it, but he had yet to hear from Donnie and had no idea where he was. Donnie would agonize over what happened to Colletta. He would counsel Jimmie on how to respond in this time of her great need.

But there was no Donnie Shand to lean on. Jimmie was unsure of himself. He felt helpless and hopeless.

The more he tried to reach Colletta, the more she pushed him away. Day after day he tried to see her, but day after day she refused to be seen. She'd send Hunter to the door to tell him she was away, or sick and asleep and couldn't be disturbed. He dared not talk about this with anyone, because Colletta was steadfastly determined that no one know of the unspeakable occurrence that awful afternoon at Grandma Freeman's house and he was afraid he might inadvertently betray her secret.

If only Mr. Saylor had shot Jaybo as he intended, or better yet that Jaybo had died a long time ago, before he got DJ started pushing drugs and before Colletta got hooked on his pills, and before he did this terrible thing. Jimmie and Ray-Gene and Colletta and Donnie Shand had made their own beds to an extent, and Jimmie couldn't escape a strong sense of guilt, but without Jaybo's evil acts their world would not have been turned upside down and left spinning out of control the way it was now. He felt an indescribable emptiness without Ray-Gene, and he was hurt and confused over Colletta's growing rejection.

He agonized for Colletta most of all. What pain she must be going through, given her ghastly experience, and now she had lost her daddy, too. Mr. Saylor wasn't much of a father, maybe, but Jimmie knew that Colletta loved him and his conviction for Ray-Gene's murder would be heart-breaking for her and Hunter and their mother.

The old team. How they'd all pitched in and worked to fix things when one of them was in trouble! But there was no team now, and Jimmie felt that he was facing an uncertain and hostile universe, alone.

Mack Brown had taken the Buick, with its blood-stained front seat, and said he'd ship it off to a wholesaler who'd have the seat replaced and get Jimmie something better. A Cadillac this time. That was a promise.

But there were too many other reminders, all the places he had been with Ray-Gene, all the things they had done together. He couldn't step out of his own front door without looking down the street at Grandma Freeman's house and remembering. Ray-Gene should be coming to meet him, or waiting for him on the sidewalk, sitting on the curb, his face lit by that magical smile. And they'd meet Colletta and DJ and the whole planet was theirs for another day.

And Colletta. So many times she'd needed him, and he had done everything in his might to be there for her. Why couldn't he help her now? He needed her, too, as a constant in his life even though their familiar world was gone and never would be again. How could he manage without her?

Too many memories. Too much pain. An impulsive urge to flee. The Army recruiting station, with its slogans and opportunities, the future it offered away from Conway, an escape from the bitter past. He signed his name and there was no turning back.

Popeye Broder took the news stoically. Jimmie's mother saw it for the best; the Army would let him see more of the world than South Carolina, she said, and maybe teach him skills he could use the rest of his life. She only wished he had a little more time before he had to report.

Mack Brown was astonished. He simply never would comprehend how Jimmie could throw away the opportunity of a lifetime. Mack came around in the end, though, and wished him all the best. He said he always had regretted not serving, himself. And Jimmie would make a fine soldier, wearing the proud uniform of Uncle Sam while some of the other local boys would most likely end up in prisoner's britches on the chain gang, picking up roadside trash. And a man who had served his country would be an outstanding business partner a few years down the road.

Colletta would be the most difficult. How could he leave

269

her, and would she even let him see her to say goodbye?

She did, and stood impassively as he delivered his news.

"I don't care," she announced bitterly. "I'm going to Wilmington and live with my aunt. We would never be together anyway."

"I promise to write to you every day, Colletta," he told her. "And when I get time off I can come see you. We can still get married, it will just have to wait a little longer."

"I won't marry you, Jimmie," she said coldly. "We were just children playing games. Don't bother to come looking for me. I probably won't live in Wilmington very long. I'm going to go to New York or someplace, where nobody will know me. You'll never see me again."

She closed the door in his face.

Jimmie turned and walked away from the Saylor house heart-broken and confused. He had lost Ray-Gene and now Colletta was slipping away. He did not look back. Hunter stood at the window and watched till Jimmy rounded the corner at the end of the block.

❧22❧

HE CORPORAL was insistent: "They want you right now, up at division, Sergeant Broder. Colonel Hewlett sent me after you." *Must be something big if they sent a driver.* Broder had been worried since his last session with Hewlett, when he'd said too much and angered the colonel, and now he dreaded to have to go back and face the music. Not that he cared much what happened anymore, with his future in the Army already washed out, but Hewlett had the rank and position to make his life miserable for the rest of the time he had to serve.

The driver had nothing to say on their ride to division HQ. Broder tried to make conversation but soon gave up. It was a trip of no more than ten minutes.

When they arrived at headquarters he was sent directly into Colonel Hewlett's office with the admonition that he was late. How could he be late when he hadn't known he was expected? That mystery was cleared up soon enough; the driver was supposed to have gone looking for him an hour earlier, but got sidetracked by a command to pick up a colonel's wife and chauffeur her to the residence of the commanding general.

Colonel Hewlett was amused by the mixup.

"It's not your fault, Broder," he said, and laughed. "We have too many field-grade officers around here who are afraid to put on their pants in the morning until their wives approve the color of their government-issued boxer shorts. Anyway, I'm glad you're here."

"A phone call would have done it, sir."

"I know. But I didn't want every man in your detachment to know I was looking for you. You and I left some unfinished business the other day and I wanted to clear it up."

"Sir, I apologize for my attitude. I didn't mean to be insubordinate. I had been under some stress, as you very well know."

"No apology necessary, sergeant. I was off base as much as you."

Superiors didn't apologize, and this was the last thing Broder would have expected from a lieutenant colonel. But Eldon Hewlett was a different breed, as he had known from the outset. He had good feelings toward the colonel again and regretted the flap over his phony clearance to jump.

"I have two quick things on my agenda this morning," the colonel went on, "and the first one is something you're not going to be happy about."

"Sir?"

"It's Captain Oates, sergeant. Sorry as I am to have to say it, people way over my head have offered the good captain a deal that will make him come out looking like a hero."

"That's hard to believe, colonel."

"I have a hard time with it, myself. But the captain is going to play ball with the feds and help them ferret out the top echelon of an organized ring that's been smuggling all kinds of illicit goods into this country through military channels, and using military personnel to distribute and sell them to the highest bidder. The pre-Columbian art you delivered was only one modest example. There's already a serious flow of ancient artifacts from Iraq. We're also talking about drugs and, worst of all, weapons. It appears to be a very large and complex operation."

"Then I guess it's a good thing somebody's on to it."

"Just one more thing about Captain Oates, and then the subject's closed. He gets a promotion and a new assignment, so if you happen to see him before he's gone he'll be wearing his new eagles as a full colonel."

"You're not serious?"

"Like I said, sergeant, that subject is now closed."

"I understand, sir."

"Now the other thing, sergeant." The colonel paused to emphasize a change of topic. "Your future. You're a good man. I hope we can keep you, even if you can't jump. I can get you a good assignment, if you're interested."

"I appreciate that, colonel. But I've decided to get out. That bad jump caused things to happen that have changed my outlook a lot. I don't mean just the Army, but my whole life."

"Have you got plans?"

"Not really, sir. There are some loose ends that need to be tied up, and then I'll just see what comes."

"I wish you the best, Sergeant Broder. You've got a few weeks left on duty, and we'll see that your leg is coming along as it ought to be before we let you go. You might be entitled to some limited disability pay, but it won't amount to much and god knows how long it will take to find out."

"That's not a problem, sir. I'll be able to make my own way. I appreciate your concern."

Their goodbyes were simple and formal. The two men had great respect for each other. Under different circumstances they could have been friends.

Broder declined the offer of a ride back to his unit by the driver who'd picked him up. It was a nice day. He wanted to walk. Fort Bragg had come to feel like home and he would not have a great deal of time left on the post. He already knew he was not going to miss it. Whatever his future held, wherever he went, he would remember his Airborne years as something of value and something to look back on with pride, but he was ready to move on.

He walked away from division headquarters thinking back to his first contact with Colonel Eldon Hewlett and the tough reputation that preceded the colonel. He wondered why Hewlett had put faith in him to help corner Captain Homer Oates. And the dismaying outcome of that effort. Captain Oates not only would escape punishment, but he also would get a big promotion for sleeping with the devil.

Broder, meanwhile, would have to contend with the threat by agents Schuler and Hines that his own involvement in that same illicit operation, minimal as it was, would hang over his head like the ancient sword of Damocles. Might he even yet be called to account because of misdeeds in the past? *You have a choice between right and wrong, Jimmie, and your conscience knows which is which.* But this time he'd done right. Life wasn't always fair.

The brightest star in his firmament during the days since his bad jump had been Rondell Wilson. He couldn't leave Fort Bragg without saying his heart-felt goodbyes to Wilson, and maybe go out for another of their infamous nights on the town. He went by the medical center and found Wilson in familiar surroundings.

"Walk down the hall with me, Broder," Wilson said. "I'll be on duty all day, but I get a break soon."

Broder waited in the same lounge where he and Colletta had talked during the one visit when he had felt that they were coming to an understanding. The space had seemed wonderfully comfortable then, compared to the tedium of his room, but now it felt oppressive.

Wilson joined him after a few minutes.

"I've come to grips with my future, to a point," Broder told him.

"And?"

"And I'm going to go civilian. This life isn't for me, Wilson. Not anymore."

"I envy you," Wilson said. "I've got have another fifteen months to go."

"And then what? You'll go home to Philadelphia, go to school? What?"

"All of the above. Yeah, I'll go back to Philly. And I'll get to school sooner or later. It's the rest of my life we're talking about, and it's still a ways off. But what about you? Going back to South Carolina?"

"I don't know. I'll go visit my folks for a little while, but after that I don't know. I can't see myself ever settling down in Conway. It's a good town but like somebody said, there are too many ghosts."

"Biggest ghost of all is Colletta, right? What about her?"

"I don't see any point in trying to talk to her again. She checked me out and decided it'd never work. But you know that."

"Broder, you are one stupid sonofabitch!" Wilson flashed anger that Broder had not seen before and it was unexpected. "If you ever cared for that woman, how can you give up that easy?"

"But she doesn't want to see me again," Broder said. "You read her letter. It was a kiss-off, once and for all."

"And she'd done it before, right? Before you marched off and joined the ranks?"

"Yes. Now that you mention it, she had."

"And you still haven't figured out why?"

"She was very upset after what had happened to her. I understand that."

"Jesus Christ, Broder. The woman had been raped! You cannot begin to know what she was going through. She needed you to stand by her for months and years, not give up after a few weeks. Now you've got a second chance. This time don't screw it up."

* BRODER FOUND a parking place across the street from the Mexicana, conscious that the high-visibility red Mustang was easy to spot. He needed to see and talk to Colletta face-to-face, not have her run at the sight of his automobile in the parking lot. He'd driven there early in the morning, earlier than she could possibly expect to pick up her paycheck, to be sure he wouldn't miss her. Now it was a simple matter of watching and waiting.

He held her letter, gingerly, and read it for the hundredth time: ". . . somewhere deep down you'd always blame me for the things that happened. . . . I know it was wrong for me to try to come back into your life." This was not a letter of rejection, it was a letter of guilt. Was that what Wilson had been trying to tell him?

The sun climbed higher and the morning air was growing sultry. Broder watched the Mexicana parking lot, careful to check on anyone coming or going, afraid to look away. Maria said Colletta would have to come sometime during the morning. It was after ten. What if she didn't show up?

He had tossed and turned all night, slept very little. It was hard to keep his eyes open, squinting into the sunlight.

The Mexicana had been open for four hours and traffic in and out of the parking lot had grown heavy at times. There had been a rush during the breakfast period and after that business slacked off substantially. The early lunch crowd was beginning to arrive. Broder wondered if he had made a mistake by parking so far away; if several people came at once, Colletta might mix with the crowd and slip in and out without him seeing her.

But he was being paranoid. She did not expect to see him there. She was not trying to avoid him. She would not be hard to spot. He merely had to be patient.

All night he'd worried about what to say when they met. This was Colletta, the little girl he had loved as a child and never stopped loving, the woman-child he had planned to marry, who had promised to marry him. And it was the woman who had said she would never see him again, then come back into his life at a time when her mere presence had helped give him hope.

He looked at her letter again: "It was wrong for me to try to come back into your life . . . think of me sometimes and know I'll always love you."

She had tried to come back into his life. These were her own words. He wanted her back in his life, but he had not told her that.

A dilapidated Toyota turned slowly into the Mexicana parking lot. A woman and child got out and started toward the restaurant door. It was Colletta, and for the first time Broder saw Jacob. They would be inside before he could get there, but he hurried across the street and slipped into a booth at the back of the Mexicana, near the door. Colletta was nowhere in sight.

A waiter came and took his request for coffee. He really didn't want anything but since he was taking up a seat he felt obligated to order. He might have needed coffee on another day, after a nearly sleepless night, but not today. He was alert, excited, anxious.

Colletta saw him the instant she came out of the manager's office. Broder tried to read her face for signs of approval or rejection, but her only look was surprise. She walked to him, Jacob close against her leg.

She said, "Jimmie, I didn't expect to see you."

"I wanted to see you. Maria said you'd come."

"This is Jacob. You've never seen him before."

"I know. He's a beautiful child."

"You shouldn't have come."

"Please sit with me and talk. Or we can go somewhere else if you'd rather."

Colletta slipped into the seat opposite him, with Jacob at her side. She looked tired and worn. He wondered if she had slept at all over the last few nights. For a brief moment he might have been looking into the dirty face of a little girl in Conway, playing beneath a chinaberry tree or scavenging scuppernongs under the backyard arbor. That was the way he would always remember her best, as if there had been no intervening years.

"We can talk here," she said. "But I don't think there's a lot to talk about."

"I love you Colletta. I want you in my life."

"Did Wilson give you my letter?"

"Yes, of course. I have it with me. But I don't understand it. Having you come back into my life was the best thing that ever happened to me. I don't want to lose you again."

The waiter brought Broder's coffee, heard just enough of his words to be embarrassed. Broder asked him to bring coffee for Colletta, too, and something for Jacob if he might want it. But Colletta said no, she didn't want anything and the child had just been fed, and the waiter quietly slipped away.

"You don't have me to lose, Jimmie," she said. "We were children in love, but that was a long time ago. Our lives have taken different paths."

"It wasn't so long ago, Colletta. We can't go back, but we could go from here and start over."

"I thought that, too, in the beginning—like things could somehow be the way they were. I saw you in the hospital and you were so needy and helpless and my being there seemed like a good thing for you. I tried to fool myself that it was like the old days again. You were always such a sweet boy and you've grown into a good man. But I was thinking with my heart and not my head. We're different people now, and all the wishing in the world won't change that."

"But things really are not all that different, are they? I mean, we're still who we are and we still have time to make a life together."

"I have Jacob now. He's the center of my life."

"I could love and care for him like my own. Look at him. He's adorable."

"You can see it, of course?"

"See what?"

"The resemblance."

"Yes. He looks like Ray-Gene."

"And you know why."

"Yes, he's Jaybo's child."

"I didn't want to have him, but I was little more than a child myself, in a strange place with no one to help me. I didn't know where to go and what to do and Aunt Edith thought it was a sin to not have the baby. And then when I finally found out what to do, it was too late."

"But you love him now, like any mother loves her child."

"Yes. But no matter how much I love him, he would always be there to remind you, Jimmie. That's what I've come to realize after seeing you again."

"What does that matter, Colletta?" Broder looked into her eyes and hoped she would understand the earnestness of his plea. "There is nothing I didn't know before, and I loved you then. Why would it matter now?"

"I can't have other children. Jacob is the only child I'll ever have. You'd try to love him, and in a way you would, but it wouldn't be the same. You'll want children of your own and Jacob would always remind you of something ugly and, deep down, you'd blame me. You ran away from it before and I'd always be afraid you'd run away from it again. I won't do that to you, Jimmie. I won't do it to us."

"I would never blame you, Colletta. I never have blamed you."

"You've never said it was my fault, but we both knew I caused my own problems. I can't forget that, and I wouldn't expect you to."

"For all these weeks now," Broder told her, "I've had an image of us together, and it seemed right. I'm getting out of the Army and I don't know where I'm going or what I'm going to do, but I had that image of us together and so the rest of it didn't matter."

"We can't truly foresee the future, though. And when we were together we never talked about it. We talked about the past, and we can't escape it. We can only imagine the future, but the past is real. I saw you in the hospital and imagined that things could be good again, but then I went home and there was Jacob and all the pain came back and I knew there was still too much to overcome. Maybe someday . . ."

"I don't know what to say, Colletta. Now that I've seen you again, and felt close to you, it was like we belonged together. I don't know what I'll do without you."

Colletta's eyes filled with tears. She reached out to him, placed a soft hand on his.

"Go back to Conway, Jimmie. You can be anything you want to be, there. Sell used cars for Mack Brown, be a cop or a banker, whatever. If you want to pick up cans along the road for a living, that's okay, too. You'll always be Airborne, and soldiers will always be heroes in Conway."

"Conway is still home," Broder said, "but there are too many ghosts. Too many bad memories, Colletta."

"Then you should understand what I'm talking about, Jimmie."

She squeezed his hand very hard, slid from her seat and leaned in and kissed him softly on the forehead. She picked up Jacob in her arms, then turned and pushed through the brightly painted door that was the Mexicana's entrance and was quickly gone from Broder's view.

Other Books by Robert Hays

Fiction
Blood on the Roses
The Baby River Angel
The Life and Death of Lizzie Morris
Early Stories from the Land
(editor)

Non-fiction
Patton's Oracle
Editorializing 'the Indian Problem'
A Race at Bay
State Science in Illinois
G-2: Intelligence for Patton
(with Gen. Oscar Koch)
Country Editor

About the Author

Robert Hays has been a newspaper reporter, public relations writer, magazine editor, and university professor and administrator. A native of Illinois, he taught in Texas and Missouri and retired in 2008 from a long journalism teaching career at the University of Illinois. He has spent a great deal of time in South Carolina, the home state of his wife, Mary, and was a member of the South Carolina Writers Workshop. His publications include academic journal and popular periodical articles and ten books, including his collaborative work with General Oscar Koch, *G-2: Intelligence for Patton*, and one published in paperback edition under a different title. Robert and Mary live in Champaign, Illinois. They have two sons and a grandson and share (long story!) a cat named Eddie with the family next door.

www.ingramcontent.com/pod-product-compliance
Lightning Source LLC
Chambersburg PA
CBHW022145170626
46807CB00005B/2085